FONTANA

Visit us at www.boldstrokesbooks.com

FONTANA

by

Joshua Martino

2012

FONTANA

ISBN 10: 1-60282-675-7
ISBN 13: 978-1-60282-675-5

This Trade Paperback Original Is Published By
Bold Strokes Books, Inc.
P.O. Box 249
Valley Falls, NY 12185

First Edition: July 2012

Credits
Editor: Cindy Cresap
Production Design: Susan Ramundo
Cover Design By Sheri (graphicartist2020@hotmail.com)
Rap Lyrics By Lew Titterton

Acknowledgments

I owe my fondest gratitude to Lukas Ortiz and Philip Spitzer, literary agents renowned for relentlessness. Both of them—especially Lukas, who never takes off his rally cap—knew that they would find a home for this novel. I thank Len Barot and her staff at Bold Strokes Books for taking a chance on a first-time author. Len leads a loaded roster of authors and publishing experts. Foremost among them is my editor, Cindy Cresap. Cindy's improvements to this novel are immeasurable, as is my appreciation for her patience and careful eye. The staff at Bold Strokes Books believes not only in the cause of good writers, but also the mission of this novel to move a few stubborn minds. Ricky Fontana is safe at home.

I humbly thank teammates who supported me long before this novel was to be published. My friend Jon Simpson, a talented writer, read this manuscipt in numerous drafts, improving the work each time. I'll be proud to see Fontana on my bookshelf alongside the novels of Griffin Hansbury, who guided me through crises of confidence and writer's block. Kevin Smith, a friend and mentor, encouraged me to publish this novel when it was just a few sloppy chapters. Quick-witted, rhyme-spitting Lew Titterton wrote the rap lyrics in Chapter Four, which I'm certain most readers (myself included) will find to be the funniest part of the novel. Rod Hernandez pitched in to make this book look fantastic and somehow forgave a fellow Yankees fan for writing an entire novel about the Mets.

Since I was old enough to listen, my father read to me. No kiddie-lit fluff—he always insisted that I read good books. My mother is a fighter and a fixer who will stop at nothing to make her children happy, which is no small task when your son is easily discouraged. My sister, who excels at everything I do well, looks up to me nonetheless. I wouldn't have put my thoughts to paper without their love.

My first reader was Fred Schade. He trusted me as a close friend since we were four years old, and I trusted him to read this manuscript before anyone else. I wish he were here to hold a copy of this book, which is dedicated to his memory.

Last here but first always in my thoughts is my wife, Jessica Kovler. She read this manuscript between our second and third dates and decided to marry me anyway. I must be doing something right.

Dedication

To Jess, my lifelong teammate

For Fred, who left too soon

Chapter One

"Fontana? That kid's the best hitter I ever saw."

The old man stopped, considering his next words, trembling in his chair, and I watched his fingers clench the armrests, and I remembered those knuckles, that grip, decades younger, squeezing each grain of pine in his bat and sending ripples running up his wrists, forearms, and biceps. As a little boy, I imagined I could hear the wood groaning as the camera zoomed in tight on his hands and then, with a mighty swoosh, he swung.

"Good, powerful line drive hitter, yes," Bob McCarty continued. "His stance, the way he keeps his feet so far apart, that reminds me of Stan Musial. Didja ever see him play?"

"No," I admitted.

"How about Duke Snider? Ever see him play? Or Mays?"

"A little before my time." I tried not to sound impatient. For a first ballot Hall of Famer, Bob McCarty didn't have many visitors in his retirement. His room was without greeting cards, photos, and "World's Best Grandfather" mugs. But then, who would schlep to a nursing home in the middle of nowhere? Who wants to climb three flights of stairs because the elevator is full of shrunken, hairless men and women, and even if they doddered aside and made room, who could endure their lonesome smiles, their stares, their confusion, and the music they piped into every piss-reeking room? Not me. Not even while my father's favorite baseball player lived here and would die here. As would many others, and soon, I thought as I reached the third floor and peered into a waiting room where three women had fallen asleep watching soap operas. It's the bottom of the ninth for these codgers, there are two outs, the count is 0 and 2, and Rivera is throwing his cutter.

I needed one more quote from Bob McCarty about Ricky Fontana, right fielder for the New York Mets who, astoundingly, at one point during the past summer, his rookie season, was batting .401. No player had hit over .400 (averaging four hits every ten at bats) over a full season in over sixty years. McCarty had come close in 1956 during his prime as a sweet-swinging outfielder for the Brooklyn Dodgers. Though Fontana also fell short, his outstanding performance thrilled fans. Readers of my sports column hounded me online and even in person for stories about the ascendant hero.

I'd always disliked spring training. We sportswriters have little to write about in February except for human interest features like the one that took me among the dying to talk baseball with a long-forgotten star.

"Can he do it?" I asked. "Can Fontana hit four hundred?"

"Absolutely," McCarty said without hesitation. "And he can break DiMaggio's streak, too."

Now I had a story. A huge fish fry dinner, five margaritas, and a terrible hangover no longer bothered my assistant, Tony, who smiled at me, suddenly alert. We could beat the Yankees to the back page.

"Are you saying that Ricky Fontana can hit four hundred *and* hit in fifty-six consecutive games?" The great Joe DiMaggio had accomplished the legendary hitting streak in 1941, the same year that Ted Williams batted over four hundred.

"You betcha," McCarty said. "Like I said, that kid's as good a hitter as I ever seen."

Later, in the car, Tony said between chugs of Pepto-Bismol, "How about that?"

"I can see the headline: '*Brooklyn's Bobby Foresees Fontana Four Hundred.*'"

"Don't cast your Hall of Fame ballot yet, man. Fontana will never do it."

"Bobby McCarty seems pretty sure. And he played with some great ballplayers."

"But you're talking about two records that haven't been broken in over sixty years," Tony explained. "And McCarty says that *one* man will do it?"

Tony drove. I opened my Mets media guide. Ricky Fontana smiled on page eighteen. The next Derek Jeter. Several other New York sportswriters compared Fontana to the Yankees captain, and Fontana earned the praise. Any hack could name their similarities. They were great ballplayers, fan favorites, and sex symbols. But Fontana treasured his privacy, and he avoided sharing his feelings with the press, rare in this age of confession. And he lacked Jeter's exuberance, never to be seen on highlight reels pumping his fist or flaunting that handsome grin after a decisive victory. But then, the Mets usually have less to smile about than the Yankees.

Fontana had two advantages over Jeter. He was a better hitter— even Jeter acknowledged it—and he led the majors in marriage proposals. Men cheered for his batting eye, and women serenaded him for batting his eyelashes. Once, during Fontana's first season, Earl Driggs, Executive Sports Editor for *The New York Eagle-Tribune* (my boss), sent me to Citi Field to sort through fan mail with Fontana. I gazed at my byline, clipped and stacked with dozens of stories in my growing manila "Fontana file."

FEMALE FANS FOND OF FONTANA
by Jeremy Rusch

NEW YORK -- After a long day of shelling National League pitching, Mets rookie sensation Ricky Fontana heads home alone in a rusty sedan that he inherited from his mother. Still, a gaggle of Gotham girls would gladly fill his passenger seat.

"He's absolutely adorable," said Mandi Shapiro, 15, of Hauppauge.

"The sexiest man alive," added Susan Miller, 19, of Brooklyn.

Manhattan's Angela Epistolero, 32, asked, "Is he single?"

She's not the only curious female fan wondering if New York's most eligible bachelor is still hers for the taking. Fontana, however, won't tell.

"I'm flattered by all the attention," he admits. "But from February until October, I've got one thing on my mind: winning the World Series."

October can't come quickly enough for some ladies. Two weeks before the All-Star break, Fontana is batting over .360 with 20 home runs, 52 RBIs and 62 marriage proposals. That is, until the mailman arrives at Citi Field with today's fan mail.

"Dear Mr. Fontana," writes Samantha. "You are my favorite Met. With you on the team, this could be our year. I'm a 24-year-old, single non-smoker with no children. And I'm your biggest fan! Marry me, Ricky!"

Make that 63 proposals, a staggering stat that impresses some of Fontana's teammates more than his league-leading batting average. Mail arrives at Citi Field shortly before the Mets take batting practice before night games. As the Mets button up their practice jerseys, reading Fontana's fan mail gets the team loose.

"This one sent photos!" shouts shortstop Jackie Rios, and the team gathers.

"I hope all these stories about girls going gooey for Fontana ended last season," I said, closing the folder. "I hate asking these questions more than Ricky hates answering them."

"He was Rookie of the Year. You expect the attention to die down?" Tony scoffed. "Just wait until he's seen in Soho with some actress on his arm. Next morning, we'll be picking through his garbage for used rubbers."

❖

The ballpark was almost empty. Tony and I arrived in Port St. Lucie, Florida, at nine thirty a.m. for the first team practice of spring training and found that the other Mets beat writers had beaten us there. Long-necked and paunchy like a wading bird in shorts and orange sneakers, Dick Rule of the *Daily News* greeted me. The *New York Post*'s Paul Callahan was there, his soft, round Catholic features pinking in the sun even though he'd only been in Florida for two days, and he gave me a toothless smile—his fleshy face rarely offered more. Budd Crane covered the Mets for *The New York Times*. He sat atop the visitor's dugout next to an open box of donuts. Oddly dignified in sandals and white socks, with the sort of flared nostril patrician face that grandchildren of Irish and Italian and Slavic immigrants imagine when they hear the word "American," Crane looked regal in the pink Oxford shirts he wore so often to the ballpark. He pointed to the donut box. "Jerry, ya hungry? Tony?" We helped ourselves.

We greeted one another after a long winter apart. Catching up, we spoke about our wives, our editors (the drunk bastards), and we talked baseball. Crane asked how many wins rookie fireballer Oscar Ferrera would throw. Rule wondered what would happen to manager Grey Mason if the Mets missed the playoffs again. Callahan asked how many homers Fontana would hit this season. In the season before, Fontana had missed Mark McGwire's rookie record of forty-nine homers by five. But forty-four were enough to lead the league, and his .361 batting average was best in baseball. Only his runs batted in total—142—prevented him from winning the Triple Crown. And the RBI leader, Fred Mercer, faced tired pitchers in the thin atmosphere of Colorado's Coors Field.

"My mother can drive in one fifty in Denver," Crane said. Our gang laughed dutifully.

"Fontana could drive in two hundred, but who cares?" I asked. "And anyone can hit home runs these days, in these tiny ballparks, with these lively balls, on these drugs. I think it's his average we oughta watch." I looked at my comrades, wondering if I should reference my own scoop. And I did. "You guys saw my article, what Bob McCarty said. Fontana can hit four hundred. He can break DiMaggio's streak. He can do both. He's better."

They absorbed my effusiveness for a moment. Crane sat silently, powdered sugar clinging to his suspended lip. Then he laughed. The others joined.

"Whoa there, Jerry!" Crane said. "Are you the guy who messaged me on Facebook last week and asked for a lock of Ricky's hair?" Tony squeezed my arm. I laughed along.

We watched as a few minor leaguers took the field and began stretching, jogging, and reacquainting themselves with their teammates and their crisp new uniforms after five months apart. Nineteen years before, the coach of the Syracuse University varsity baseball team cut me from the squad. As those kids bent and stretched, I missed the game, the grass, the clay. Sunshine and stadium lights don't shine as brilliantly upon the press box.

The big leaguers drifted onto the field. Cameras snapped. Tony fumbled with the memory card on his camera, leaned forward, and began shooting. I thought with a grin how New Yorkers in boots and wool hats would see Tony's photos tomorrow, and they would be reminded that summer would come. The sight of baseball would relieve not only noses chapped in winter cold; the game's return was also a welcome distraction, I imagined, during the bitter presidential primary season. Like children of divorcees, Americans watched with skeptical resignation as their caretakers bickered for control of an ominous future.

Ricky Fontana strode out of the dugout smiling, sharing a joke with Mick Kelleher, the backup catcher. The pulse of the camera clicks doubled.

I checked my media guide again. The Mets listed Fontana at six four and 220 pounds, but anyone who had met the man would dismiss these claims as fiction. In his uniform and spikes, Fontana was proportionally superheroic. And though his shyness and his dark Italian features might have inspired some moviemaker to cast him in a Western as a distant, brooding gunslinger, a mysterious antihero whose intentions are ambiguous until the final scene, Fontana was a champion to the Mets beat writers. He remembered our names and the names of our children, our wives, and our assistants, which stirred so many of us to wax elegiac about the man even though he was "just a fucking jock," as Driggs liked to remind me. Fontana waved to us, and we all waved back as he reached the infield grass.

Two years earlier, Fontana was swatting stadium-length homers in tiny ballparks in Durham, Louisville, and Toledo for fans who had never ridden the 7 train, braved the Grand Central Parkway, or paid six dollars for a hot dog. The red uniform of the Triple-A Norfolk Tides looked nothing like the orange and blue worn by the Mets. Still, when Fontana first buttoned New York's striped home jersey (#6), pitchers recognized him. His highlights, their nightmares. During his final minor league season, New York newscasters slipped clips of Fontana's titanic clouts between their nightly Mets and Yankees recaps. As his legend grew, national sports networks joined the craze. Between reels of hardball highlights beamed nationwide from Wrigley Field and Fenway Park, ESPN sneaked in clumsily filmed footage of a home run from Slugger Field in Indianapolis or McCoy Stadium in Pawtucket. Fontana's barrage against minor league pitchers inched closer and closer to the top of the broadcasts until one night in June. Some poor sap on the Pittsburgh Pirates was seven innings into a no-hitter, but *SportsCenter*'s top story at eleven p.m. was a 600-foot home run that left P&C Stadium in Syracuse and landed in the parking lot, smashing the windshield of the ballpark organist's Oldsmobile. Before he reached the majors, before his name was sold on T-shirts at Mets.com, before he took enough at bats to qualify for the Rookie of the Year Award that Vegas bookies had four to one odds he would win, everyone knew that Ricky Fontana belonged.

His rookie season was also mine. Days after the Mets announced that Fontana was to be next season's starting right fielder, the *Tribune* promoted me to daily columnist, a beat writer's dream. Suddenly, I was somebody, and fans recognized me and stopped me for news and rumors or to complain about my opinions. I was even appointed an assistant, Tony, to manage a blog on the newspaper's website featuring a heavily doctored headshot of yours truly. Fontana filled that summer with days of wonder that I remember with giddy nostalgia. His rookie performance made my working life more exciting than I could have imagined. When February comes and ballplayers arrive in Florida, rooters of last season's runners-up confine past failures to history; optimism rules. I remember the rookie season I shared with Fontana as ballplayers in August remember spring training: the carefree times when anyone could be champion.

We met one year to the day before my interview with Bob McCarty. When I introduced myself, I admired Fontana and understood why girls sent him perfumed letters. He was tall, very tall, and in his pinstriped pants, his lower body seemed endless. Though his legs were thick and muscular, he had delicate ankles and feet. When he moved, he was quick and capable of explosive power. He set his spikes far apart when he batted and generated torque with a concise stride—only a few inches—and a severe twist of his hips, so he seemed to dive into the ball when he swung, shifting his weight so drastically that he almost stood on one foot when bat met ball. Fontana could flick an outside pitch over the right-field fence with only his arms, thick and corded with muscle like shipping rope.

"Hello, Mr. Fontana," I said, offering my hand. He took it. A crushing grip! "My name's Jeremy Rusch. I'm a rookie, too." My line was rehearsed. I had to have something clever to say the first time I met Ricky Fontana. Even if he was a nineteen-year-old kid, expectations for his career were stratospheric, while I was just another writer for a New York tabloid that lagged far behind its competition in the race for readers. I could only imagine how he saw me, six inches shorter, decades older, with thinning hair like rusty steel wool, not quite red or brown, blue eyes between freckles and worry lines, a long, crooked nose, yellowed teeth (I smoked fanatically in college) and a permanent five o'clock shadow. I would not have blamed him if he preferred to admire his reflection in the hairless patch atop my head.

In that reflection, he would have seen glossy black hair, heavy-lidded eyes that gave him an almost oriental appearance, a long, thin nose, perfectly straight except for a slight crook at the end, an imperfection that, so I am told, made him that much more accessible and adorable to the female fans who cheered and even wolf-whistled, and a mouth full of straight and brilliant teeth.

He insisted that I call him Ricky. Everybody does, he told me. And before I could ask him about being the youngest player in the major leagues, he asked me how long I had been a writer, where I lived, did I come from New York, where did I go to college, and how I thought the Mets would fare that season. I was stunned. Most athletes offer minimal responses to reporters and dismiss us when they've had enough. The days when sportswriters traveled, ate, and hit the town with players ended decades ago. Nowadays, the relationship is cool, I thought, if not antagonistic. But as a rookie, Ricky was exceedingly friendly. By August of his first season, I felt comfortable enough to ask him why he tried so hard.

"A coach once told me that if I'm polite to you guys, you'll save the tough questions for other players," he said. Charmed by his frankness, I laughed and told myself that from then on, I would save my worst for his teammates.

While the players stretched and admired the brilliant, high Florida sky, Fontana bent down to the infield grass. He grabbed a fistful of dirt and rubbed it into the center of his mitt, and then he pressed his palm to the webbing of the glove, which bent unwillingly.

"Top story on every backpage tomorrow: 'Fontana Breaks In New Glove,'" chuckled Tony.

The coaches followed the players out of the dugout and called the team together for a meeting. As Manager Grey Mason finished his lecture, Tom Simon, a rookie, rose, donned his cap, and reached for his glove. Several players glared. Sheepishly, he turned back toward the circle of teammates and took off his cap. The rest of the team stood and huddled together. Henry Monan, a left-handed reliever, led the team prayer.

"Praying before practice? That's new," Tony exclaimed.

Crane quipped, "Yea, though we walk in the shadow of the valley of third place, we fear no bad hops for we hired new groundskeepers," to titters from the gallery.

Prayer completed, the players broke apart and scattered across the field.

❖

My nerves danced. My mind rattled. So before bed that night I poured two hearty shots of whiskey from the travel flask that I inherited from my father. Still, my mind was a mess. I worried. Would any of our readers care about the baseball prophecies of a withered old man? Another lackluster story for a sports desk that lagged behind competitors in newsstand sales and website visits. I didn't sleep much. When I did, I slept restlessly. At six o'clock, the phone rang, and I awoke, sure my mother was dead, sure my sister was finally pregnant, sure that my literary agent had finally sold my mystery novel. But it was my wife.

"I hate it here. I want to go home," she complained. "I hate my job." She was about to leave for work. She always got glum on a Monday after a long weekend. Tara taught at an elementary school in the South Bronx. In the springtime, Yankee Stadium's shadows kissed the school's playground, and during day games, she closed the windows to drown the noise of the crowd. Once, a student stole money from her purse. Another kid pushed a teacher, Tara's closest friend, down a flight of stairs. Two men, two among many drifting, purposeless young men in that forgotten neighborhood, hollered at her every day when she bought lunch at a nearby bodega with a fraying awning. "*Roja! Roja! Señorita Roja*," they called, "Miss Red," for her rust-colored hair. Once, when I reluctantly visited her school, she introduced me to a man with soft, deep wrinkles who sold sliced mangoes from a pushcart near her school. Now she complained mournfully that the old man had died and the woman who took over his pushcart spoke no English and greeted her with a sneer and sold mangoes that were too chewy. But my wife had not yet mentioned her friend Sara, "who has two beautiful daughters," or Rachel, "who is swelling up like a balloon—she's due in March," and I was grateful.

"It's lonely here when you're gone," Tara continued. She paused for a few seconds, and I knew something big was coming. "I was thinking of quitting," she blurted, and then rapidly, "Quitting and staying with Mom in Rochester until spring training is over and you come home and then I'll look for another job in New York. Sara's a paralegal. She said they are always looking for extra help at her firm."

I told her to stay. I told her to suck it up. I told her I would be back in New York in six weeks and then we would be together. She told me that she was over forty and childless and married to a drunk. Then she hung up.

I had little time to brood before good news arrived over breakfast. Driggs loved my interview with Bobby McCarty. That morning, the *Tribune* ran on its back page a photo of the old coot in his chair, clinging to life and his La-Z-Boy armrests. Crane, Rule, and Callahan dismissed the claims of the ancient Dodgers shortstop. ("Pitchers will find Fontana's weakness," Rule predicted. "High fastballs, inside junk—he'll never hit forty homers again."). But readers were fascinated. Tony maintained a blog with my analysis on the *Tribune* website, as well as a Twitter feed. Followers and blog readers ardently debated McCarty's claim. Look out, Splendid Splinter! One side, Joltin' Joe! Driggs, the wily bastard, had tracked down McCarty at that dreary assisted living facility in Boynton Beach, and I had gone reluctantly. But my story had created two quests for Fontana that would captivate readers throughout the season: Could he get a hit in four out of every ten at bats, and could he hit safely in fifty-six consecutive games?

Of course, a follow-up story was in order. Fortunately for *Tribune* readers, I had an inside track to Fontana. Last August, I had spotted a book in Fontana's locker: *350 Easy Italian Phrases*. Not long before I hired him, Tony graduated with a film degree from NYU's Tisch School of the Arts. Like a lot of nineteen-year-olds with ambitions to be the next Fellini and a foreign language requirement, Tony had studied Italian. During a semester in Florence, he refined his fluency and his taste for European women, who were fascinated by the young black American who spoke Dante's mother tongue. But even compared to Florentine coeds, Ricky Fontana was a pushover. He warmed to me the moment he saw Tony reading a magazine on Lamborghini racecars (in Italian, of course) in a corridor near the locker room during a rain delay. The magazine was my idea. Tony prefers sci-fi paperbacks.

Scoring an impromptu interview with Fontana, great-grandson of immigrants from Calabria, who had fond memories of his grandma singing in Italian as she worked in her garden, had not been a problem since.

After the Mets ended their first spring training practice, I spotted Fontana sitting on a locker room bench unbuttoning his jersey. He was alone and unoccupied, so I thought then was the ideal moment to tell him about Bobby McCarty's predictions. I walked toward him determinedly, and he noticed me and I saw in his eyes an expression that I had never seen before: fear. He grabbed his glove and his spikes and began to walk away.

"Wait! Ricky, wait!" I hollered. "It's me, Jerry."

He stopped. His shoulders sagged and he turned slowly. He had tried to stifle his look of alarm, yet I still read fear and anger—violation?—in his gaze.

"Ricky! Did you think I was some autograph-seeker or something?" I asked.

"Sorry," he said, regaining his composure. "How are you, Jerry? Did you go anywhere fun this winter? How's Tony?"

I answered his questions, and then he offered me his hand.

"Well, it was good talking to you," he said.

"Wait! Do you have time for a few of my questions?" I asked.

"We aren't going to go through my fan mail again, are we?"

Fontana tumbled into a chair and leaned forward, elbows on his knees. He smiled with broad lips and brilliant teeth that could melt the frostiest woman into a puddle of desire. For a moment, I hated him. Envy, yes, I envied his youth, his looks, his talent, his wealth, and the legend he was certain to become, the Cult of Fontana spawned by my bylines and growing until his face was everywhere like a totalitarian, on razor commercials, gossip columns, anti-drug posters, and spinning on his laminated baseball card stuck in the spokes of some kid's bike until he retires and a letter arrived from the Writer's Committee asking me to hang his idol in Cooperstown. Sure, I envied the skills he had developed and the talent with which he was born, but I loathed the casual way he wore his success, handsome even in his sliding pants, knee socks, and a stained undershirt. Unlike Bobby McCarty, Fontana's last days would be spent in his bed surrounded by loved ones, and when the breath left his body, presidents, professors, and plumbers would remember him—surely he knew that. Why didn't he love every minute of this life? I should be angry at the world, I wanted to shout at him. I'm more likely to die in a place that reeks of formaldehyde while some peppy Phil Collins tune is broadcast through the halls. Nobody will note the death of this paunchy, balding sportswriter who never drew a second glance except from his creditors, his widow (the only woman he's ever slept with), and a bilingual blog assistant.

"No fan mail, Ricky. Cross my heart."

"All right then," Fontana said, and he leaned back in his chair. "Fire away."

CHAPTER TWO

My mother calls me a product of the Summer of Love. I was born on April 10, 1968, appropriately, my wife says, on opening day. Mom, a part-time nurse, and my father, who owned a Chevrolet dealership near our home in Bensonhurst, Brooklyn, didn't care that the Mets lost that afternoon 5-4. They were Dodgers fans.

But I loved the Mets. When I wasn't pounding hits (and Devil Dogs) as the chunky third baseman for my Little League team, I was sketching my favorites, Lee Mazzilli and Ed Kranepool, in the margins of the scorecards I kept of almost every Mets game. At first, Dad didn't get it. How could I root for the Mets? Still mourning baseball in Brooklyn, he considered the Mets a poor substitute for "Dem Bums," the Dodgers. His team had been sold to a new owner and moved to Los Angeles in 1958. But Dad came around, and eventually, he looked forward to "Jerry's play-by-play," as he called it, the blow-by-blow accounts that I would read to him from my scorecards of games that we couldn't watch together. I was a freshman at Syracuse University on October 27, 1986, when Dad called me in tears. The Mets had won the World Series, and I promised my overjoyed father that I would name his first grandson William after Billy Buckner, the first baseman for the Boston Red Sox whose improbable error allowed our Mets to win.

My dream of playing third base in the majors ended at age eighteen. At five ten and 235 pounds, I was too fat to play ball for the Syracuse Orangemen. My replacement dream was also quickly dashed. The head of the university radio station said, "You've got a face made for radio, Jerry, but your Brooklyn accent is hard on the ears," so I couldn't call the play-by-play for the varsity ballgames.

Dad took pity on me. He bought me an electronic word processor, and the following semester I joined the school paper. Now I had new heroes: Red Smith and Ring Lardner, every sportswriter's idols.

I was twenty-five years old and looking for work when my father one day sold a brand-new Chevy Camaro to Vincent Hunter, then the Executive Metro Sports Editor for *The New York Eagle-Tribune*. "By the way," Dad said as he handed Hunter the keys, "My kid's a sportswriter, too. Take a look." He motioned to the wall behind his desk where he had pinned to a bulletin board every article I had written in college. Hunter was impressed (he was also an obsessive Mets fan), so he got me a job as an office clerk at the *Tribune* Metro Sports desk. My first job was to transcribe a reporter's nearly illegible shorthand interview with Darryl Strawberry, who was then my favorite player and perhaps the best hitter who ever played for the New York Mets.

That is, until Ricky Fontana came along. He quickly became my new favorite. Being a sportswriter ruins baseball for many of us. Watching games is our job, and it becomes like any job— unglamorous drudgery. Following Fontana, however, was pure fun. We cheered like little boys as Fontana amazed us, jaded writers who thought they'd seen it all.

Like the fawning lady fans, I wanted more of Fontana than an interview or an autograph. I wanted to know him. Toward the end of his rookie season, I invited Fontana to join me, Crane, Callahan, and Rule at our favorite pub. "Tomorrow's an off day, so me and the beat guys are going to meet for a few drinks," I told him after a lazy August afternoon loss. Then I realized he wasn't old enough to drink. "Maybe you'd like to come and have a Coke or something?" I sounded like an idiot, so I don't blame him for refusing me. Too bad! Even though I would have breached professional etiquette, I would have liked to call Ricky Fontana my friend. But of course he had better things to do. He was wealthy and famous and good-looking.

He had twenty-five teammates for companionship. Women waited in hotel lobbies and outside the players' entrance to the ballpark for the chance to entice him with a desperate shout or shake. All he'd have to do is smile.

But Ricky Fontana seemed at age nineteen too reserved to exploit his rising fame. He would have made an unlikely chum for four hard-drinking newsmen. He didn't drink—his tender age aside, he said that alcohol dulled his batting eye. A millionaire in a city with ten thousand restaurants, Fontana's favorite food was plain cheese pizza. The four of us and the SNY-TV crew that followed the Mets knew little else about him. He rented a small house in New Jersey that he shared with backup catcher Mick Kelleher. He had spent only two seasons in the minors, the first as an unknown busher, but the second as the most highly touted prospect in the game. One year later, he was chasing .400 in the major leagues. His ascension would have jaded almost anyone, but the rookie Ricky didn't walk or talk with a star athlete's world-is-mine cockiness. We knew him well enough to know he was different, but we didn't know him well enough to know why.

Truth be told, the sight of Ricky Fontana hearkened my school days spent admiring charismatic jocks from my far-flung corner of social insignificance. Despite his modesty, Ricky Fontana was a conspicuous reminder of everything I'd never experience. He seemed to be the perfect man. All that is celebrated in masculinity is expected of baseball stars. The game requires players to balance physical aggression and cunning restraint. But off the field, we permit (perhaps even expect) athletes to demonstrate the worst of maleness lived loudly. That's why I loved the game; that's why I wanted to play, and when I couldn't, the carefree loutishness of baseball men fascinated me. That's why I twice turned down an offer to take over the *Tribune*'s sports column because the promotion would mean less time at the ballpark. I was a birdwatcher obsessed with fantasies of flight.

People often ask me what the lives of major leaguers are like. I tell them to imagine what a teenager would do with fifty million dollars, no parents, and near-constant admiration. The stories passed from clubhouse attendants, agents, and other hangers-on still amaze me. Rules don't apply to professional athletes. Players pampered friends and family with tickets and transportation. Some squandered their salaries on private masseurs, publicity gurus, or image consultants. One Mets slugger took his personal trainer on every road trip until the team discovered he was actually a medium who had convinced the ballplayer he could end a slump by contacting the spirits of Babe Ruth and Hank Aaron. Apparently, the medium never told the player that Aaron was alive.

The seedy stuff was always the most fun, the stories I relished hearing and telling. Some ballplayers treated women as if they were dishes in the catered postgame buffet. The very first words spoken to me by a major leaguer were, "What the fuck do you want, man? I'm about to go and stick it." He was a celebrated Mets infielder of the late 1980s, with his car keys in one hand and the other draped over the shoulder of a young woman who seemed unhappy that her trip to a BMW in the Shea Stadium parking lot had been interrupted by a pimply reporter.

A benighted minority of ballplayers are, of course, good church-going lads. Still, many major leaguers are living aloud the fantasies of ordinary fans. Inevitably, I thought, Ricky Fontana would become just such a professional party boy. He'd outdo his comrades' hedonism as he surpassed their hitting, all the while sending half his paycheck to his mother and baby brother in Rhode Island. Then I'd envy him all the more.

Still, I couldn't help but like the kid. After all, he didn't have to give me an exclusive interview about Bobby McCarty. So once I assured him we weren't going to go through his fan mail, he smiled and invited my questions. While Fontana spoke, a groundskeeper approached. He escorted a little boy in a mustard yellow Little League uniform. The kid removed a baseball from his tiny mitt. The groundskeeper handed a pen to Fontana. Without skipping a beat, Fontana signed the ball, handed it back to the boy, and gave the kid a friendly pat atop his cap. "Thank you," the groundskeeper mouthed as he walked away.

While Fontana and his mates shagged fly balls and swatted practice pitches, I typed my article. Crane, Rule, and Callahan joshed me for ignoring my buzzing cell phone twice, three, four times when my wife's name appeared onscreen. I didn't care; Fontana's name under my byline was more important than returning their jibes. Practice ended. The Mets drifted off the field, and the media men exchanged pleasantries and dinner plans in the parking lot. Back at my hotel, I deleted a voice mail from Tara and stumbled into a nap.

Tony's tittering woke me.

Sitting at the desk, bent over my laptop, Tony giggled. The door was open to the adjoining room, where the *Tribune* had stashed Tony for the first week of spring training, ostensibly as my right-hand man, though I knew the boss expected Tony to report back if I spent more time drinking than writing good copy.

Fat chance, I thought, propping myself up on my elbows. I had written one helluva follow-up. "Whatcha think?" I asked Tony.

"Ricky never answered the big question," Tony said. "Looks like you answered it for him."

"Whaddya mean?" I asked.

"Check the transcripts from your interview," Tony insisted. "Read it on the way to dinner, man. I'm hungry."

I read the interview four times on the drive to the restaurant where Tony and I were meeting Crane and Rule for surf, turf, and what always ended up being one margarita too many. My eyes kept drifting back to one section of the transcript. A fact that I had overlooked during my initial reading became clear as I read it again and again. Like most men who love the game, I admire baseball players. But Ricky Fontana—his talent, his charm, his stature—can turn that appreciation to awe. And in his presence, thinking about my exclusive interview and the excitement it would inspire, I did not realize that Fontana made an ass of me.

JR: Did you read my interview with Bobby McCarty?
RF: No, but the rest of the team did. I've been catching hell all morning.
JR: Do you think you can hit .400?
RF: Yes.
JR: Really?

RF: Why not?

JR: Because no one has done it in over sixty years.

RF: It could happen again. Why not me?

JR: Can you break Joe DiMaggio's consecutive hitting streak?

RF: Yes. For the same reason.

JR: You're saying you can do both in the same season, as Bobby suggested?

RF: Look, you're not asking if I can write a novel or find a cure for cancer. I'm a ballplayer. I try to be a good one.

JR: Will you do it? Make a prediction.

RF: I predict that I will put up better numbers than last season. I'm more familiar with the pitchers and what they'll throw in certain situations.

JR: Is Joe DiMaggio an inspiration to you as an Italian-American?

RF: You know what inspires me? He won nine World Series.

JR: Would you be proud as an Italian to break DiMaggio's record?

RF: Yes indeed. I'd also be proud as a Swede or a Zulu to hit in 56 straight games.

JR: [chuckles] So if you break DiMaggio's record, can New Yorkers expect to see you with a modern Marilyn perhaps?

RF: No. I have no interest in fashion or celebrity. I just want to win the World Series.

Then I noticed. "The son of a bitch never answered the most important question. He never said he can break both records this season."

"No dumb jock is Ricky," Tony said with a smirk.

I thought quickly. "Fontana said he could hit four hundred. And he said he could break DiMaggio's streak. If he believed he could do both, why not assume he means in the same season?"

"I don't think that's entirely ethical," Tony said. He was parking our rental car outside of a Palm City restaurant called Mickey Maco's Bar and Grille.

Rule and Crane were leaning against an SUV parked nearby. They approached as our car stopped. "We're starving! You're late," said Rule.

The next day, the *Tribune* ran my interview as the top story in the sports section. The back page featured a photo of Ricky Fontana taken during his first year as a Met. He is leaning on the top step of the dugout, his bat slung over his shoulder like a rifle, gazing over the field calmly, confidently. Above his blue cap, a headline declared: YES I CAN.

For two weeks, Crane and Rule and Callahan fed and watered the little seed I had planted, and the goddamn non-story grew. Speculation, wild and unfounded crystal ball gazing and nothing more, became headline news not only for the *Tribune*, but for the other New York dailies. None of my colleagues doubted that Fontana was capable of breaking both records, and no readers wrote in to ask that we newsmen cover some actual news—such was the public perception of Fontana's abilities. Even if he would not claim he could outhit the greats, DiMaggio and Williams, everyone who read the sports pages had already decided he could. Newsstand sales for the *Tribune* soared in February, and for the first time since V-J Day, our bottom-feeding rag outsold the *New York Post* and vaulted into third place among the New York dailies. My story had the most hits of any on the *Trib*'s website for the three days following its publication.

Not every reader appreciated my predictions. Some bloggers scoffed at me for using outdated statistics like RBIs and batting average. The new generation of baseball analysts touted stats like fWAR and OPS+. Don't ask me what these letters stand for. I never bothered to learn. Analysis is for statisticians. Writing is for writers. I've always seen my job as telling stories. Still, a writer for Fangraphs.com sneered, "I understand why Bob McCarty trades in old fart statistics. He was born during the Hoover administration. But why is a professional sportswriter in the twenty-first century using batting average to measure greatness?" I responded in my column that these numbers have far-reaching resonance. Many who don't follow baseball have heard of Ted Williams's batting average, and anyone can appreciate the consistency of DiMaggio's streak. Men with sports bylines are purveyors of nostalgia. We depict an America that no longer exists (or never existed) by connecting modern ballplayers to the saga of their forbearers. Familiar stats like batting average are a measure of baseball achievements across generations.

Four days before the first exhibition game of the new spring training practice season, a producer from SNY, the Mets television network, invited me to appear on *The Hot Stove Report*, a preseason miniseries where the beat writers forecast the coming season. It was my first invitation. (Crane and Rule had appeared every year since the program's inception.) I called my mother and father and my literary agent and my wife with the news: Jeremy Rusch was to be a television personality. If I held my own, the producer suggested, I could appear on the network during the regular season for *The Amazin's Hour*, a weekly Mets highlights show, an unimaginable boost to my pride and my byline.

Tara called me every few days. And she sent letters, a romantic gesture that would have moved me had she not also enclosed clippings from the real estate sections of New Jersey and Long Island newspapers. Each carefully cut clip featured a cozy house above which she had notes that read, "Isn't this one nice?" or, "Look, it's close to the beach." I crumpled them up, all of them. "Think about it," read her final note in February, written above a white colonial with blue shutter boards three miles from the Long Island Sound. That too I sent to the trash. I had long ago made up my mind never to leave Manhattan and strand myself in the suburbs. I made this decision clear to Tara when we moved in together, and only now she seemed to regret it.

If my wife was hurt that I didn't discuss her would-be home in a sleepy commuter town, she didn't say so when I called to ask her to record my TV appearance. Crane, Rule, and Tony watched *The Hot Stove Report* live over mojitos (my treat) at Mickey Maco's. I had offered cash to the cameraman to cut off the frame above my potbelly, Rule teased. Tony snickered while I explained how much makeup they slathered on my face to make it lens friendly. Even so, seeing myself on television had made me feel like less of a nobody. And it was all thanks to Ricky Fontana.

I have always preferred not to eat at the same restaurant on consecutive nights when I travel. I discovered early in my working life that I am not cut out for routines. I am grateful that my job allows me to travel and keeps me from the rhythmic life of a man with an English degree pushing fifty in publishing, public relations, or marketing, which is where my friends outside the game spend every baseball season and the months in between. And my work allows me to continue my first and only true romance, a love that began on my fifth birthday, when my father gave me a batting tee, a Whiffle ball, and a plastic bat. During the winter months, Tara always seemed to grow weary of my restlessness, when I sat at home waiting for spring. She tired of me, my complaints, my unwillingness to cook when I grew weary of the dozen recipes that she could reliably prepare. Every baseball game is unique; there might be one hundred games each season won by a 1-0 score, yet the way each pair of teams reached that outcome is singular. But dinner at our home— and the time between meals—was predictable. I knew exactly what would be on our table and what she would tell me between forkfuls of one of her specialties and what she would say when she turned off her bedside lamp. Still, it's hard during spring training to find a new restaurant every night because I'm in the same town for nearly two months. So I returned to Mickey Maco's alone the next evening because I was hungry and the food was good and because the drinks were cheap, and I felt like I needed a few of them.

Like many seafood-serving tourist traps in Florida, Mickey Maco's has a nautical theme. A ship's wheel, a sextant, and rope tied in sailor knots decorate the walls. The bar of polished cypress wood is guarded by Ernest, the restaurant's mascot, a five-foot plastic swordfish depicted in mid-thrash, his buggy eyes warning boozing patrons to tip the bartender generously each time he pours a sudsy beer or crushes fresh mint. Someone spoiled Ernest's piscatorial majesty in 2003 by fixing a Florida Marlins cap to the peak of his dorsal fin. But Mickey Marino, owner of the restaurant, is a dedicated Marlins fan and left the cap undisturbed to commemorate his team's World Series victory.

Mickey's is filled with old-timers from baseball towns like Cleveland, Detroit, and St. Louis who yap about the day's Grapefruit League action and their journeys south in days past to see Rocky Colavito, Al Kaline, and Bob Gibson play the season's first game of catch amidst the palms and saw grass. They wear khaki shorts and polo shirts, wrinkled and reeking of mothballs from a long winter in the attic. They carry too much in their bulging shoulder bags and fanny packs: cameras, film, sunscreen, maps, and the various items they will need to collect autographs, like baseballs (still in their packaging), yearbooks, and scorecards. Even though their better instincts tell them that Alex Rodriguez, Miguel Cabrera, and Ricky Fontana wouldn't be caught dead in a place like this, it's February, the state is crawling with ballplayers, and it never hurts to be prepared.

I too carry a felt-tip marker and baseball cards in my breast pocket. They are for my young nephew, I tell myself, but I always carry doubles of my favorite players and triples of Ricky Fontana, whose autograph is worth my daily salary to zealous New York collectors. But he shouldn't be at Mickey Maco's, I thought, even if he couldn't get a table at the steakhouse near the team hotel or a seat at the Seminole Club, the ocean-side resort where the Mets were honorary members ever since the team's owner financed golf course renovations in 1998. He should be at a nicer restaurant or ordering room service or eating a plate of scrambled eggs prepared by one of the pretty tramps who troll the hotel bar and want nothing more than to take home a real major leaguer, let alone a superstar like Ricky Fontana. He shouldn't have been at Mickey's, but he was there when I walked in on my second night, sitting across from Eusebio Hernandez, a recently retired infielder for the New York Yankees.

When Fontana noticed me, his eyes blazed: first recognition, then panic, then fear. The same look he had given me weeks before. He quickly looked away.

Fontana was wearing a beige baseball cap with no logo. Tucked into the collar of his black T-shirt was a pair of wrap-around sunglasses. But even if he had been wearing them, nothing could hide his famous face, that Hollywood jawline, his surgeon's model chin, and his lean, sculpted frame. I had been at the restaurant for thirty minutes before I noticed him. Five margaritas down, I didn't recognize Fontana at first—then again, I might not have recognized Jesus if Mickey Maco's had been the site of the Resurrection. Fontana's table was twenty feet away, tucked into a corner. He remained undisturbed while I tried again to catch his gaze and wave hello. The two tables nearest to him were filled by families from Montreal, chatting in French about their tans and how dark they would look compared to the Quebecois who didn't fly south that winter.

Finally, he shot me a quick glance. I offered him a wave and a smile. Fontana stood. Oh good, I thought. He's coming to say hello! I wished that I hadn't had so much to drink, and I hoped I was presentable. I buttoned my top button and brushed some crumbs off my table. Just when I expected Fontana to reach me and take the empty seat, I looked up and saw a black and beige blur whisk past me toward the front of the restaurant, out the door, into the tropical night.

I turned to Fontana's table. His seat was empty. Eusebio Hernandez was talking into his cell phone, waving to the waitress.

Sloppy and surprised, I stood. I must have wobbled for a few minutes before gathering myself. Hernandez was still on his phone. He signed his check, stood up with pen in hand, phone at his ear, and headed for the exit.

I lurched after him, calling, "Seb, Seb!" The Yankees infielder didn't seem to hear. I caught him near the door. I tapped his shoulder. He turned to me, sunglasses hiding his eyes. He pardoned himself in Spanish to the caller on his phone, and I started to speak.

"Sorry to interrupt—" I began.

Seb snatched something from my hand. In my woozy haste, I had taken my napkin from my table. With a quick swipe, Hernandez slashed his pen across the paper. He stuffed it in my breast pocket and gave my shoulder a friendly pat. Then he barged out the door, jabbering into his phone.

A waitress sauntered past, the same server who brought Hernandez his check. I cornered her and asked, "Did you wait on Ricky Fontana's table?" She looked confused. I grunted impatiently, "He's only the best hitter in the major leagues. The two men at the corner table."

She nodded. "Yeah, that's my table."

"Did you hear what the two men were talking about?"

"Why? Friends of yours?"

I took twenty dollars from my wallet and handed her the bill. "Yes, old friends."

The waitress smirked. "I heard nothing 'cept the Spanish guy says to the other one, 'No one is stopping you from doing what you want to do.' That's all I heard."

The five margaritas churning in my bladder determined my next move. In the men's room, reasonable excuses came first. Maybe Fontana had an upset stomach, I told myself. But my reporter's inquisitiveness didn't buy it. What did Fontana have to fear from being recognized, I wondered. Afraid of going hungry at the expense of needy fans? A word to Mickey Marino—and perhaps an autographed photo—and he would see that meddlesome moochers were ushered away from Fontana's table. Why shun the fame, the admiration, the awe of these people? Why hide his face if the sight of him will inspire them to tell everyone they know, "I sat near Ricky Fontana at dinner!"

The urgency with which he protected his privacy prickled me. He should know I wasn't about to announce to the room that Ricky Fontana was sitting at table ten. Why should he need protection from me, who portrayed him so admiringly to the world?

Chapter Three

No need for a wake-up call from the front desk; I've got Driggs. No need for a wife to turn life's shortest hurdles into ten-foot barbed wire fences; I've got Driggs. You've got your boss; I've got Earl Driggs, who proudly tells anyone who will listen that he never wears a tie, runs a five-minute mile, and remains undefeated at the staff lounge pool table.

A curious child—but who isn't at age seven?—I once asked my father for a sip of the whiskey he was enjoying one night. He obliged me. "One sip," he said, "but no more." It burned. He laughed at my grimace, which only made me determined to drink more, to be grown-up. My old man put away two tumblers full of scotch before dinner, so when he left the table to watch the headlines, I took another full sip. If Daddy drinks two glasses, I thought, a little more won't matter. Later, he went to piss and abandoned his drink, so I had more. Finally, he went into the kitchen to help my mother with dinner, and I finished the glass. My poor mother. Proud chef that she was, she deserved better than watching her son regurgitate bacon-wrapped meatloaf across her clean tablecloth. When I woke the next morning with a terrible headache, she explained that God was punishing me for having too much to drink.

Driggs woke me at six thirty a.m. on the morning after my Fontana sighting. My head was throbbing and my muscles ached and my stomach churned, and all I could think about was my mother and her folksy explanation for a hangover. So I said to Driggs with my cracked lips and sticky tongue, "God is punishing me."

"What? What the fuck are you talking about?"

"Never mind."

"We're fucked," said Driggs. "Did you hear?"

The *Tribune* was sinking fast. Blame classified ads moving online, or blame apathy, illiteracy, or the recession—no matter what, our circulation had tumbled every year for the past five. Few readers downloaded the *Tribune*'s smartphone and tablet apps, and the company refused to pay the outlandish fees to publish an e-reader edition. I kept plugging away while advertisers fled with droves of readers. What else could I do?

Driggs wasn't calling to tell me all that.

"We could be going under, Jerry. The Rudolphs are tired of losing money, and the scuttlebutt around the corner offices is that they're ready to concede to the other dailies."

The Rudolphs—siblings Herman and Esther—were the current owners and publishers of the *Tribune*, which had been in their family since their great-great-grandfather, Francis Rudolph, published the first ten-page issue of the newspaper in 1845. My booze-addled brain conjured an image of Frankie, as we referred to the mutton-chopped man in a boardroom portrait, heroically bent over his handiwork, scouring the pages for errors, lest a mistake sully his reputation as the finest journalist in New York, and the first newsman in the city to demand the abolition of slavery.

"But the history, the tradition," I stammered.

"Fuck it!" Driggs shouted. "Two more advertisers just made it official. Gone! That's the bottom line." His voiced softened. "I just wanted you to hear it from me. Before Joe or Tony told you something that isn't true. The fourth quarter numbers came in, and, well…they aren't pretty. The paper's in trouble; that's all I know."

"Thanks, Earl," was all I could manage. I said good-bye, got dressed, and left for the ballpark.

I trusted only one man to allay the fear of losing my job. That night, after the first Mets exhibition game, I called Joe Lippincott, the *Tribune* columnist covering the Yankees. Joe and I had been colleagues for nearly twelve years. Before his sports career, Joe had written a popular sex advice column for an alternative weekly. He called those days his "cliterary career." Then, not long after joining the Metro Sports desk, Joe heard the good news: Jesus Christ would soon return to reward the righteous and judge the rest. Joe became a Christian. Born again, he lost a lot of friends. New York journalists are a cynical and skeptical bunch, and most of us stopped calling Joe when, in his enthusiasm, he would ask if he could tell us about his Lord and Savior. Most of us told him to fuck right off.

I didn't. I listened. Joe was a good friend and a great sportswriter. I would not judge him for his devotion, though I seldom attended church. "There is no God but Torre," I told Joe when he asked if I was a Christian. "And Jeter is his prophet." Joe laughed at my blasphemous joke and hadn't bothered me again about my drinking and my godlessness. Thank God!

Maybe Joe would know something about the plight of our employers. Certainly he'd know more than I did about Ricky Fontana's dinner partner.

"What can you tell me about Eusebio Hernandez?" I asked him.

"Seb? Besides the obvious?" Joe was referring to the appearance by Hernandez in the Mitchell Report, the 2007 dossier on steroid users in baseball. A lab technician in California told investigators that he sent human growth hormone to Hernandez in 2005. Hernandez admitted the indiscretion, but claimed he used the performance enhancers only to recover from a knee injury.

Joe said, "Seb was a loner. Always kept to himself. Why?"

"I ran into Hernandez eating last night with Ricky Fontana. That was the first time I've ever seen Fontana with another player outside of the ballpark."

"That *is* strange. I've never known Seb to fraternize with his teammates. Except for team meetings and travel days, the only time I ever saw Seb with the team was on the field. I think he didn't want to tarnish the younger guys with his past."

"Did Hernandez know Fontana before they reached the pros?" I asked.

"Probably not. Seb's twelve years older and signed straight out of the Venezuelan leagues. Where is Fontana from? New England, right? That's a long way from Caracas. Could be they were pen pals."

We laughed. "Speaking of long-distance relationships," Joe continued, "did you get a panicked call from Driggs today?"

"Yep. Should we be worried?" I asked cautiously.

"No, no," he said. "Driggs predicts disasters like this every few weeks." He affected Driggs's gruff baritone. "Print media is frickin' dead, Joe! The bloggers! The bloggers! They're coming for us, Joe, straight from their mamas' basements!"

I laughed at Joe's spot-on impression. "True," I said. "The boss needs to take his Zoloft and let us worry about writing good copy."

Joe said placidly, "Whatever happens to the *Trib* will happen for a reason. It's all part of God's plan. The paper may indeed shut down. If that's what the good Lord wills for us, so be it."

No deity who'd take my job could be called "good," I thought, but I said nothing. To believe he had a soul that had been saved was Joe's way to cope with being ordinary. Good for him. But I needed my byline. As much as my name caught thousands of eyes each day, I couldn't shake the feeling that I was just a generic and talentless man like any other. That is the worst fate of any.

The closest icon to godliness in my life was a liar. He lied to my face. Two days after I saw him at Mickey Maco's, Ricky Fontana tried to tell me he hadn't been there. Of course I had to ask him—there might be a front-page story in the secretive dinner between Hernandez and Fontana. A meeting between an up-and-coming slugger and a needle-plunging pariah could make for sexy headlines, I thought, though I needn't jump to conclusions. Fontana could dine with any of 800 major leaguers, and odds are good he would have been sitting across from a juicer.

But when I caught him after the next day's practice, he simply lied. He paled, his eyes gaped, and then he lied. I knew he was lying, and he knew I knew. But he did it anyway.

"Wasn't there," Ricky said coolly. "I don't know what you're talking about."

"Are you sure? I'm quite sure it was you."

That look again, fear and shame. "I just told you I wasn't there."

"Okay, Ricky, my mistake." I shrugged. "Good game today!"

❖

If Ricky Fontana wanted to avoid the spotlight, he didn't help himself by making a mockery of every pitching staff that opposed the Mets during spring training. He went hitless in his first exhibition game, but the following day he went four for four against the Cardinals. Facing the Orioles, he had two hits, and the next day he added two more against the Indians. In Fort Myers, he hit a home run off of Pete Thryft that traveled over 500 feet, according to a groundskeeper. The cameras beaming the game back to the Red Sox faithful in frigid New England caught Thryft mouthing the words "Holy shit!" as he watched the ball sail away.

In March, he swung the bat with the confidence of a player hitting his summer stride. That spring, I speculated in one column that Fontana spent the winter someplace warm playing ball, studying video of every pitcher he might face, scrutinizing their pitching motions for any advantage (Miller tips his curveball by holding his glove higher during the set; Santana's knee bends less when he's going to throw the changeup) so that when he arrived in Port St. Lucie it was as if he had already faced the men who had the unfortunate task of throwing a baseball past him.

After another powerful outburst (four for four against the Marlins), I asked Fontana how he spent his winter. He demurred, at first. Why did I want to know? I explained that I suspected he had not taken the winter off. Did he travel to Venezuela or the Dominican Republic—the only places major league-quality pitchers are throwing during November, December, and January? Did he go to Cuba and play under a pseudonym, raking deadly forkballs and curves that will never be seen by a prime-time audience thanks to Castro? I asked, *"Se habla español, Señor Fontana?"* He laughed. No, he said, he had not left his mama and baby bro alone on Thanksgiving, Christmas, and New Year's Day. He spent the off-season at home in Rhode Island. Poring over video? No, he assured me that he had not been watching tapes of Yankees pitcher Timon Torres, even though Fontana seemed to know Timmy was throwing a fastball in the first inning and a curveball in the third, for he drilled both pitches over the outfield fence at Steinbrenner Field. Just a lucky guess, Fontana said. Two lucky guesses, I reminded him.

Fontana's increasing timidity (and the Hernandez incident) tempted me to ask Driggs for permission to fly to Rhode Island and interview Celeste Fontana. Of course, the moment I set foot on her front lawn, I would never again be granted an exclusive interview with the man whose every movement I was paid to follow. And what could Celeste tell me about the abilities of her son that dumbfounded forty-year baseball veterans? I had interviewed the parents of pro athletes before. Besides baby photos and cute anecdotes, I learned nothing that would interest *Tribune* readers. And, after two years, I already knew Ricky Fontana better than any other sportswriter in New York. Maybe even better than his teammates.

Which is to say, I knew little more than nothing about him.

His height, his weight, his birthday, and his minor league statistics—the Mets made little else known to the media about him. The team drafted Fontana weeks after his high school graduation. He was seventeen. As a senior, he batted over .600. He was an average student at Ladley Senior High School. Four years there produced one cute story, which I squeezed from Fontana's high school coach during his rookie season. On the day Fontana was scheduled to take his SAT exam, the Ladley Browns had a game against a rival school. The coach told the Browns he would reschedule the game. "Don't bother," Fontana piped up. "I don't need the SATs. I'm going straight to the major leagues." The anecdote was repeated hundreds of times. It was the only story radio or TV commentators had to fill in the many moments of inaction during a baseball game, when Fontana stepped out of the batter's box to clean his spikes, take practice swings, adjust his gloves, or look lazily toward the third base coach for a sign.

None of us who covered the team had ever seen him outside the ballpark. None of us knew what music he enjoyed, what movies he watched, or his favorite TV shows. We didn't know who he dated. One year before, the blogs blazed when Fontana arrived at the ESPY Awards to be crowned Best Breakthrough Athlete. On his arm was Mindy Kennedy, star of FOX's *SoCal Nights*. But though the eager paparazzi searched, Fontana and the starlet were never again spotted together. Kennedy's publicist said the two "were just good friends."

I had never seen him socialize with teammates, which is why after I spotted him at Mickey Maco's, I asked Tony to help me answer questions that puzzled me after our accidental run-in. How did Fontana know Seb Hernandez? Why were they dining together? What was the significance of Hernandez's inspiring charge to Fontana? *"Nobody is stopping you from doing what you want to do."*

"Be obsessed," I told Tony. "Dig up whatever you can. There is a mystery to this guy. Let's figure it out!"

I expected Tony and I might come to a disturbing conclusion: Ricky Fontana was using performance-enhancing drugs. What other secret would a ballplayer guard so warily? Perhaps in retirement, Eusebio Hernandez had taken on the role of steroid supplier to the stars. He had motive (his total career earnings were a paltry $2.2 million), he had a past suspension for HGH abuse, and he had connections—in many South American and Caribbean nations (like Hernandez's native Venezuela), steroids and hormonal cheats were available in street corner pharmacies. If Fontana indeed snapped the modern single-season batting record and broke DiMaggio's streak, then these achievements, like Barry Bonds's home run records, would be tainted with suspicion if my hunch were correct. Disaster for our game! Though such a discovery could boost my career, I ached to be wrong.

Throughout March, Fontana sent baseballs soaring through the Florida sky like rockets from Cape Canaveral. But high batting averages in spring training mean little to sportswriters who have followed the game for decades. So some, including Budd Crane, continued to scoff at Fontana's lofty statistics. "He's facing minor league pitchers in meaningless exhibition games," Crane protested. "And we all know that hitters have the early advantage because pitchers take longer to reach regular season readiness." Still, many media men who followed the team—including my friends Rule and Callahan, who were once skeptical of an aging ballplayer's claims about Fontana's fantastic abilities—began to whisper: He just might be able to do it.

Fontana's final gaudy line for the spring: In thirty games, he batted .417 with nine homers, nineteen runs batted in, and, of course, two marriage proposals. A fan in Tampa and another in Port St. Lucie held aloft signs for Fontana that read, "Marry me, Ricky!"

❖

Bad news, it had to be. She wasn't there when I arrived at our apartment wanting her and my bed and her in my bed. I inhaled the smell of her, still heavy on the air. She hadn't been gone long. I drew in that scent, that milky, organic scent, to replace the dry air from the jetliner's cabin, and suddenly, I felt clean and warm and home at last. My suspicions faded, and I sat in my armchair, took off my shoes, and opened a book. My mind drifted, though, and soon my imagination offered better entertainment: Plans, wicked plans of what I would do with her, to her, once she arrived and had to her satisfaction followed the requisite re-acquaintance routines that her unyielding sense of decorum demanded.

Time passed. My arousal passed, replaced by impatience, then frustration, then anger coupled by a throbbing compulsion to pleasure myself. Instead I poured a drink and refilled it. When I was done, I refilled again with heartbeat regularity for the next two hours. Meanwhile, my mind blundered into anxious thoughts. She was having an affair, I concluded. She woke up this morning facing the portrait of me that she keeps on her nightstand and she felt no joy—in fact, she had wished instead to be asleep again, back to a vision of falling or escaping a pursuer or public shame that was somehow a respite from her waking life, her marriage to a very ugly and small man. I fell asleep, but it wasn't long before the rattle of keys awakened me.

"Where were you?"

"At Sara's."

"But tonight is my first night home. Why are you home so late?"

"I was hoping you'd be asleep."

"Why?"

Now she began to turn red. "Because I'm mad, Jerry, and I didn't want to spoil your first night home with a fight."

"A fight about what?"

"I don't want to talk about it."

"Too late."

She sighed. "I want something else. I want a child, a baby. I want two or three! I want to leave Manhattan."

"We've talked about kids and how hard it would be with both of us working. I was only promoted two years ago, after all, and until then we didn't have enough money."

"So you want to have a baby?"

"No, I didn't say that."

"Why?"

"Because I would make a lousy dad."

"Why?"

"Because I'm just not cut out for it."

"Why?"

"Because. Just because," and now I was shouting. "Kids, they're like water. They start out clean, but mix them with shit like me, and they get fucking brackish, you understand?"

An ugly truth crossed her face. "You're drunk."

"I'm not." But I was.

"I know this routine. You come home and get wasted and all you want is to…" She seemed to search for a word. "Fuck. Not even make love to your wife. To fuck."

"That's not true." But it was.

"You're an asshole."

"No, not so."

"I'm sorry. I didn't mean that," she said with her head in her hands. She sighed. "Yes, I did. I do. Maybe it would be better if I slept at Sara's tonight."

"Don't bother," I said. I left with my unpacked suitcase and checked into a hotel near Herald Square and emptied the minibar. The next morning, I wandered into the midtown crowd and admired the city. And I fell in love again.

I'm a rare New Yorker. Not many in my hometown stop to admire the city, to smell its breath, to hear its pulse, which I think is a little like making love to a beautiful woman with your eyes closed.

Despite the jarring events of the previous night and my grating hangover, I found comfort when, as usual, I was the only rider in my subway car unoccupied by a newspaper or smartphone except for a young woman leaning over a baby carriage. Smiling, a new mother stroking her first child. Her first—I knew it was because she touched the baby clinically, almost without affection, brushing his head with the back of her hand tentatively, counting his breaths and confirming that he was still warm, all the while astonished that she had produced him, and with nervous excitement considered the work and care his breaths would require as they accumulated. I smiled. Produced in pleasure and delivered in pain, the child was a proof-of-purchase to his parents, a receipt that verified both man and woman had lived and would be remembered. Nearing my fifth decade and still childless, I would live forever in my bylines. My name would endure.

I watched the other commuters carefully. There are four million women in New York, and most of them are beautiful—and that morning they seemed suddenly accessible. I admired them. I observed what they were reading. That morning a pretty blonde in a short skirt and tan pantyhose and a tall, dark-skinned teenager in a Rangers jersey were reading my column. She chewed gum while she read, and her head bounced like an outfielder chasing fly balls in new cleats. The teenager read while standing, squashed into a corner, and every few words he spoke silently to himself. Both seemed engrossed; I had done my job well. My final column of the pre-season predicted the Mets would finally catch the Atlanta Braves thanks to the pitching of Oscar Ferrera, the scrappy base stealing of Jackie Rios, and, of course, record-breaking offense from Ricky Fontana.

It's a funny thing to be a public figure and yet so unrecognized. More than a few times, I've stopped myself from approaching a reader to ask, "Are you enjoying my article?" I admit that I've conspicuously opened the *Tribune* to my byline and laughed aloud to earn a few over-the-shoulder readers. But, alas, nobody acknowledges me except for a few aspiring school-age journalists who want advice or fans who disagree with my baseball opinions.

And even if I had approached the teen or the blonde, they would have thought I was crazy. Only drunks or lunatics or tourists talk to strangers in New York.

Only a lunatic, I think, could root for the Yankees, the overpaid, overexposed foils to my Mets. Still, on the subway that morning, a man in a Yankees cap and jacket was bent over his iPhone. When I peered over his shoulder, I saw my face. On the phone's tiny screen, I was speaking to the other panelists on *The Amazin's Hour.* The host was asking me why Ricky Fontana, now the face of his team, made fewer public appearances than his teammates. The night before the show's taping, Fontana had skipped the annual Mets Welcome Home dinner and charity fundraiser. Why should he be so mysterious?

A clue came two days later.

Tara had not answered my phone calls, and she had instructed her friends to lie about her whereabouts. Yet she remained in New York—she had come home periodically while I was at my office to remove her clothes and books from our apartment—and she was on my mind constantly until Tony called on the day before opening day and life, as it inevitably does, changed irreversibly.

Before Tony called, I didn't know anything about Carlos Jackson. His name was meaningless to me, as he was a minor league ballplayer who spent his career on buses between 5,000-seat ballparks. I would soon learn from Tony everything there was to know about Jackson that could be determined from Baseball-Reference.com. Born in 1986, Jackson was six feet tall and weighed 210 pounds (although Tony said the team was flattering the portly third baseman, whose uniform seemed uncomfortably tight in the few photos Tony found online). Raised in the Dominican Republic and later the Bronx, Jackson was selected in the thirty-third round of the 2007 draft by the Washington Nationals. After two sub-par seasons, Jackson toured the country in a wild series of demotions, promotions, and trades that saw him wearing the home uniform in Durham, Las Vegas, and Walla Walla. It was during his time in Durham that he had an encounter with an up-and-coming outfielder named Ricky Fontana that compelled Tony to call me.

"Fontana's no choirboy," Tony said.

"What do you mean?" I asked. "Is he a juicer?"

"I thought so at first. Two years ago in the minor leagues, Ricky Fontana was suspended for five games. But not for PEDs. He belted some guy in the head—another player, his name is Carlos Jackson."

"Why the hell would he do that? Ricky's as cool as they come."

"Jackson was harassing Fontana's teammates. That's all I got out of their manager, Jeff Steig. He's still the skipper down in Durham."

"No shit."

Violence and the emotions needed to inspire it were not part of Fontana's character. In a game during Fontana's first season, a Mets pitcher clocked a batter for the Atlanta Braves in the elbow with a fastball that made a sickening crack on impact. Fontana was first up for the Mets in the following inning. The Braves pitcher threw subtlety aside and a fastball at Ricky's head. Long before fans at Turner Field heard the earflap on Fontana's helmet crack, even as the ball was rolling off the pitcher's fingertips, and maybe as soon as the pitcher began his windup, everyone in the ballpark knew that Fontana was going to get beaned. Shocked and momentarily deafened, he fell over backward.

As if a bugle had sounded, the Mets dugout emptied. The Braves players also charged to the field. How many millionaire bare-knuckle boxing champs are there? None. That's why punches are rarely thrown at the ballpark. The clash between Mets and Braves, like most baseball scrums, was a mosh pit of threats, cursing, and shoving inspired more by fraternal obligation than rage. Still, in the midst of the brawl, Fontana was nowhere to be found. While the testosterone surged and the crowd jeered and the umpires dove into the crowd of players to separate the most energetic pushers, I spotted Fontana standing on first base. Calmly, he motioned to the bewildered batboy to bring him another helmet.

Punch another player? Not Flushing's Fontana.

According to Tony, Carlos Jackson had a ballgame to play in Spokane later that night. He would be batting sixth and playing third base and thus would be difficult to reach between the hours of seven and eleven p.m. Fortunately, I phoned his agent at five and placed a call to Jackson's cell phone at five fifteen, just as he was stepping off the team bus, which had been stuck in traffic, Jackson told me.

He didn't have to answer questions about being the loser of a one-punch fight four years ago. Then again, his name in the papers could only help his going-nowhere-except-Spokane career.

"Yes, Ricky Fontana hit me. Why you wanna know?"

I could have told him the story of the Braves beanball. To keep things simple, I explained that Fontana is known in New York for keeping his cool.

"His team was dissing me. Rios, Reynolds, those guys. I lost my temper and I yelled back at them."

"What did you say?"

"I don't know."

"Why did Fontana hit you, then?"

"Defending his teammates, I guess."

"Are you sure you can't remember what you said to them? Did you use any ethnic slurs?"

"Huh? No. Rios, he's Dominican, too."

"What about Reynolds? What did you say to him?"

"I dunno. Yeah. I called him a faggot."

"Are you sure?"

"Yeah. That fucking fag would rather fuck me than fight me. Fontana was protecting his faggot teammate."

CHAPTER FOUR

The slur meant nothing to me. I didn't bother to investigate whether Greg Reynolds, the target of Jackson's epithet, was gay. Working around ballplayers had numbed me to the vocabulary of the casual bigot. As Joe DiMaggio's teammates had affectionately referred to him as "Daig" (short for "dago"), the ballplayers I had known casually peppered their speech with racial slurs. One almost expects to hear such talk in a locker room, especially among an increasingly diverse group of players who, in order to avoid offending anyone, offend everyone equally. To many black players, "nigga" was a multipurpose word: an exclamation, a pronoun, a term of camaraderie. White kids were "rubes" and "crackers." Latino players used a vast lexicon of epithets that I couldn't decipher; each player seemed to be an ethnic taxonomist with a slang term for players from other Latin American countries, and each nation seemed to have its own colloquialisms. I had heard "fag" thousands of times, and more often than not, a ballplayer was using the word as a catchall insult, when "asshole" just wasn't quite right.

His demeanor as macho as his hitting was mediocre, Jackson was the kind of insecure man who used the word as an unspecific derision and as an anti-gay slur. I'm sure he spat the syllable toward a pitcher who had thrown too far inside or used it as an accusation if he felt he was getting too much attention in the locker room. A batboy who threw awkwardly, a fan who stared too long, a reporter who asked too many questions. These were all loose definitions of "faggot" to Carlos Jackson.

Fontana must have known that. Perhaps, I thought, he was resisting a cruel double standard. If a player had publicly called another "nigger" or "chink" or "kike," he would be kicked off his team or at least suspended. But athletes use "faggot" with few consequences. Even if he'd called Greg Reynolds a fag in front of TV cameras, Carlos Jackson could expect only a petty fine.

A gay ballplayer would make for huge headlines, but I can't say that I'd ever been driven to investigate rumors that a player might be gay. And there were always rumors. For years, I'd heard whispers about certain major leaguers and even a few retired stars. But fans cared more for sports-related scandal than sex. Readers devoured steroid rumors. We loved turning up cheaters. There is more dignity in chasing down urine sample results and pharmacy shipping receipts than investigating who your team's shortstop is fucking. Whenever a player broke the law, we sportswriters were there to document his fall. Yet even in the media culture of gossip and confession, only the seediest blogs broke stories on the sex lives of sports stars.

I thought I had reached a dead end. I told Tony I believed Carlos Jackson was hiding something, a past injury to Fontana that inspired Fontana to belt him. "Or maybe Jackson wasn't lying," Tony suggested. "Maybe Ricky was just defending his teammates."

Or he was having a bad day. He had a headache, a sore arm, a hangover. A fight with his mother over the phone had upset him, or he hadn't gotten laid in weeks. There could be innumerable reasons for Ricky Fontana to step outside of himself one night and strike another man.

A good reporter knows that the truth is always more complicated than what he writes under his byline. Eleven years after he first heard the word "faggot," Fontana told the story that follows to Mick Kelleher, his teammate and roommate. Kelleher, backup catcher for the Mets, agreed to be interviewed for a series of columns on Ricky Fontana that I used in writing this book.

He'd always felt like an outsider, Fontana told Kelleher, even before he knew why. Then one word crystallized his separateness, a word Fontana learned at age eight. Far from the schoolgirl's pinup he would become, in third grade, little Ricky was chubby and bucktoothed. His cocoa-colored hair was straighter then, and his mother thought it would be cute to let it grow, so Ricky wore it in a shoulder-length mop. His clothes—also chosen by Celeste—were mostly hand-me-downs from a cousin. He was to his classmates an awkward, nerdy fop.

At lunch one day, Ricky wandered his school playground aimless and friendless, as he often did when he finished Mama's tuna fish sandwiches. He spotted Adam Edgar, a sixth-grader, and a group of his friends squatting in one corner of the playground and laughing. Ricky had long admired Adam from afar; the older boy was tall, a giant to Ricky, and he had recently sprouted little black hairs from his knees to his shins that fascinated Ricky, who absentmindedly rubbed his knee while he watched Adam and his friends. Not feeling particularly courageous, mostly curious, Ricky wandered to where the older boys were playing until he was close enough to view what he admired most about Adam, a white badge that read "Character, Courage, Loyalty" sewn onto the black Little League jersey that he wore unbuttoned with a white T-shirt underneath.

"What are you looking at, Chubbo?" Adam demanded. Ricky had been unaware that his dreamy walk had ended only a few feet away from the boys. They were sitting in a circle and using twigs to poke a series of anthills that served as entrances and exits to a colony built by the tiny black bugs below the pavement.

"Nothing," Ricky said shyly.

"Well, what do you want?" Adam asked.

Ricky quaked in his sandals. "You play for the Hawks?"

Adam beamed. "Yep, that's right. I pitched in our first game on Sunday. We won nine to four. Mike had two hits." He nodded toward a sandy-haired boy busily filling in an anthill. Mike looked up, nodded, and then went back to work.

Should he dare? He did. "Could I play for the Hawks?" Ricky asked. Now stunned by his own courage, Ricky kept talking. "I play center field. I can hit, too. I practice at the cages at the arcade. I never miss a pitch."

"No way, Chunky," Adam said. And with that, his friends burst into laughter. "You've gotta be at least eleven to play Little League."

A girl's voice interrupted them. "What are you doing?"

Another sixth grader, a blonde in jeans and a ponytail, was peering into the center of the circle of boys.

"Playing with these ants," said Mike, and he held up a twig swarming with them.

"Ew," said the girl. "You guys are total dorks."

"Be careful, Cindy," said Mike. "You might get ants *in your cunt*!" And Mike heaved the twig toward the little girl. She stumbled backward on her heels. The stick bounced off her jeans.

Cindy fled, all the while repeating, "Ew! Ew! Ew! Ew!"

The older boys laughed. Ricky watched them and decided he should laugh, too. Adam stopped giggling for a moment, and Ricky's curiosity got the better of him.

"What's a cunt?" he asked.

The rest of the boys, recharging from the last comedic episode, burst into hoots and snorts again.

"Dude, you have got to be kidding me," Adam wheezed. "You don't know what a cunt is?"

He knew he shouldn't answer honestly. But he did. Ricky shook his head.

The cackling grew louder.

Adam could barely explain between guffaws. "It's the part on a girl where your dick goes, stupid."

Now amazement trumped self-consciousness, and Ricky asked, "Why would I want to put my dick in a girl?"

Two of the boys collapsed into giddy, spitting convulsions of surprised laughter. Adam had fallen to his knees and was hugging his chest to keep himself steady.

"What's so funny?" Ricky asked, trying to chuckle. "I don't get it." Adam couldn't answer, so Ricky took him by the arm and shook him. "What's so funny?"

Adam stopped laughing and yanked his arm away. "Don't touch me, fucker."

His friends stopped laughing.

"No," Ricky said, jabbing his finger toward Adam's face. "It's not nice to laugh at people."

Then Adam pushed Ricky. He fell over backward and landed on his rump. "Fuck off, kid."

Ricky felt his throat tighten and the back of his eyes grow heavy with tears. He swallowed and blinked hard to stifle them. He kicked at Adam, and landed his sandaled foot squarely in Adam's chest.

Adam and Michael dove at Ricky, still on his back, and punched and kicked him, pulling at his hair. "Faggot!" Adam screamed. "You fucking little faggot." And then he clubbed Ricky with his bristly knee.

❖

Adam Edgar remembers the fight. When I interviewed him for this book, Edgar was twenty-five, an assistant manager at a restaurant in Providence, Rhode Island. His memory of the playground tussle surely improved with Fontana's fame (or infamy). Still, Edgar tells the story of introducing Fontana to the slur that would change his life without boasting. He even made sure to explain that he has friends who are gay and his girlfriend's sister is a lesbian.

I never had the chance to ask Ricky Fontana about Adam Edgar. But eleven years later, when I asked him about another fight over the word "faggot," he turned bright red. I asked him about Carlos Jackson and Fontana cursed at me.

"Where the fuck did you hear that?" Ricky was in a T-shirt and sliding shorts. He stopped oiling his glove when I mentioned the incident with Jackson. He flipped the cap shut on the linseed oil bottle and angrily stuffed his glossy mitt into his bag. He turned his back to me as he grabbed clothes from his locker.

In retrospect, I am amazed at my composure. It was the first time I had ever heard him swear.

"Oh, lots of folks remember that fight. It was the only instance that Jeff Steig remembers seeing you lose your temper."

It was opening day. He had gone two for four with two runs batted in against the Cardinals. He had answered dozens of questions already about the curveball he drilled for a double in the fifth inning and his expectations for the season ahead, his performance, his team's performance, but unlike that hook from Jake Lieber, Fontana had not seen my question coming.

"Carlos Jackson is a—"

His Adam's apple bobbed as he swallowed his conclusion. And he forced a smile.

"That was a long time ago," he finally said. I grinned at the absurdity of a twenty-year-old with a retiree's regrets. "I was a younger man. I made a mistake. I never should have hit him."

He had done it again, the son of a bitch. Fontana charm waylaid another prying reporter.

"Okay, Ricky. Good game today, by the way."

There were many more good games to come.

Barry Bonds called that April for Ricky Fontana "the greatest hitting performance I have ever seen." Willie Mays swore to reporters that he had never hit so well for so long. Pete Rose joked, "I've got ten grand on Fontana for MVP." And when reached for comment, Mike Schmidt, Mark McGwire, and Tony Gwynn began their quotes with the same word: "Wow." A *Boston Herald* columnist wrote, "Somewhere in a freezer in Arizona, Ted Williams's head must be spinning."

I asked someone in the Yankees front office if he was disappointed that a Met was stealing all the local headlines. "Hell no!" he exclaimed, "I've got Fontana on my fantasy team."

That is to say nothing of the hyperbole with which every baseball writer, from grizzled columnists to amateurs with no-name blogs, covered Fontana's record setting pace during April in his second season. If the writers had their way, Fontana would have been the first twenty-year-old elected to the Hall of Fame. Folks who didn't follow baseball had to wonder why so many grown men had lost their minds. After all, only lunatics could earnestly refer to a ballplayer with words like "epic," "majestic," "heroic," "awe-inspiring," and, my favorite, "godlike." After a CBS newscaster described a Fontana home run with breathless admiration, a female anchor remarked, "I wish my husband talked about me like that."

My counterparts fed the cult of Fontana with their own worshipful pieces:

"Amazing is a word used too often and too casually to describe the New York Mets. It's even used as the team's nickname. But Ricky Fontana changes the meaning of the word with each at bat."—Dick Rule, *New York Daily News*

"Anyone and everyone who has watched Fontana during April has no doubt that he is on pace to record the best season in the history of Major League Baseball."—Paul Callahan, *New York Post*

Suddenly, the hottest story in New York City was on my beat. Fontana slugged. Fontana walloped. Fontana mashed. And he did it all with mechanical efficiency, day in and out, a joy to watch, reviving me, beaming life into me each time his eyes widened in that beautiful moment when he recognized an incoming pitch and the destiny of a mitt-bound baseball was altered forever. After midnight on the morning of May 1, Budd Crane called me. He knew I would answer my phone. The Mets had beaten the Dodgers in extra innings, and both Crane and I were struggling to find unused adjectives to describe Fontana's game-winning home run to our readers. "Titanic?" I asked. "No, too cliché. How about mammoth?" "I dunno. I try to stay away from dinosaur-related adjectives." "But mammoths were mammals." "Never mind. No. How about towering?" "I used that to describe his eleventh homer." "I know. That's what I called number thirteen." "No shit? Okay, then let's call this one…supersonic." "Maybe if it was more of a line drive, but tonight's homer wasn't as far as it was high." "I like the space theme, though. How about rocketing, soaring, blast-off?" "Not bad, actually. Something about the ball now being in orbit…" "Stratospheric?" "Good one! Back to earth for a sec. Booming, resonant, thunderous?" "Thunderclap—that's a cool synonym for a homer." "Forget it, that one's mine." "Fair enough. How about meteoric? Asteroidal? Comet-ish?" "Are those real words?" "I don't know."

"I need a new thesaurus," Crane said. We laughed.

"I better get back to writing. Talk to you later, Budd."

I was about to hang up and then I heard Crane's voice, distant and tinny, "Jerry? Jerry?"

"Yeah?"

"Still there?"

"Obviously."

"I wanted to ask you, do you still think he can do it? Hit four hundred, I mean. And break the streak? Because I am beginning to think he can. I really do."

At that moment, I also began to believe.

Tara didn't answer my calls. She didn't respond to my e-mails. I was waiting for the divorce like Fontana looks for a fastball on a 3-0 count, but it never arrived. No papers served, no lawyers calling—a pitchout. Fine. I was too busy to dwell. Fontana's star blazed, and my byline reflected its glow. There were bubbles in my booze. My connections to Fontana were well known in Bristol, Connecticut, where an ESPN program director called me to offer analysis for *One Amazin' April*, a TV special on Fontana's fabulous month. Now my Twitter followers included the best in the business, top sportswriters whose nationwide influence I had for years envied, in addition to a tidal wave of fans who hung on the statistical nuggets that Tony prepared and tweeted every night. My Facebook page gained 25,000 friends.

In a column in early May, I coined the term "Fontanarama" to describe the city's reaction to Ricky's sophomore spring. The word was fun to say, and I thought there should be a name for the event, the nightly craze to follow Fontana's performance, the astonishing proliferation of Fontana merchandise—the most newsworthy pop culture happening in Queens since Beatlemania. The word appeared in newspapers, on television, and even the video scoreboard at Citi Field, which lit up with cartoon fireworks and "Fontanarama!" whenever Ricky hit a home run and the famous apple in left field rose from its hiding spot.

That word, and the baseball craze it described, would spread across the country as the season continued. I really felt like I had hit the big time weeks later when a female rapper named Elli recorded a song containing the lyric:

Ain't seen lines like this since outside Shea in '86
Wrappin' 'round the block and givin' Doc a case of coke dick
It's sick, this Dago bro be gettin' hits in every game
Magic new DiMaggio, he conquered and I came
Shreddin' fuckin' fastballs like the ax of Chuck Santana
Smoothest kid inside the box, my boy Fontanarama

Elli was from Jamaica, Queens. She was a huge Mets fan, she told *The Source* magazine, and also admitted, "I think Fontana is totally fuckable."

I'd never felt so hip.

Fontanarama enraptured jaded journalists, too. At the offices of *The New York Eagle-Tribune*, Tony and I were suddenly in demand. Everyone at our weekly editorial meeting grilled the men who captured the handsome Italian in words and on film.

"Where does he live?" demanded the real estate editor. "I want a story on his apartment."

"I've never seen him *anywhere*," complained our gossip columnist. "Does he order pizza every night?"

"Is there anything unique about his swing?" asked the science and technology editor. "Does he have fantastic eyesight?"

"Does he play any musical instruments?" asked our arts editor. "You must remember that feature we did on Bernie Williams and classical guitar."

"You know Ricky Fontana?" inquired copyeditors, deliverymen, mailroom clerks, the ombudsman, the layout staff. "What's he like?" Truthfully, I knew him no better than I did before he became a national hero. That didn't stop Tony and me from telling every Fontana-related anecdote we knew, and when we exhausted the true tales, we made up a few. Even though the baseball season was only a month old, the cult of Fontana flourished, and colleagues treated our Fontana fiction as gospel.

There were two men in New York unmoved by Fontana's fantastic April. The first was Hank Steinbrenner. The Yankees won eighteen of their first twenty-six games, but the Mets and their slugging right fielder won more daily coverage. Joe Lippincott said

Steinbrenner was furious. "Fontana was a third-round draft pick. Why the fuck didn't we sign this guy?" he raged to his assistants.

The second was Fontana himself. As the days passed in April, he withdrew. He was short, even surly to the newsmen he once charmed with smiles and friendly chatter. As his batting average soared, his mood sank. The swarm of reporters around his locker seemed to swell nightly. As the frontrunner in a horde that approached him after a victory over the Nationals on April 28, I saw that fear again in his eyes. He had whacked a double and a triple, helping the Mets defeat the Nats three to one. His brief, toneless responses to reporters were becoming conspicuous.

What was that pitch you hit for a double?

"A slider."

What do you think of Garcia's performance tonight?

"He was great."

Did you hurt your elbow when you dove in the fifth inning?

"No. I'm fine. No more questions, please."

He made our jobs difficult. All the Mets writers acknowledged that in the last thirty days, Ricky Fontana had become the most distant player on the team. But we didn't care. We gratefully gobbled his meager three-word quotes and reported them to fans starving for Fontana. And we didn't realize that we were his tormentors.

"He's so locked in right now," said Callahan, "He is the picture of focus and concentration."

"You know ballplayers and their superstitions," said Rule. "I wouldn't talk about the streak either."

I should have known that something more than the pressures of breaking a record troubled him. But I also attributed his dark mood to stress. He'll snap out of it, I thought, when he stops hitting. "But what if this carries on all year?" Crane asked me one night. "What if we can't get a quote from the best hitter on the team? We're fucked."

When April ended, Ricky Fontana was batting .443. In twenty-seven games he amassed fourteen home runs and thirty-four runs batted in. And he had reached base in more than sixty percent of his plate appearances. Perhaps Fontana had taken to heart Eusebio Hernandez's encouragement: No one is stopping you from doing what you want to do. He seemed to drive the ball with the force of his undaunted will.

I could picture Bob McCarty in his nursing home reading the box scores and wheezing and croaking triumphant laughs. Ricky Fontana had struck a base hit in every game in April. He was halfway to breaking Joe DiMaggio's streak of fifty-six consecutive games with a hit. McCarty's prophecy could come true in a month.

April 30 was a day off for the Mets. At *Tribune* headquarters, I was polishing another column when Tony called me to his computer. "Here, have a look at this!" He pointed to a tweet from a friend in midtown. The posting read: *"#rickyfontana hitting baseballs in bryant park! got me an autograph! it's #fontanarama here!"* Clicking the trending Fontana hashtags led us to more posts from Bryant Park. No hoax, we thought, grabbing our coats and huffing and puffing from the *Trib* offices near Herald Square to 42nd Street.

We heard the crowd long before we reached the park. Rising and falling, cheers bursting like waves against a dam, the sound crashed, only to rise again in anticipation. And preceding every cheer, a loud crack. Unmistakable, the sound of bat and ball. None more resonant than the smash of a Ricky Fontana swing. Atop an eight-foot stage, the idol in uniform. In pinstripe pants and his black warm-up jersey, Fontana stood with a bat propped against his hip, ankles crossed, signing a baseball. Then he took up the bat in one hand, tossed up the autographed ball, and thumped it into the squirming, cheering mob that stretched from the stage near Sixth Avenue to the back of the public library.

His fly ball skimmed outstretched fingertips and disappeared into the crowd. A dozen heads ducked into a scrum for the prize.

Fontana was hitting for a cause. Give Kids a Chance was a preferred Major League Baseball charity whose aim was to raise funds for needy children with chronic illnesses. Most of the baseballs he slapped gently into the crowd were unsigned. For a twenty-dollar donation to Give Kids a Chance, fans who retrieved the baseballs could have them personally inscribed by Ricky Fontana at the end of the event. While he stroked soft line drives around Bryant Park, Fontana's teammates Oscar Ferrara and Mick Kelleher, signed autographs at the foot of the stage and passed a donation box. The fitful crowd was ten times larger than the NYPD had expected. Fontana's unexpected last-minute appearance had turned the event into a mob scene.

❖

Nothing could have stopped Fontana's ascendance to baseball immortality—certainly not a new page on the calendar. He kept hitting. In the first seven games of May, he batted over .500, but on May 9, the streak almost ended. Astros pitcher Glen Flemming kept the Mets off-balance with cut fastballs and curves for seven innings. In the bottom of the ninth, Fontana, who was hitless in three at bats, led off against Felix Niñero, the Houston closer. There was no score.

Flemming had hardly fooled Fontana. In his first at bat, Ricky popped out meekly to the shortstop, but moments earlier, he had bashed a fastball down the left field line. The ball curved foul, missing the pole by four feet. In the fourth, he lined out sharply to third base. In the sixth, he slapped a grounder to the right side that almost eviscerated the first baseman, who somehow snared the ball and beat the sprinting Fontana to the bag. The Citi Field crowd groaned, and the home fans near the Astros dugout speculated loudly about the paternity and sexual proclivities of the Mets' opponents.

As Fontana stepped in against Niñero, all 34,645 paying customers rose to their feet. I leaned out of the press box and noticed all of Fontana's teammates were also standing, leaning against the protective screen in front of the dugout. Below me, a vendor wriggled out of the shoulder straps holding his foamy wares. The drinks at his feet sat unnoticed. Squatting behind the tarpaulin, the groundskeepers peeked out onto the field.

The first pitch to Fontana was a ball, outside.

The second pitch was a ball, too low.

The third pitch was a strike, lower inside corner.

The fourth pitch was a ball, outside.

The fifth pitch was a home run the moment it left the bat.

If only a leather and yarn ball could enjoy its blessed ride to glory! Hundreds of flashbulbs illuminated its flight and the gleaming faces of thousands of New Yorkers wished the baseball onward with expressions of hope and elation, urging the stitched sphere higher in its trajectory and farther in its objective. Had any ball hit at Citi Field inspired so much anxiety during its journey? I don't know. But there was no need for concern. The ball traveled 457 feet, landing safely in the bullpen.

Although following Fontana was not my charge until long after his Little League and varsity days, I suspect that he has never once stopped to admire a home run. He was running briskly around second base as the first of his teammates leapt from the dugout. He beat most of them to home plate, where a handful of the quickest Mets were waiting to embrace him as he scored the winning run in New York's 1-0 victory and, more importantly to the stunned men and women in the press box, ended the thirty-fourth consecutive game with a Ricky Fontana base hit. The streak survived.

Despite his reticence, Fontana would be at the ballpark answering questions for hours, I assumed, so I journeyed to the visitors' clubhouse to interview Glen Flemming and Felix Niñero. How did it feel, I asked, to almost break Ricky Fontana's streak? "I'd like to have that fastball back," admitted Niñero.

I asked Flemming, "Do you have any advice for Roy Rodriguez, tomorrow's starting pitcher?"

"Yes," he said. "Get a good night's sleep."

Fontana was gone. I arrived approximately fifteen minutes after his home run cleared the left field fence, but Fontana had disappeared. Callahan said, "He left after answering a few questions with the same jock cliché bullshit responses. 'I'm just glad we won the game.' 'Whatever it takes to help the team.' Then he excused himself and left. Motherfucker. Doesn't give me jack shit to work with, does it?"

"Fuck him," snapped a voice behind me. Several of the Mets players stopped their celebration. "Fuck Fontana!"

Ed Stanley leaned around his locker. "Hey, watch it!" snarled the Mets first baseman.

"No! Fuck Ricky Fontana!" Crane yelled again. Red-faced, panting, the slight reporter showed no fear as several players in various stages of undress encircled him.

"Watch it, man," warned Oscar Ferrera. "That's our man, Ricky."

Two TV cameramen fumbled with their equipment to catch the rest of the outburst. But Budd had regained some of his composure.

"I'm just trying to do my fucking job," Crane said, a half-whimper, half-shriek.

Callahan and I each took an arm and led him outside. The fresh air calmed him. But a beer did more good, and Crane described what happened after the game as we drank at a nearby Flushing bar.

Crane was a clever son of a bitch. Even though he had more experience, more readers, earned more, and wrote better than other Mets writers, Crane worked harder to get his stories. He wrote much-ballyhooed bios of players, detailed features on Mets personnel (including a two-part profile of the grounds crew), and often caught up with players in the off-season to update baseball-hungry fans on the off-field lives of their favorite major leaguers. Rule, Callahan, and I simultaneously resented and respected his work.

Years ago, Crane discovered the preferred cigarettes (Marlboro Lights) of Manolo Ortez, the head of security at the Shea Stadium players' parking lot. Although he quit smoking in the eighties, Crane carried a pack of Marlboros every day. Many a listless postgame recap was saved by quotes gleaned from players strolling to their cars. They were relaxed then, ready to face the drive home, and although they were surprised—even miffed—to find Crane leaning against their car or chatting with Manny at his security post, they spoke to him candidly. Crane realized early in his career that a player would say more to one reporter than to a gang of men with microphones and tape recorders.

"Fucking Fontana," Crane said sourly. "The moment we reached the clubhouse, Paul and I saw that he was in no mood to speak."

So Crane sneaked out of the stadium and, fishing through his pocket for a lighter, found Manny in his usual post by the entrance to the players' lot. He offered Manny a smoke. He figured that the reporters would soon tire of Fontana's monotonous responses and leave, allowing him to slip away. He was right. Ten minutes later, as Manny finished his second Marlboro Light, Fontana walked by, nodded a silent greeting, and strolled to his car. Leaning against the driver's door was Budd Crane with a pen, a notebook, and a shit-eating grin.

"Hi, Ricky. Do you have a second to answer a few questions?"

Fontana did not move.

"What was that pitch from Niñero? It looked like a slider."

Fontana said, "Get away from my car."

Crane stepped away from the car. "Okay. Sorry. So, were you thinking about the streak during your final at bat?"

At first, Fontana's mouth didn't move, but his eyes scanned Crane and settled on his breast pocket, bulging with his digital recorder.

"Please leave. No more questions. Don't follow me outside the stadium."

"I didn't follow you, Ricky. I was having a smoke with Manny. I've spoken to several of your teammates out here. And I speak to them at the golf course, at their charity events, at their apartments, so I don't—"

With the precision of a lunging cobra, Fontana's arm swung toward Crane, snatching his digital recorder from his pocket. He dropped the gadget to the ground and smashed it with his heel.

"Listen to me. And listen good. Don't follow me around outside of the ballpark. Do you understand?"

Crane nodded. It was only as Fontana sped away that Crane's anger erupted.

"So what? He broke your recorder," Callahan said. "The Old Grey Lady will buy you another. I remember once I had to interview Albert Belle. Now *there's* an asshole."

"The recorder is not the point," Crane said, pounding the bar with his fist and rattling our glasses. "It's our job to report what these fucking jocks do and say. To guys like Fontana, we're a nuisance at best. At worst, we're parasites. But without us, ballplayers are just nameless millionaires with numbers on their backs. In the era of free agency, players with eight-figure salaries come and go every season. Why should fans root for these men? Half of them don't even speak English. I'm doing the players a favor, putting their personal stories into context, reminding fans that these guys are human beings. Right? Right, Jerry?"

I could hold no grudge against Fontana. I felt no regret for showering attention on a private man. But as I watched him during the first weeks of the new season, something became clear: Ricky Fontana was not having fun.

Better writers than me have written thousands of paeans to baseball comparing the game to religion, sex, war—whatever men are supposed to love. But at its heart, baseball is a game, a boys' game played by men. Exuberant moments like the locker room celebration after Fontana's game-winning home run remind the professionals who play the game (or write about it) that baseball is fun.

After Fontana's homer, the Mets returned to their locker room hooting and hollering and laughing. Someone played rap from portable speakers. Finicky veterans who usually ate their late suppers at posh Manhattan nightspots rushed the post-game deli spread with the rookies. The team's three born-again Christians— Henry Monan, Adam Carlest, and Luis Esperanza—postponed their post-game prayer and gleefully hoisted cans of cola when Grey Mason raised a beer to toast Monan's hitless relief appearance. The players joked and teased and laughed and lingered in the clubhouse until after midnight, watching the Braves lose to the Giants on TV. The Mets had moved within two games of first place.

But Fontana skipped celebrating a victory that he alone secured. He met his raving teammates at home plate with the thin-lipped smile of a traveler who learns that the flight he missed has crashed. And before most of the Mets had their spikes off, Fontana was gone.

"This joyless play, is that what makes him so good?"

As my mates considered my suggestion, Crane quipped, "If so, trade him to the Yankees."

Poor Ricky Fontana, I thought. The thrill of being a Major League Baseball player had worn off in only a year. Even in victory, he found no peace.

❖

How much is too much? The question crossed my mind before Callahan, Crane, and I washed it away that night. One beer became two and then three, and then Callahan, affecting his father's Irish brogue (which he does when he's drunk), proclaimed, "Let's switch to whiskey, lads!"

"Hear, hear!" cried Crane, and three whiskeys were poured, which became six, and then nine. Callahan fell asleep with his head on my shoulder in the taxi, which was disarming and funny until he began to drool. I was the last to reach home, a one-bedroom apartment on the Upper East Side. My apartment seemed to shimmer and fade like the road on a hot day when I closed the door and stumbled into bed. "Good night, Mr. Met," I said. An effigy of the Mets mascot—a working telephone, actually—stood on my nightstand. The mascot is a man with a giant baseball for a head wearing a tiny cap. Mr. Met's shoulders and head lift off his torso to become the receiver. Thankfully, no one ever calls my home number; the phone's ringer is a shrill screech that suggests that my miniature mascot is having a seizure. Until the jarring ring awoke me four hours after my drunken collapse, I had not heard the baseball man shriek in months because everyone calls my cell phone except for Earl Driggs's secretary, Louise, who never entered my cell number into her contact list.

"Hello, Mr. Rusch. Earl wanted me to ask you to come into the office today. There will be an important meeting at three p.m."

"Aren't sports desk meetings usually on Mondays?"

"Yes, Mr. Rusch. But this is a company-wide meeting. The Rudolphs will be there."

Too much is never enough when the future is as empty as a drunkard's glass. I had plenty of time to develop this and other metaphors for the ruin of my life during a binge that began the next night. The Mets left for St. Louis, but I stayed in New York and drank. I have never been able to handle bad news as well as I handle liquor. "No hope," I sobbed to myself at an Irish pub on 93rd Street (three whiskeys). "No future," I was heard mumbling at a dive on Second Avenue (four bottles of beer). "It's over," I said in a German *biergarten* on York Avenue (two tall steins of lager). If I were as good at newswriting as I am at self-pity, I would have surely won the Pulitzer Prize.

As a refuge from anxiety, alcohol is a poor choice; if I swung the bat like Ricky Fontana, I too would have been underneath Busch Stadium taking batting practice and losing myself in the rhythmic whoosh and crack. The stress of being a sports sensation stiffened his shoulders and his back, but with each swing his secret became easier to keep. Soon the bat felt too heavy to lift. Ricky declared his practice finished, tired enough to go back to the hotel, order dinner, read the Cardinals scouting reports, and fall asleep. But I was always a lousy hitter. So I emptied my flask on the flight to St. Louis. I went through the minibar in my hotel room over the next three days, which were successful for the Mets—who swept a series from the Cardinals—and Fontana, who continued his streak and hit two more home runs. I don't remember the flight to Milwaukee, and I'm sure that Tony rewrote most of my coverage of the series against the Brewers, bless his heart! I was sober for the first two games in Pittsburgh, but drunk on getaway day, when the Pirates beat the Mets, but New York rejoiced because Ricky Fontana got a base hit in his fortieth consecutive game. In less than twenty days, Fontana could break Joe DiMaggio's record. But in thirty days, I would lose my job.

The meeting with the Rudolphs had not gone well.

"There is no easy way of saying this," Herman Rudolph said, pinching the lapels on his jacket nervously. "But we've done everything we can to stay afloat. It wasn't enough. Online news services, cable news channels, and the aggressive campaigns by our competitors to lure away our readers have winnowed our market share to less than half of what this company needs to be profitable."

Two hundred pairs of eyes stared back in disbelief, each pair enclosed by dark rings—those eyes had stayed open long into the night, night after night, to produce *The New York Eagle-Tribune*. But the newspaper was no more. Our last issue would go to press on June 15.

"You all know Heather Merdieu from Human Resources," Rudolph continued. A young woman wearing too much makeup stood up beside Rudolph. She nodded, never losing her look of practiced solemnity. "Heather will explain your severance packages and can answer questions regarding overdue pay and benefits. I wish you the best of luck in your future endeavors."

The room was silent as Heather, with appropriate sighs and frowns, began her recital. I couldn't concentrate. I was nauseous and achy from booze, feelings I had come to know well in the weeks past. Indeed, the days I spent on the road with the Mets drinking myself stupid would have been better spent looking for another job. But I didn't want another. Covering the Mets and Ricky Fontana seemed like the best job I would ever have.

Some folks have psychologists to whom they can whine. Some have spiritual gurus to help them find their chi and align their auras, and some have men in black dresses who pass prayers up the ladder. I've got a guy in a smock who sells lager. I needed a bartender's company on that night of sobering news. I began to drink at five p.m. An hour later, I had assigned to each scrubbing bubble in my glass a mission beyond the usual memory wiping that booze accomplishes in large volumes. That mission was to finance courage that I couldn't afford while sober to call my wife and ask her to take me back.

After my sixth drink, I called. She didn't answer. I called back fifteen minutes later. No answer. After the third no-go, I pressed the redial button again and again, not even listening for a ring right away, just enjoying the feel of pushing and pressing, and when I brought the phone to my ear, rings, endless rings, but no answer. I pressed the dialer forcefully to the tune of Beethoven's Fifth Symphony while I sang the notes aloud—"Ba ba ba BUM!"—over and over again, conjuring an image of what the composer himself looked like pounding away at his piano, wild-eyed, frantic, hair in knots and shirt unbuttoned, little black shoes with big silver buckles kicking the pedals of his instrument, and I almost put my own foot through the bar as I stomped and pressed and screamed "Ba ba ba BUM!" and called my wife again and again, but she didn't answer, even though she had no right to refuse me—she was my wife, after all, I thought—still, in a historic instance of matrimonial inadequacy, she refused to hear my contrition and keep a promise to her husband—made in front of a judge, no less, who upheld the rule of law, the foundation of civilization, these marriage laws—still she refused to keep her promise to stick with me through the worst, can you believe it? The bartender, unsympathetic, asked me to please stop kicking the bar, and I did. But I kept calling Tara, and after an hour, she finally answered.

"Jerry, please stop," she said in a big voice I didn't know or like.

"I want you back."

"Grow up."

"Come back."

"No, clearly, you're drunk."

"You got your wish. I lost my job."

"Oh," she sighed and paused, and then she answered in her old voice, the little, quiet one that sounded to me like the silence between the notes of a beloved song. "I'm sorry."

"Come back, then? I need you."

"No."

"Then why no divorce?" I asked, now getting loud. "What is this game?"

"You don't need a divorce. You need to get well. You need to get sober and get another job."

"But I don't want another. Covering the Mets and Ricky Fontana is the best job I'll ever have."

She said good-bye and turned off her phone.

CHAPTER FIVE

The streak saved my life; I'm sure of it. Ricky Fontana was the only excuse I had to put down my flask. For the next two weeks, when he came to bat, the world stopped.

Not only for me, of course. Everyone remembers those momentous weeks when baseball was the only thing that mattered.

In 1941, bandleader Les Brown and his orchestra recorded a brassy, toe-tapping tribute to a ballplayer whose consistent greatness on the baseball diamond thrilled Americans during the last summer before war. The Fontana craze officially began when a DJ for CBS-FM in New York found that song, "Joltin' Joe DiMaggio," on a CD compilation of baseball tunes. Minutes after Les Brown made his triumphant return to the airwaves, the phones began to ring at the station. Callers, e-mails, and Twitter followers demanded: "Who wrote that song?" "Where can I buy that record?" "Play it again." It was May 7. That night, Ricky Fontana hit in his thirtieth consecutive game and the soundtrack of the spring changed for good.

Suddenly, the Mets were the most popular team in New York. Not often before that season had their royal blue caps outnumbered navy Yankees headgear on Manhattan street corners. The irony was, of course, that the Mets had always been lovable losers. Even when they won, their victory was seen as a miraculous fluke, a once-in-a-generation triumph for a perpetual underdog. Ricky Fontana—relentless, mechanical, and utterly without flamboyance—was better suited for the Yankees, the symbol of consistent success. If

Hank Steinbrenner was furious in April, he surely ground his teeth to powder in May when a lowly Met threatened to sink the great Yankee Clipper.

After the fortieth consecutive game, the nation took notice. Talking heads on the cable news stations interrupted their political back-and-forths to update fans when Fontana was at bat. The moderator of a CNN political talk show interrupted the proceedings to announce, "I've just been told that Rick Fontana has another base hit." One of the talking heads corrected him with a laugh, "Everyone calls him Ricky."

When the streak reached forty-five, the networks cut away from their programming to broadcast Fontana's at bats live. His batting results were top stories in towns where baseball rarely rated above rodeo, racing, and wrestling. More often than not, anchors relayed only the news of another Fontana base hit—who in Boise, Billings, and Birmingham cared whether the Mets won? On June 1, the Mets website crashed from the increase in Internet traffic. The value of autographed Fontana baseballs on eBay was $45 in April, $60 in May, and $5,000 in June. Even so, I never sold mine.

Did he get a hit? That seemed to be the question everyone asked if they were far from a TV or a computer. People would ask strangers, "Did he get a hit?" No further explanation needed. "Yes, a single to left field." A sign outside a deli in Brooklyn read, "Streak Special: Free Coffee Until Fontana Stops Hitting. Get It While He's Hot!" On the last day of May, a bum fell into a drunken sleep in Union Square Park next to a cardboard sign that read, "I need tickets to see Fontana hit #57." A few hours later, he awoke to find sixty-one dollars in the Mets cap he had set upside-down between his legs.

Les Brown's ode to DiMaggio quickly moved from the jazz and oldies stations to Top Forty radio. Of course, the song's popularity came with a price. A clever YouTube user remixed it with a new chorus: *Joe, Joe DiMaggio, you're no Ricky Fontana!* The singers of the doctored chorus drew out the first A in Fontana to mimic the whining New York vowels in the original version. On May 27, Fontana strode to home plate for the first at bat of a game against the Rockies. All of a sudden, the song boomed from the Citi Field speakers. When they heard the alternative chorus, the crowd cheered uproariously. Even Fontana couldn't fight back a smile.

On May 28, the Israeli prime minister visited the White House. He and the president were answering questions about peace in the Middle East when an aide sitting among the press corps waved frantically to the president, who leaned forward, squinting anxiously and lifting his glasses. His aide gave the thumbs-up. The president smiled. "Ladies and gentlemen," he announced, interrupting a reporter's question. "I've just been informed that Ricky Fontana has hit safely in his fiftieth consecutive game." The Rose Garden gallery applauded.

Ricky Fontana was a national sensation. A nation weary of war, anxious about the economy, and cynical about the faction on the other side of the red-and-blue-state divide found in this statuesque small-town slugger the ingredients for an American icon. After all, Dick Rule wrote in his column, who better to fill the shoes of astronauts, presidents, and war heroes than Ricky Fontana? Here was a fellow with the humble charisma of Lou Gehrig and the sex appeal of John Kennedy who was nearing a record as unreachable as Neil Armstrong's lunar footsteps. Athletes make lousy role models; so many are archetypes of arrested youth: over-privileged, self-indulgent, and inarticulate. But when Ricky spoke, he spoke well, and when Ricky's paycheck arrived, he sent most of it home to Mama.

America needed a champion, so we chose Ricky.

America chose a gay man.

The gay man chose privacy, and he had his way. Considering that millions of Americans obsessed over the streak—"Ricky Fontana" was the a top-ten search on Google and a trending Twitter subject throughout June—Fontana's ability to maintain his wary distance from the media and public was as miraculous as his hitting streak. Privacy costs money. Fontana spent it willingly. Although he earned $500,000, nearly minimum wage by baseball standards, he paid thousands to two key clubhouse attendants. In return, they ensured that the New York media could not find Ricky Fontana if he did not want to be found. The two team employees (they asked me not to reveal their names, and I promised to oblige them) told Fontana they would gladly serve as coconspirators for free.

But Fontana insisted. "I'd feel better if I paid you," he told one of the attendants.

One of the clubhouse employees would scout the corridors under the stands to find an unwatched exit. The other attendant would be waiting outside with Fontana's car running and ready to go.

His most clever trick I learned well after the streak was over. When the game ended, he would throw on his clothes, a beige cap, and a little cologne to mask the smell of nine exhausting innings. Then he would sneak through the groundskeeper's tunnel, stroll onto the field, and then into the stands. He would leave the ballpark with the straggling fans. On the way to his car (he often parked in the fans' lot after his encounter with Crane), he would sign autographs and shake hands with fans who occasionally recognized him. He was happy to be among people who asked only for his signature, not opinions, answers, and personal details.

So I might as well have kept drinking. For the last three weeks of the streak, I staggered between the locker room, the clubhouse, and the players' lounge for any sign of Fontana. The rest of the Mets media contingent had no better luck. Finally, one night after Fontana had almost single-handedly defeated the Brewers with two homers, Budd Crane had enough.

"Fuck Fontana," he said, repeating his locker room refrain. "He expects me to quote Esperanza and Kelleher and Rios, who had one hit between them tonight. He's carrying this team. I look like an asshole if I can't get this guy to talk."

Mets Media Relations Director Jason Meyers was short, skinny, and nervous. Balding and perpetually damp with sweat, he constantly carried a pocket handkerchief, yellowing cotton with the Mets logo fading from mopping his wrinkled brow. Poor fellow! Fontana blessed the front office by swelling sales of tickets and merchandise and guaranteeing national coverage for his team. But Fontana was the bane of Meyers's career. For he had the objectionable task of explaining to frustrated newsmen why Fontana was unavailable. Fontana's secrecy was mysterious and beguiling to readers; that he wasn't beamed live from the locker room offering post-game assessments of his performance made his talent seem almost magical to fans. But the members of the media did not recognize the appeal of baseball's own J.D. Salinger. We needed a story, and since April we bombarded Meyers's office with complaining phone calls and e-mails. Crane was the first to confront him in person.

"Jason, we need to talk," Crane said urgently. He had entered Meyers's office without knocking, but Meyers looked more frightened than angry. Dick Rule and I followed, ready to wrench Crane's hands from his neck, if need be.

"Budd, if this is about Ricky, I told you already that—"

"I know, I know. You've spoken to him. Well, it didn't do any good. I still can't get a word out of this guy. He's always had a good rapport with Jerry, but even he can't find Fontana after the game."

"We're worried, Budd," Meyers said. "This streak is the best thing that's happened to this franchise in decades. If I ask Fontana to do something that makes him uncomfortable and the next day he goes 0 for 4, I'll get the blame. Ballplayers are superstitious, you know."

"What am I supposed to do, ask Jackie Rios what he thinks of Ricky Fontana's streak? What do I do the next day? I'll ask Ferrera. And then? There are only twenty-five guys on the team. Should I move on to the coaches? The groundskeepers? Maybe the guy selling peanuts has some insight."

Crane's face was red. Meyers was pale and sagging.

"Let me see what I can do," he said without enough conviction for Crane.

"We're losing readers every day to television and the Internet. Look what happened at the *Tribune*. The networks can cut together extra in-game footage to compensate, but to our readers, the lack of Fontana is glaring."

Meyers set his jaw and straightened his back. "I understand. Let me see what I can do."

The next day, I arrived at the ballpark a little tipsy. But I thought I might be hallucinating when I reached the clubhouse and found a swarm of reporters around Fontana's locker. Callahan and Rule grinned at me from the middle of the mob. Rule waved to me with the hand that wasn't thrusting his tape recorder toward the middle of the crowd where I saw, sure enough, Ricky Fontana sitting on a bench somehow timid and defiant simultaneously, a man who has lost a battle but refuses to concede victory.

He stank of menthol. The bruises on his arms and shoulders from slides, bumps, and the occasional beanball were healing, some purple, some blue, some yellow. His almost-black hair, longer and wavy on top, and shorter on the sides and back, stuck out from beneath his cap, which sat crookedly on his crown. His hands were clasped tightly— his fingertips seemed to dig into his knuckles, and when he freed his hands to fix his cap, I saw elliptical white calluses on his palms.

The barrage began.

"You've hit in fifty-one consecutive games. Do you think you can break DiMaggio's record?" asked a local TV sportscaster.

"Yes, I do," Fontana answered.

"What would it mean to you to outdo Joe DiMaggio?" asked another.

"The streak's given me even more respect for DiMaggio." Fontana looked like he had finished and the press began to bark out questions, but then he continued. "To do what he did in the era before expansion, before each team had a masseuse and a nutritionist and personal trainers, when teams traveled by trains—that's amazing to me. I'm no Joe DiMaggio."

"Where have you gone, Ricky Fontana?" Crane asked with a smirk. "I am wondering why you have made yourself accessible today after leaving the ballpark so quickly recently."

The response came through gritted teeth. "I am…sorry I haven't been…available. I need to concentrate on my hitting to help the team win."

Shit, Crane. You're going to fuck this up for all of us.

"What are you going to look for at bat against Padilla tonight?" I asked quickly, and I felt relieved as the muscles in Fontana's jaw relaxed, and he almost smiled at me as he answered.

"Fastballs early in the count. Great heater, comes in at ninety-seven. I'll try to take it the other way early and then look for the change or the slider later to pull."

"I wonder what Jason said to him," Rule said later when the gang bang was over.

"Whatever he said, it worked," came my response.

I found out later Meyers resorted to begging. He pleaded with Fontana, please speak to the media, even if only for a few minutes, please, just do it for the team. This was brilliant psychology—an order from the front office would have insulted Fontana, but to invoke his sense of team resonated with Fontana, who had played baseball since he was old enough to hold a bat. Thus, he agreed to meet with the press every day for no more than ten minutes and only before the game, never after. Few of us complained.

Nobody knew until after that eventful June the price of the streak for Fontana. One could imagine, of course, the frustration of fame to a privacy fetishist. Roger Maris lost his hair in clumps due to the strain of breaking Babe Ruth's single-season home run record in 1961. Fontana's streak also took a physical toll. After his pre-game interviews, reporters whispered about the circles under his eyes, the glint of determination gone, dulled by exhaustion. The source of his anxiety was not the daily struggle to outsmart the opposing pitcher; no, that was simple. Even on days when he was hitless until his final at bat, he came to the plate and took his practice swings blithely. Undisturbed by tension, he never swung desperately. Instead he waited for the right pitch to larrup into the outfield, and when he reached base, no matter the dramatic circumstances of his hits, he never celebrated. It was as if he expected to be there.

The uneasiness set in when the game ended. Who was going to follow him home? Who had been watching the last time he went out to a restaurant? Who was going to phone his friends or his mother and pester them with questions until they relented? How long could he keep his secret?

Joe DiMaggio had a few lucky breaks during his fifty-six-game hitting streak. Grounders trickled past infielders and bloops dropped in front of outfielders. But Fontana had been hitting the ball hard since spring training, and games in which he reached base only once were rare. Still, he realized that his luck would soon run out. Someone was going to find out he was gay, and that inevitability twisted in his guts. On the day of his forty-third consecutive game with a hit, Fontana found blood in his feces. He was dying, he told his friend Seb Hernandez; surely this was colon cancer eating him alive. Although he found relief in his doctor's diagnosis (a stress ulcer), there was no chance of following the doctor's advice (avoid stress). The illness couldn't stop his hitting. After the forty-ninth game of the streak, he called Hernandez again. "Not bad for a guy with a bleeding asshole," Fontana told him.

The Mets protected their teammate. Although he distanced himself from them, they believed that once the streak ended, Fontana could be himself. The veterans, especially those who had played in New York for several years and knew the intensity of the local media, defended Fontana's quick exits from the ballpark. Some of the Mets enjoyed watching Fontana's daily attempt to escape Houdini-like from reporters. Adam Carlest and Mick Kelleher followed his post-game getaway with glee from the final out until Fontana fled through the dugout to the safety of the stands. Kelleher recalled, "It was like rooting for a mouse to find his way through a maze. Ricky always got that cheese!"

One day, a photographer approached Carlest and struck up a conversation with him about life in the big city. He spoke casually about his apartment in Soho and asked Carlest about his neighborhood. Carlest, an Indiana boy, complained about the prices on the Upper West Side—four dollars for a half-gallon of milk! Hoping to bait Carlest, the photographer asked, "Don't a few other Mets live in your neighborhood? Isn't Fontana near you?"

Carlest was not fooled. Red-faced and spewing threats, he chased the paparazzo from the locker room. Fontana was long gone, but the next day during batting practice Carlest warned him that reporters were looking for his home. "Everyone wants a piece of you, Ricky," he said. "We're all praying for you."

Hours after Fontana scorched a base hit in his fifty-second consecutive game, Paul Callahan took Lucy, his French bulldog, for a walk near his home in Rochelle Park, New Jersey. While Lucy paused to sniff a fire hydrant, Callahan yawned and gazed around the street, quiet and gloomy at one thirty a.m. Then, a black car came around the corner and slowed farther up the block. The door opened. Callahan froze. Stepping out of the cab, maybe ninety feet away, was none other than Ricky Fontana. Fontana was wearing his beige cap and street clothes, but there was no mistaking that jaw, the chin, the face of a man on the cover of a romance novel and those dark brown eyes that darted about nervously and spotted— horror!—standing on the curb with a little dog was the red-haired reporter from the *Post*, who recognized Fontana immediately with a sheepish grin.

"Hi, Ricky!" called Callahan. Fontana lunged back into the car and told the driver to go. Slumped in the backseat, playing a game on his cell phone, Fontana waited nervously as the cab idled in the parking lot of a nearby mall. After thirty minutes, he asked the driver to return him to the house where he roomed with teammate Mick Kelleher, a cozy brick home that sat a few yards from the hydrant where Lucy had her fateful sniff.

The next morning, I later learned from one of his friends, Fontana stopped in the vestibule before he opened his front door. There will be people out there, he thought. A crush of reporters will be waiting for me. *They will know.*

Shaking off (most of) his doubt, Fontana thrust the door open and, with a confidence that surprised him, stepped outside to face his pursuers. *Fuck you! I'm Ricky Fontana, the best hitter in baseball.*

But no one was waiting except the black car he hired to take him to the ballpark. Smirking awkwardly, he greeted the driver and stepped inside.

The next day, the sunny suburban street was empty again when Fontana peered through his front door. Nor were reporters stalking his house on the next two mornings. When Fontana left home on the day he tied Joe DiMaggio's fifty-six-game hitting streak, he was alone. The reporters were waiting for him, yes, but we waited at Citi Field, preparing our most purple prose for the next day's morning editions, issuing update after update on Fontana's arrival and batting practice results, and writing very little about the Mets game against the San Francisco Giants. Only Fontana's trips to home plate mattered.

He was surprisingly relaxed when he reached the ballpark. "Yo, Grey!" he called to his manager, as he walked into the clubhouse.

"I was thinking maybe I should take the day off. You know, give [rookie outfielder Sam] Caple a chance to play. Whaddya say?"

His teammates laughed louder than they meant to, Kelleher told me later. "But we were so glad to see Ricky joking, and we figured that we were right all along. Now that he had reached number fifty-six, Ricky was back to his old self. Getting there had been the problem."

Ricky Fontana abandoned his knack for drama with his first swing off Giants pitcher Al Schmidt. The pitch, a fastball designed to nick the outside corner of the strike zone, met Fontana's bat before it reached home plate and the impact sent the ball over the shortstop's head and into left field—a clean single.

A few days earlier, the Mets front office argued about how to treat the tie. Meyers told me he was against an on field celebration. "He wouldn't have truly bested DiMaggio yet," he said, surely echoing what Fontana would have said about the tie. "We should wait until he breaks the record."

General Manager Lewis Daniels disagreed. "What if he doesn't get a hit the next day? We won't have recognized his remarkable achievement in front of the fans." So as Fontana rounded first base after the historic single, the umpire stopped the game and the groundskeepers scurried onto the field to erect a podium. Daniels and team owner Wilbur Allan presented Fontana with a Swarovski crystal plaque recognizing his achievement. Then the game resumed. The Mets lost four to two.

The following evening, I was more excited to go to the ballpark than I had been since my first game at age six. I pictured the scene around the nation: Americans dropped whatever they were doing to watch. At seven p.m., families from New York to Ohio, Maine to Florida, rushed to the television with their dinner. At four p.m., men and women at work on the West Coast interrupted their afternoon labors and crowded around computers and TVs in conference rooms. And Americans between the coasts tuned in during their commutes to watch and listen to history made live on national television. It seemed so perfect. The shy, handsome boy from small-town Rhode Island was about to transcend sports and become a national hero.

For the first time in months (years?), I felt happy enough to convince myself that I wasn't miserable. The portent of losing my job and the grief of my pending divorce was far from my mind. This is why you became a sportswriter, I told myself as I stepped through the press entrance to the stadium, to witness baseball history, so you can say in fifty years, "I was there."

Many Americans, I think, felt the pull of history's gravity as Ricky Fontana stepped to the plate in the first inning. There were two outs and the Mets were losing by one run. To a blinding burst of flashbulbs, Fontana swung at three pitches and missed them all, a strikeout, perhaps the most talked about strikeout since Casey came up empty. The crowd groaned.

The Mets were down 2-0 in the fourth inning when Fontana came up again. Everyone stood. The television announcers were silent. Again, like a million tiny supernovae, flashes erupted in the stands. Somehow, San Francisco pitcher Frankie Hernandez ignored it all and threw a cut fastball that fooled Fontana, who hit the pitch weakly with the handle of his bat. First baseman Jervis Gomez snared the pop-up.

The score was the same in the seventh inning when Fontana came to the plate again with two outs. Luis Esperanza had singled and Morgan Shellock had walked, but the next two hitters grounded out. Hernandez had stifled the Mets lineup, and unless the team rallied in the eighth inning, Fontana would not bat again. "Jesus H. Christ, Jerry, I'm shaking," said Crane hoarsely. "Give me your flask."

Two pitchers began to throw in the Giants bullpen as Hernandez threw the first pitch to Fontana outside for ball one. The next pitch was a strike. Fontana watched it without concern. The third pitch looked low to everyone in Citi Field except the umpire, who called strike two. While the crowd showered the umpire with deafening jeers, Hernandez threw ball two, outside. The catcher tossed the ball back to him, and Hernandez caressed the stitches as he considered his next pitch. "It was supposed to be a slider," he later said of the most famous pitch he would ever throw. "But I guess it didn't slide."

The crack of the bat said it all. Fontana swatted the next pitch deep into center field. It soared and soared until it came down, finally, on the giant apple in the center field stands, a long, long home run.

From the television booth, Fox announcer Joe Buck issued the most famous home run call of his career. "Here's the two-two pitch. Oh my goodness, there it goes. Gone! Gone! Gone! He did it! Move over, Joe DiMaggio; Ricky Fontana is the consecutive base hit king!"

Pandemonium in Queens. The Mets rushed to home plate to greet Fontana, and they weren't alone. Ignoring the extra policemen on hand to provide security, scores of fans rushed the field. Three young men scurried past the cops guarding the left field stands. They skipped over the fence and ran to meet Fontana as he rounded third base, following him on the last leg of his trip around the bases. Patting him on the back and shoulders, desperate to touch their hero in the flesh, they cheered him on for ninety feet ("Attaboy, Ricky." "You're the man, Fontana!") until they disappeared into the crowd of his teammates and other determined well-wishers who had stormed past the police, three nameless celebrities forever part of baseball history on film.

"I remember thinking about Hank Aaron as I rounded the bases," Fontana told reporters after the game, his iridescent smile reflecting the glow of camera lights. "When he broke the home run record, Aaron said 'Thank God it's over.' That's exactly how I felt when the ball left the bat."

Ricky Fontana bubbled and bragged and smiled and smirked and gushed and guffawed for hours after the game during interview after interview with the same questions. I was proud—after all, we broke in together, Ricky and I—and rueful—after all, he was now a living legend, and I was a lonely and soon-to-be jobless drunk. Watching him after the game from the outskirts of a swarm of reporters that seemed to be ten men deep, admiring the reappearance of that movie star grin, I thought that I might never again see the scowl to which I had grown accustomed. His problems were over.

Chapter Six

I met my wife during college. She was a freshman and I was a senior at Syracuse when we started dating. A knock-kneed, freckled redhead, she was fair enough to catch a passing glance. But to me, a short, bespectacled frump with hair like a Brillo Pad—not much handsomer then than the portrait above my column in the *Tribune*—she was utterly unattainable. I thought so even as we explored each other's lips in shadowy corners of the campus. What is she doing with me, I wondered. Is she some dream of a Celtic goddess I created while smoking pot after my British history class, dreaming cloudy thoughts of Stonehenge and listening to Black Sabbath? The sorority girl and the school paper nerd sounds like the contrived ending to one of the teen sex comedies popular when we were undergrads. I joked that she dated me only to fulfill her sorority's community service requirements. I was surprised when she agreed to leave her home near Rochester and move with me to New York City after she graduated. Until my first major league byline, that was my greatest accomplishment, achieved in spite of the typical obstacles to college romances: a pregnancy scare, long summers apart, and roommates who commandeered our dorm rooms for their own sexual dalliances.

Reliable for setting afloat long-sunken memories and drowning new ones, my bouts of drink led to thoughts of my wife. Tara was on my mind two nights after the streak ended when I spotted Ricky Fontana kissing another man. But lost in nostalgia, I didn't immediately register what I was seeing: the most precious secret of a man I followed obsessively, the explanation for his furtiveness, a scoop from a reporter's dreams. Bobby, I thought. Bobby the Queer kissed his boyfriend like that. I caught them at it so many times when I brought Tara back to my room hoping to get her into bed but instead settling for cautious kisses on the quad because my roommate, Bobby McNamara, was gay and couldn't very well smooch another man in public.

I was never one for protests and sit-ins during college. My contribution to social justice was befriending Bobby McNamara. I fought the good fight by surrendering my room to him and his boyfriend, Sam. Slightly built and soft-spoken, he opened up to me during our first week together with a plea for acceptance. "I'm gay, Jerry. You would've found out sooner or later. If you want me to move out, I will. I understand. I won't tell the dorm proctor why." Even though behind his back I called him "Bobby the Queer," macho posturing to show my friends that I wasn't turning into some politically correct sissy, I felt sorry for him. His honesty moved me. Whenever another student tittered at his just-slightly-effeminate stride or inflection, I confronted them angrily. Still, to Tara and me, he was always Bobby the Queer. We had four friends named Robert, so the title distinguished Bobby McNamara and, of course, inspired some giggles. "Bobby's flitting it up again," we'd snicker to each other as we walked out of my dormitory and searched for a dark alley where I could slip my hands underneath her skirt and lose myself, a feeling in spite of my empathy for Bobby that I could never imagine living without.

Just like Bobby. Watching Fontana kissing the slender blond man on the screen of my smartphone, I thought of my old roommate. And I wondered if what I saw was some fiction bubbled up by booze. I asked the cab driver, "Is that Ricky Fontana over there?" I gestured to the stoop bathed in orange streetlight. Two men sharing an embrace. The cabbie shrugged. Even if I'd been sober, the driver's name was unpronounceable except to friends and family he'd left behind in a nation without baseball. He wouldn't know Ricky Fontana.

Drunk, bold, and self-righteous, I considered forfeiting my cab and approaching Fontana for a better shot or even to say hello. But what would I tell him? Congrats on being gay! I couldn't even consider congratulating him for the streak. I knew he was furious that it had ended two days before at sixty-two. He bested Joe DiMaggio by six games. And he was leading every other ballplayer in all major offensive categories. He was batting .414. He had socked twenty-seven home runs. He had driven in eighty-two runs and reached base in fifty-four percent of his at bats.

Still, when the streak ended during an interleague game in Cleveland, Fontana did not congratulate himself. He was outraged. Fontana flew out twice and smacked two hard ground balls—sure base hits, he thought—that Indians third baseman Kip Karey snatched, throwing him out at first both times. "Fuck!" he kept screaming after the game as he bashed the concrete wall of the visitor's' clubhouse with his bat. Dripping hot sweat and tears, Fontana finally surrendered his bat to three teammates.

One of them asked, "Why are you upset, Ricky? You broke the streak and then some."

"I really thought it could last forever," Fontana said.

The day after the streak ended, the Mets had a day off. Fontana took a cab down to Mulberry Street and accepted an award from the Italian-American Society of New York. I scribbled cute headlines in pidgin Italian and Tony snapped photos as the IASNY gave Fontana the Amerigo Vespucci Award for "Outstanding Contributions to National Life by an Italian-American." After a quick lunch—Tony got a great shot of Fontana with his fork in midair, twirling spaghetti—the new consecutive hit king took a private cab to LaGuardia Airport. He flew to Washington, where DC police and White House aides met him at the airport. That afternoon in the Rose Garden, Fontana handed the president a personalized Mets jersey with the number sixty-two. The president gave him a plaque, a special Presidential Award Recognizing Outstanding Achievement. "Congratulations, Ricky," the president said. "Your consistency is an inspiration to us all. You have broken a record once thought unbreakable. You are a true role model who reminds all Americans that nothing is impossible."

"Thank you, Mr. President," Fontana responded. "I'll do my best to start another hitting streak tomorrow against the Cubs."

"Watch out for those curveballs," the president said, a rejoinder suggested by his chief of staff, a Chicago native. "That Miguel Oliver has a wicked one."

Ricky later told Mick Kelleher that the presidential award meant more to him than any baseball accolade; he finally felt like a hero.

He returned to New York that evening, brimming with pride. His agent called. Was he available? David Letterman, Jay Leno, Conan O'Brien, *Good Morning America*, *Good Day New York*, ESPN, *The Daily Show*—they all wanted him. The following morning at Citi Field, a camera crew filmed Fontana using his bat to chop through a seven-foot poster of the number sixty-two. Then he stepped through the tear and took a few swings at the camera, reenacting Joe DiMaggio's famous publicity newsreel from 1941. The clip was shown on the scoreboard that night to raucous applause as Ricky Fontana stepped to the plate for his first at bat. He rapped the second pitch from Miguel Oliver—a curveball, of course—into left field for a single. A new streak began, though the Mets lost five to four. After the game, Fontana hurried out of the ballpark as usual, and I did not expect to see him again until the next day's game. But there he was on a stoop in Brooklyn kissing another man.

My journey to that moment started, unsurprisingly, at the bottom of a glass. Absolutely fucking ratted, I knew all the same that the man who sauntered past the Carrickfergus Pub, where I was on my seventh black and tan, was Eusebio Hernandez. He was less than four feet from my blushed nose when he passed. I left my seat by the window and stumbled into the street. The retired Yankee, the steroid washout, and Ricky Fontana's erstwhile dinner partner— he was getting away. His brisk, athletic stride outpaced the traffic choking 45th Street. Shuffling, huffing after him, I had no trouble keeping a stalker's distance from my target. He was sixty feet ahead when he stopped at the corner of Ninth Avenue. Hernandez put his phone to his ear and started talking. I ducked into a doorway and watched. Two minutes later came a short, skinny man dressed all in black. The boyish blond in glasses gave Seb a quick hug. Then Seb threw his arm aloft. A cab stopped. Both men climbed inside. I pulled myself forward into a jog. At the corner, I waved down another taxi as I folded the license plate digits of Hernandez's ride into my addled memory.

The meter spun as my taxi followed Hernandez and his friend downtown. I was less curious about our destination than the embrace. More than friends, Hernandez and the blond. There was something girlish about how the little man had risen on his toes to squeeze the rangy jock. Beneath the spires of the Williamsburg Bridge, the thought occurred to me that Eusebio Hernandez was gay and the shorter man was his lover. An interesting story, I thought, but I'm not in the gossip biz. Not even the sports pages would be interested in the sex life of Eusebio Hernandez. Poor hitting and the taint of cheating scuttled his career years before.

Then, up through the foam came the reason I ought to care about the company he kept. I fished my phone from my pocket and turned on its camera.

Beyond my wildest hopes, he was there. Over the bridge, off the highway, we plunged into Williamsburg, Brooklyn, streets alive with weeknight revelers wandering between bars and cafés, eyes on one another and their reflections. Except for one man. He searched every passing car until the cab carrying Eusebio Hernandez stopped before a brownstone on Bedford Avenue. The little blond man stepped from the cab and ran into the waiting arms of Ricky Fontana.

My camera captured the reunion frame by frame, though I hardly believed what I saw.

He was gay. All the barriers he erected between himself and teammates, fans and followers in the media were built to protect this secret. Now, he unwittingly and unwillingly shared his secret with me.

Stepping outside even for a moment was an unbelievable risk for Fontana. The television ratings for the record-breaking game exceeded the Super Bowl. During the streak's final week, the Mets had been swarmed everywhere. The cities they visited provided a police escort. Crowds greeting Fontana at the airport followed the team to their hotel and often camped in the lobby. Autograph seekers, adoring women, newsmen, amateur paparazzi, and a bizarre coterie of strangers with something to sell or hustlers who claimed to be Fontana's long-lost father—they were the subjects of a feature I wrote for ESPN.com on Fontana's fame. An obsessed teenager attempted to climb down to the balcony of Fontana's room from the roof of a St. Louis hotel. Two determined fans in stolen utility uniforms slipped past hotel security in Atlanta and knocked on Fontana's suite until he obliged them with an autograph.

Pro athletes wander in the shallows of celebrity; most go unrecognized without their uniform. Yet Ricky Fontana's talent had dragged him past the breakers to fame's deep waters. His was the most photographed face in America. Did he really think he could smooch his boyfriend—boyfriend!—in public and not be discovered by the likes of me?

No, of course not. Ricky Fontana was coming out of the closet, I thought. He might make an announcement to that effect tomorrow at Citi Field. Maybe tomorrow, or maybe next week. Maybe when he had fulfilled the second of Bob McCarty's prophecies and became unassailable, a god, gay or not. But I could have the story that night, an exclusive.

An exclusive story on the most famous man in America. Under my byline. In the *New York Eagle-Tribune*. The *Tribune*'s last issue was three days away. A story like that could save the paper. It could make my name, make me the most famous journalist in New York. Everyone with a byline would think of me with envy and respect and speak to me in the reverent tone they save for the really-matters we interview: politicians, pop celebs, and superstar jocks. Could Tara refuse me then? Once I accomplished so much, would she still insist that I am an alcoholic? No, I decided. Not once she became easily replaceable. Not once my story was everywhere and she was in Rochester.

It seemed like a good idea at the time.

So as the taxi idled, I called Tony. "Are you drunk?" he asked. "Jesus Christ, it's two a.m. How drunk are you?"

Much more than I knew. After the game, Crane and I took the 7 train to Times Square and ducked into a Chinese restaurant for lo mein and mai tais. Then we switched to black and tans at Carrickfergus, an Irish pub frequented by Budd's *New York Times* buddies. Crane left at midnight. I had been drinking steadily for four hours when Eusebio Hernandez—and the biggest story of my life—passed right under my nose.

"Tony, listen. He's gay. Ricky Fontana is gay." I explained how I came to a stoop where Fontana was kissing a fair-haired stranger.

"Well," said Tony. "That explains a lot."

"No kidding."

"Wow. Who woulda thought?"

"And I got the pictures to prove it."

"What for?" asked Tony.

"The *Trib*."

"What? Are you fucking crazy?"

"No," I said. "I have to write about this. He's obviously going to come out publicly. Why else would he be out and about with his boyfriend? Boyfriend! Ha!"

"Jerry, are you out of your fucking mind?" Tony hissed. "He stepped into public view just for a second. He's not coming out. He's hiding there. He's been hiding for his whole career!"

Doubt drained a few drops from my well of resolve. But I swallowed.

"Someone will find out anyway, Tony. This is New York. Celebrities' secrets last about as long as empty parking spots." I smiled at my drunken wit. And continued. "If not us, then Crane or Rule or Callahan will get the news first. It's only a matter of time."

Tony started to speak, but I interrupted him.

"Besides, the fans have a right to know. Public figures understand the price of fame. They forfeit their privacy in public. You think Tom Cruise can walk into McDonald's and eat a cheeseburger without every bite recorded and uploaded? The gossip industry in this country is huge. You can't buy a magazine or watch TV without seeing some unknowing celeb walking his dog, cuddling with her boyfriend, taking his kids to the park."

Tony finally interjected. "But for God's sake, Jerry. Ricky is twenty years old. He's not Tom Cruise. He's just a kid who plays ball. This could ruin his life if it gets out."

"But this could save our jobs. This is the story that could put the *Trib* back on the map. And nobody's life is going to be ruined. There have been other gay ballplayers. Remember Glenn Burke? And there's the Japanese pitcher who made a gay porno. His career wasn't ruined. Isn't he still pitching?"

Tony was unmoved. "But Ricky's not just some ballplayer. He's the best ballplayer in the country. Maybe the best ever. A national hero. Captain fucking America, Jerry. You don't think there will be repercussions to him being gay?"

"Celebrities are coming out all the time nowadays. No big deal. Fontana's talent is so extraordinary that folks opposed to his lifestyle will at least respect his ability. Why, he might even be a hero for his community! An example of how much they can accomplish in a straight guy's world. Already there are Pride Nights for gay fans in at least five major league ballparks."

I stopped speaking. Tony began his defense.

"Jerry, if being gay is no big deal, then why would you put Ricky Fontana on the front page? Let him make the choice to come out. This is obviously something he wants to keep private. Why do you think he avoids us so much? Why do you think he has no close friends on the team? Why do you think he's turned down every endorsement deal thrown at him?"

At least I think that's what Tony said; I really wasn't listening. I watched Fontana and his boyfriend walk into the brownstone.

When Tony finished, I said, "Let's let Earl decide." I hung up and called my boss.

"Holy fucking shit on a dick!" Earl Driggs screamed into the phone. "I don't fucking believe it. Fuck me! You gotta get that fucking story, Jerry. By any means necessary. This could save our asses."

I called Tony. "Earl says go for it."

"I don't care what Earl said," Tony said. "I'm not gonna be a part of this."

Silence from my phone; Tony had disconnected. I threw money at the cabbie, and I lurched across Bedford Avenue. Only the third floor windows were lit, so I rang the uppermost doorbell. And I waited. I stood where Fontana had waited, waiting for him now, to come down, to come out.

Instead came the man he had kissed. His nose wrinkled, brow furrowed, confused about the stranger ringing his bell so far past bedtime.

I asked, "Is Ricky Fontana here?" I already knew the answer, of course. At the top of the stairs to the second floor, a pair of feet appeared. The blond man peered over his shoulder then back to me.

"Uh oh!" said the blond man, smiling knowingly. "An autograph seeker."

"Not quite," I said politely. "I know Ricky from the Mets. I cover them for the *Tribune.* My name's Jeremy Rusch."

I offered my hand, but the man in glasses did not shake it.

"What the hell are you doing here?" a voice croaked from the second-floor landing. Fontana, his face ashen, slumped down the stairs.

"Well, it's funny. I sort of stumbled in here accidentally. Had no idea, you know…"

I didn't continue. Fontana was reddening; now a deep red. His fingers curled into fists.

"Ricky, honey, don't do this," the man in glasses pleaded.

"You fucking bastard," Fontana whispered.

"Ricky, listen. I didn't follow you here. There's no problem with, you know, you being gay. I just wanted to talk to you about it, to see if you wanted to—"

"Let you write about it in your fucking newspaper?"

He towered over me, now, the beast. He was flushed, sweating, shaking, nostrils flared and teeth bared. The man in glasses tugged helplessly at Fontana's shirt, but got no response. He looked more frightened than I was. I barely nodded my response.

"Write whatever you want!" he bellowed. His voice and his hot breath nearly knocked me over. "Write whatever you want," he repeated, even louder. Ignoring his pleading lover, he stomped upstairs. A door slammed. The blond man followed.

My cell phone was ringing.

"Jerry! Jerry? Do we have a story?"

"Yes."

"Fucking 'ay! How did you do it?" Earl asked.

"He gave me permission. He wasn't happy about it though."

"Don't worry about it. This is big, Jerry. Too big to give up after it fell into your lap. Everyone here is walking around with a fucking hard-on for your story."

Suddenly, the air seemed thick. An urge overwhelmed me to put down my phone and run, but I wasn't sure where to flee. I thought: Who am I to capture a man on paper, let alone a man as remarkable as Ricky Fontana? He will live forever. Who will remember Jeremy Rusch? I had accomplished so little and lost so much. My mind raced. This is right. Was I sure? I didn't convince Tony. The costs are huge. He will never speak to me again. I'm drunk. This is wrong. Is it the booze? Maybe Tony is right.

"Jerry? Are you gonna get your ass to your computer and write that fucking story?"

On a warm, wet June night, I said yes.

The following article is reprinted from the *New York Eagle-Tribune*. It appeared alongside my photo of Fontana and Peter Morgenstern, his boyfriend, in the Metro Sports section the following day.

A SLUGGER'S SECRET

Ricky Fontana, the most popular athlete in America, hid his sexuality as he smashed baseball's celebrated streak.

By Jeremy Rusch

NEW YORK -- Ricky Fontana has nothing to hide. He's the best hitter in baseball, he's beloved by Mets fans, and he's a national hero. Ricky Fontana is also gay.

Last night, this reporter spotted the Mets right fielder and a male companion kissing on the stoop of a Brooklyn brownstone. When I greeted Fontana, he was shocked— even horrified—to be recognized as a homosexual. Fortunately, during his young career I have gained Ricky's confidence, and he allowed me to write whatever I wanted on the subject.

Ricky Fontana has always been a reluctant celebrity. His talent is almost as much of a curse as a blessing, for Fontana is fiercely protective of his privacy. Now we know why.

Now we know why Ricky has been an infrequent guest on Mets television coverage. Now we know why we've so seldom heard his voice on our sports radio stations. Now we know why we've never seen him in commercials for deodorant or shoes or sports drinks like so many other athletes. Perhaps he worried that we would see in his face or hear in his voice some suggestion of the identity he wanted so desperately to keep secret.

Why should someone who means so much to New York be afraid to be seen in public? Why should a man whose talent will take him all the way to Cooperstown be afraid of the news media? Why should Ricky, handsome, smart, and admired by his teammates, be ashamed to be seen holding hands with his boyfriend?

I can think of no good reason.

Ricky Fontana should be the proudest man in New York. Instead he sneaks in and out of Citi Field, avoids close friendships with his teammates, and enjoys none of the public admiration that New Yorkers lavish upon their heroes. It is my hope that by making Ricky's secret known, those who create the climate of fear and intolerance that forces many gays and lesbians to live their lives in secret will come to know the shame and humiliation they have caused.

Ricky took a risk coming out. I am taking a risk, too. I am putting my trust in you, dear readers, to treat Ricky as he deserves to be treated: as a hero, as a leader, as a great athlete, as a New Yorker. I am asking you not to think of Ricky as a gay ballplayer, but to think of him as I do: perhaps the greatest ballplayer who has ever lived.

CHAPTER SEVEN

Ever since that column, which no matter what I write will be my most famous byline, some readers have suspected that my story isn't true. I knew Ricky Fontana would be at that house in Brooklyn, they insist; I had known that Ricky was gay, and proof was all I wanted. And fame and money and all the trimmings, of course. Some will think profit is what I hope to gain by continuing to write about Fontana, even though I announced to *Publisher's Weekly* when this book was contracted that all my proceeds would be donated to the Gay Men's Health Crisis. Even now, I assume, skeptics will say that I don't need my advance and royalties because I have grown wealthy thanks to my plot to expose Ricky Fontana as a homosexual.

But nobody was more surprised than I was.

Ricky Fontana never expressed any of the supposed telltale traits that indicate homosexuality. Don't ask me what they are. Each of us has our own ideas about what makes a gesture or an inflection gay, and after thousands of letters and phone calls to the *Tribune* accusing me of homophobia, I'm not about to explain what qualities I would look for. It suffices to say that Fontana didn't have them.

I'm not a homophobe, and the accusations hurt me. Some of my colleagues, good friends of mine for years, refused to speak to me after my column. Tony sent me an e-mail the next day—his immediate resignation. "I'll never understand why you hate Ricky Fontana," he wrote. But he was wrong. I didn't hate Fontana.

I envied him.

Of course, that envy became pity when the consequences of my column very quickly and severely diverged from the expected results. But on the night before my story was published, I fell asleep thinking that Ricky Fontana could have any woman in New York (or any man) while I was wasted and alone. At the time I believed that neither condition was my fault.

The night before, I missed her. The night before, I hated her, too. Only minutes before Eusebio Hernandez walked past the pub, I had been feeding a drunken fantasy of sneaking into Tara's bedroom as she slept and shaving her head of all that lovely red hair. But in dreams that night of our early days together, I loved her still.

By the first time I spoke to Tara at age eighteen, I already knew the sound of her voice and the smell of her breath and that her palms were always warm but the soles of her feet are always cold, and I knew the way Nature had folded her navel and how her eyes can change the temperature of a room, those frostbitten glares of disapproval and sky-blue smiles that warmed my guts like a stiff drink. I had imagined all of this for six months, and by the time I had the chance to confirm my visions, to me they were already true.

You can do better, I assured myself at the bar. She wasn't perfect. Her lips were thin and always chapped, but I didn't notice until the end when we weren't kissing much anyway. She was a bony thing, and she ate and ate, gulping down second helpings of her own piss-poor cooking. Yet none of the food padded her frame and gave her a woman's softness. Still, I admit there was something satisfying about her frailty and how she flinched whenever I squeezed her skinny wrist at play or during a fight. She could crush me with a glance and drive me out of bed and into pants and a shirt over my bedclothes and downstairs and next door to the bar. But like her wrist, Tara was no more powerful than me. Just a thin skin over the tiny blue piping of her delicate interior.

Now I had another reason to envy Fontana. For the rest of his life he would never have to surrender to such a fragile creature. He would never answer to a wife.

Suddenly, unexpectedly, improbably, she appeared. When I awoke on the day that my infamous column was published, my wife was at the foot of my bed. She was folding clothes from her boudoir, watching me nervously, frowning when my eyes opened and remained open.

I croaked, "What are you doing home?"

"What does it look like I'm doing?" she asked crossly. "Need my summer clothes."

But before I could ask if she'd read the story that I'd hoped would win back her affection, or else furnish her replacement, she spat, "Well, you really fucked it up this time, eh?"

I sat up in bed, rubbing my throbbing temples. "Whaddya mean?"

"The Page Six bullshit stalker stuff about your hero. Nice going." She threw a stack of blouses into a paper bag.

"You don't like my story?"

"Oh, I'm sure it'll be front-page news for a while," she said. "But it's dirty business, making your name by talking about who's fucking who."

"He's in the papers every day," I said. Righteousness revved my bleary engine. "He can't expect privacy. I asked him for permission, and he didn't refuse. Do you know how many blogs would print a story like mine based entirely on hearsay? Every time a sports exec or athlete is rumored to be gay, it's news. This will all blow over quickly. All I've written is the first of many admiring articles about a prominent gay athlete."

Tara sneered. "What you've written is his epitaph: Ricky Fontana, faggot superstar. That's how they'll remember him thanks to you."

She gathered a swimsuit and sandals for a trip to the Hamptons with friends. Meanwhile, I followed her and tried to convince her that it was better for Fontana to be out of the closet. He could be a role model for gay kids. As Jackie Robinson showed racists that blacks could play a white man's game, Ricky Fontana would show homophobes that a gay man could best his straight counterparts in the manliest pursuits.

She ignored me. Then, packing finished, she made for the door, forsaking my pleas for her to stay. In the hall, she stepped over my copy of the *Tribune*. On the front page, a headline blared: RICKY FONTANA'S SECRET: I'M GAY. Running beside my short column was an infographic featuring gay and lesbian athletes. None of them except for tennis star Martina Navratilova were out of the closet during their careers. And besides Navratilova, none of them were very good. The only openly gay former baseball players, Billy Bean and Glenn Burke, had forgettable careers that also rendered their sexuality forgettable. But no one could ignore Ricky Fontana, his talent, his looks, and now, his sexual preferences, still exotic or disgusting or dismissed as a chosen habit by most of his countrymen.

Tara looked at the headline and shook her head. "You know, you never would have written that article if you were sober."

Fucking bitch, I thought. I cursed the day I first saw her and all the days I'd lately wished she'd come back. The smell of her was still on the air, and I wanted to follow her and fuck her, it had been so long for me and her, for me and anyone.

Ricky Fontana also cursed his fate. He'd been up all night, pacing his boyfriend's apartment, alternately yelling, weeping, and calling everyone he trusted to prepare for the day to come, a day he knew would come but never wanted to come, a day he'd only accept on his own terms, which I had denied him. I should have known he was miserable that morning as I pleasured myself in the shower. But I thought he was lucky. He was, after all, handsome and wealthy and talented and desired by everyone, while I had allowed that I would never be an object of desire. After my shower, I wondered if the lucky ones know how sexuality can be a burden to regular people. To men, especially ordinary-looking guys like me, it's an unappeasable appetite, a distracting impulse. The women that we want know they can do better, and the women we can have we'd rather not. But abstinence is a joke, I thought, and masturbation is a hollow thrill. Sex is enough to turn men like me into fundamentalists clucking missives against the debauchery of our society while we watch commercials for shampoo and perfume and tampons and become aroused dreaming of the very earthy satisfactions promised to heaven-bound barbarians after death.

Yet Ricky Fontana denied his sexuality. This secrecy made no sense to me considering the promiscuity of the gay world (as it appears to outsiders). He could get laid any time he wanted, an advantage not many twenty-year-olds would overlook. I swallowed two aspirin with orange juice as I read my notorious column and thought that maybe my piece would allow the guy to loosen up and enjoy his luck.

❖

That few people in his adopted neighborhood were reading my column that morning was no consolation to Ricky Fontana. Bulging with the weight of New York City's disaffected youth, Greenwich Village burst open decades ago and spilt on Long Island's westernmost shores a tide of students, artists, and recent grads who couldn't afford Manhattan. They made Williamsburg, Brooklyn, the capital of cool. There, Ricky Fontana found a hideaway. Among his new neighbors, he was a nameless stranger. Dressed to show how little they cared for fashion—*Look at me*, demanded their matted hair, outdated clothes, and ragged shoes—the kids fretted endlessly that others groomed and clothed themselves with less concern. So they paid no attention to a man in sunglasses and a beige cap pulled over his brow. Had they known that the greatest hitter in the major leagues bought coffee on Bedford Avenue and jogged in McCarren Park, most wouldn't have cared. To them, baseball was for red-staters, the bourgeois, the jocks who once teased them in school or the parents who stared askance at their costumes.

Sometimes it's hard for a sportswriter to imagine people who don't care about baseball, but they exist.

He had lived in Brooklyn only a few weeks, but some drivers for the local cab companies who drove him to and from Citi Field already recognized him. Fontana paid double their fee if they promised to keep his hideout secret. Still, he had little fear when he opened his front door. Williamsburg was quiet and empty by Manhattan standards, the sleepy campus for the University of the Magnitude of Me.

From the rooftop of a brownstone on Brooklyn's North 10th Street, he could see the Manhattan skyline framed in dramatic style by the Williamsburg Bridge. He stared at the city longingly. While he stretched on the roof, squatting, bending, and contorting his long frame, his eyes never left the spires, darting from tower to tower to a quiet section of the little island he one day would like to call home. Fontana dreamed of life when—if—my story blew over, while below his feet the subways carried thousands of Brooklynites to work, reading with fascination about a prestigious ballplayer who happened to be gay. It was June 16.

Pearly dawn sunlight washed him. How Ricky wished that light were bright enough to erase his face! Or if only, like a camera's flash, the light could duplicate him. Replica Fontanas to fill nightspots and daytime talk shows with his doubles, each phony Fontana with a pretty girl on his arm. Nobody would know the real Ricky.

As my marriage was ending, the first love affair for Ricky Fontana was blooming in Brooklyn. Peter Morgenstern, the short, fair-haired man pictured next to Fontana on page one of the *Tribune* that morning, was more than happy to share his two-bedroom flat with him. Fontana fascinated Peter since the two were introduced at a party by Eusebio Hernandez. No dates in public, the nervous Fontana insisted. Peter agreed. What fun! It was like high school all over again for Peter, sneaking kisses from shy boys. When Peter finally convinced Ricky to be seen with him in public, Fontana chose an anonymous red sauce spaghetti joint in a New Jersey strip mall. The condition of this date, and every other meeting between them, was "complete discretion," and Peter's vow never to tell anyone who Ricky was and what he did for a living. Peter didn't care that his food was cold or that his date was petrified. He was too busy admiring Fontana's nervous brown eyes, the allure of which had, since their increased television exposure, inspired an average of 200 e-mails each day from amorous women.

He spent most of their first public date listening. Peter told me later that Fontana seemed desperate to talk—the nights alone without a trustworthy friend had taken their toll. But a voice interrupted Peter's admiring gaze. A wispy man, loosely holding a pen and pad, asked them, "Are you interested in dessert?"

Peter eyed the waiter. *Not bad. Cute, even. But not anywhere near Ricky.* He looked back to Fontana, who eyed the waiter suspiciously. They decided to split the tiramisu.

"I know I'm new to this," Fontana told Peter once the waiter left. "Being out. Seeing men. But I don't get pretty boys, swishy boys like him. Why can't they act like men? I don't like some thirty-year-old stockbroker by day wearing makeup at night asking me at a club, 'top or bottom, honey?'"

Peter frowned. "I'm not exactly what you'd call butch."

"You're a grown-up. That's all that matters. That's why..." Fontana paused and seemed to search, "I like you so much. I'm having a really good time!" He smiled, and Peter's heart melted.

❖

While preparing a feature article for *Vanity Fair* that would become the core of this book, I contacted Peter Morgenstern a few months after Fontana's record season had ended. Although he had every reason to turn me down, he agreed to speak with me. Two days after Christmas, I found myself in Williamsburg. The delis and cafés that lined Bedford Avenue still wore lights and holiday greetings in their windows. Summoning the courage to visit Peter had been difficult. Yet thanks to his generosity, I came to know Fontana better than anyone else. For that I will always be grateful.

Peter told me he called Fontana "Slugger." "Nice shades, Slugger," Peter teased when Fontana arrived at his apartment in sunglasses to celebrate their one-month anniversary. He still had infield dirt caked under his fingernails. After Peter poured him a drink, he took off his glasses—he wouldn't leave the apartment without them, Peter explained—and excitedly told Peter about hitting in his thirtieth consecutive game that day.

To Fontana, Peter was "Bambino," the Babe, a play on Peter's height and an ironic nod to his inward demeanor, a far cry from his namesake, Babe Ruth. Peter had a vague idea who Ruth was (though I had to explain that the Yankees legend had nothing to do with the Baby Ruth candy bar). But he was happy to be called anything by Slugger, who he gleefully dragged to private parties ("discrete, nameless affairs," he assured Fontana). Million-dollar arm candy, he called his Slugger.

Since a childhood fright (a neighbor's dog broke her chain and bit young Ricky in the leg), Fontana distrusted animals. Yet he grew to enjoy the attention of Peter's Siamese cat, Frenchie. Frenchie and Fontana spent evenings together after Mets games inventing their own sports with catnip balls and bits of string. Fontana would throw a toy mouse into the air, and Frenchie, claws extended, leapt to catch the mouse with one paw, bringing it into his mouth and landing on all fours in one smooth motion. "Our infielders could learn a thing or two from Frenchie," Fontana told Peter.

Peter calls himself "a neat-freak." Mets fans—who have watched Fontana in the dugout between at bats spitting gobs of sunflower seeds—and reporters—who joked among ourselves about the chaos that was Fontana's locker—know that he was anything but tidy. So Peter got used to finding his bathroom sink lined with thick, black hairs from his Slugger's pre-game shave. And he grew accustomed to discovering socks and shirts draped over chairs and the bedspread. Still, he was surprised one day to spot a pair of size-XL boxers hanging from his ceiling fan. Peter wondered how they came to rest in a place he could reach only by standing on a chair. Mets fans will remember that Fontana had a strong, if not accurate, throwing arm.

Peter cooked. Ricky ate. For weeks, Fontana awoke to find his eggs fried and his orange juice poured over ice, as he preferred. Peter hardly expected Fontana to be much of a homemaker. But two weeks before I discovered them kissing on Peter's doorstep, Peter came home to find Ricky in the kitchen. He had not yet noticed

Peter, who watched quietly. Ricky laid long, flat lasagna noodles one by one in a pan and spooned cheese and homemade sauce (his mother's recipe, dictated over the phone that afternoon) to complete the layer. Peter applauded. Ricky blushed.

To Fontana, the flat on North 10th Street became more than home. There, he found affection that he had never known before, love that his mother could not provide; there, he shared a bed for the first time. At first, he couldn't sleep—when Fontana made two errors in right field one day in April, would fans have pardoned his miscues if they had known he had been awake all night, too nervous to sleep next to another man for the first time? Eventually, the warmth and the sleeping coughs and the slow rhythm of Peter's breathing comforted him, and he slept soundly. Peter's hair and sweat on his pillow smelled more like home to Fontana than his antiseptic bed in New Jersey. He had hired a maid to clean his apartment, and his bed always reeked of her perfume for days after. He lived in Williamsburg on and off during the streak, but once my column was published, fear convinced Fontana that reporters would find and stalk his New Jersey apartment. He moved to Brooklyn for good.

On off days and after the games, they were inseparable. He became such a familiar face around Peter's place that once Fontana left New York, Peter's oblivious friends would ask what happened to "the Italian Stallion," unaware that they needed to look no further than the sports pages, where Fontana's photo appeared every day as the most famous homosexual in the country. Still, not often while he lived in Williamsburg did a stranger stop him for an autograph, an irony that even hipsters dressed in fashionable shabbiness might appreciate.

And I ruined them. I passed judgment by judging their love newsworthy. So I visited Peter Morgenstern for more than just a follow-up story on Fontana. I showed up for penance. What could be more absurd than arriving one December morning at the home of a man I had publicly humiliated? When he opened the door, I thrust my hand into his and shook violently, and I said, "Thank you, thank you so much for seeing me today. Really, I am truly grateful. Thank you, thanks again."

Peter was the physical reverse of Fontana. Fontana was a muscled Mediterranean ox; the man at the door, eyeing me suspiciously, was a skinny Scandinavian mouse. Peter was short and boyish at twenty-seven. He spiked his corn silk hair messily and wore glasses with black rectangular frames and thick lenses that shrunk his eyes. The sunlight blanched his almost colorless eyebrows. He looked at me, wrinkled his nose twice (which made him look even more rodent-like), and invited me inside.

Peter was a graphic designer for a trade magazine publisher. He painted, too, mostly watercolors, but his home was undecorated. I wondered, shouldn't an artist decorate his home with his creations? His walls were white, plain white, and what little hung on them was functional: mail, unopened, stacked neatly on a hanging shelf, keys on hooks, sorted and labeled, plastic bins also labeled carefully ("Mittens," "Gloves," "Hats,") and umbrellas hung in height order. A stack of magazines and Playbills near the front door was the only clutter in Peter's home, spotless otherwise. Dressed in a coal-colored shirt and pants, Peter himself was the focal point of a modern art masterpiece, a black dot on a white canvas.

He directed me into a sparsely furnished living room (also devoid of decoration) to a white leather couch.

"Tea? Coffee?"

I shook my head.

"Beer? Glass of wine?"

My jaw slackened. I shouldn't, but I wanted to, and he had invited me. To drink. Now, a moment, a lifetime, and forever felt indistinguishable, and I panicked. Mouth dry, head numb, all my reproductive viscera shrank into my torso, and I panicked. Panicked because I had to shake off vital memories of happiness in a glass, the funny way the oily surface of Peter's wine would reflect my face and slake my thirst and my nervousness, the oh-my-God cringing embarrassment of showing up here with a pad and pencil, a grin, and a badge in my pocket congratulating me for three sober months.

"Thanks, but I'd better not."

He sat in an armchair, facing me.

"How are you?" he asked, frowning slightly.

This I hadn't expected. How am I? What should I say? "I'm all right."

He offered a weak smile, but said nothing else.

"So…how are you?" I offered. And then I felt stupid. For asking, for coming to his house, for not wiping my feet, for wondering how Fontana and his little mouse had anything in common, and lived, ate, and…well, yes, slept together. Because that's what all this is about: fucking, right? It's all about the curiosity, the novelty, the peculiarity, the unfamiliarity of two men fucking. Sex, of course, is what made my big scoop on Ricky Fontana front-page news. Sex is what sent reporters from every newspaper and network patrolling what was rumored to be his suburban New Jersey neighborhood, what sent a contingent of us that seemed to grow nightly to the stadium entrance, locker room, and players' parking lot before and after every game. Even though my photograph caught two men exchanging a caring kiss, they might as well have been pictured unclothed in a yin and yang tangle of dark and pale skin on the mound at Citi Field.

Getting the photos was luck, nothing more; I'm no photographer. I got the smartphone for free through the *Tribune*. In fact, I had only used the camera function once before, after Tara left, to take a picture of myself for a dating website. But my nose looked too big and my ears too small, so I gave up and downloaded the portrait next to my sports column from the newspaper website. (Nobody was reading the *Trib* anyway, according to Driggs, so what did it matter?) I gave up dating after dinner with a woman who wrote me the next day to complain, "All you talk about is baseball."

My next photo was of Ricky and Peter. A million-dollar shot. "Lurid" everyone at the *Tribune* agreed was the best word to describe the photo in my follow-up story. "A lurid photo captured Mets superstar Ricky Fontana at play with his boyfriend on Monday in Williamsburg," I wrote the next day. Bathed in shadows, the men stare at each other longingly. Fontana's head is tilted thoughtfully to one side, toward the camera, considering Peter with the adoration of Leonardo's magi. Mets fans might swear those are not their right fielder's eyes; we've all watched his glare, like a gunslinger's, the concentration, determination, and confidence when he's staring down the pitcher. But he's not holding a bat in the photo. Ricky holds Peter's small, yielding hand between his palms. The delicacy of the gesture and the emotion it suggests cannot be overstated; rub the fingertips of one hand over the knuckles of another—between two people, there is an intimacy to this simple act that we strive for during our most desperate moments of coupling.

"I'm doing okay," Peter said to me. "Under the circumstances, I'm doing quite okay."

I broke down. "I'm sorry, I'm sorry. I shouldn't be here. Not after what I've done to you and Ricky."

"Oh stop it, stop it!" he snapped. "Stop it! All your contrition will do is make me sorry for you, and I don't want that."

I apologized again, and then I apologized for apologizing. Peter shook his head and rolled his eyes. Finally, he said, "Ricky doesn't blame you."

"Really?"

"He knew he was going to be outed someday. You know, he always liked you."

"Really?" I felt wildly happy. I was disappointed when he didn't explain more.

"Yes," Peter said crossly. "To be honest, that's one reason I'm speaking to you for your article."

My first question to Peter was one that I have been asked often since I outed Ricky Fontana: Why didn't anyone suspect Ricky was gay?

"Ricky has never been to a Broadway show," said Peter. "He doesn't swish around with his wrist hanging limply from his arm. He doesn't lisp or dress like a woman. He doesn't blast disco from the locker room stereo. These are all cruel stereotypes of gay men, but because Ricky doesn't conform to them, none of his teammates knew."

I told him that I thought he was being unfair to Fontana's teammates. It had never crossed their mind because many athletes are afraid to discuss homosexuality with their comrades. And some are too afraid even to wonder who among their teammates might be gay. Most American professional athletes have since they were young teenagers lived inside an insulating sports-only culture that outsiders—even we who examine them so closely—cannot understand as a pervasive cult of competition and manhood. We imagine major leaguers as normal people. But a big league jock is no more normal than the prodigy who has spent most of his waking life sawing at his violin or pecking programs into a computer. He has probably never met an openly gay person. In school, the queer kids stayed away from the practice fields, and the gay ballplayers kept their secret close lest coaches and teammates reject them and squander years of hard work. The ones that chose to keep their secret perhaps walked away from the game happier than Ricky Fontana could ever be in the closet. But his genius was not wasted.

Peter said angrily, "Then why so much shock? Why didn't the coach ever speak to him again?"

"Coach? You mean the manager, Grey Mason?"

Peter's pupils burst wide. "You don't know?"

"Know what?"

"Nobody but Ricky knew? Nobody told the press? Poor Ricky."

I pressed him for more, and he said, "Mason never spoke to Ricky again after your article was published."

"Good ol' Grey? You're joking!"

"Nope. Never. No questions. No curses. No dirty looks. Just silence. When Ricky asked him a question, the coach would ignore him. Ricky told me that he even stopped giving him signals—err… signs—from the dugout."

There was silence for a moment. I didn't look at Peter, avoiding eye contact, staring around the empty room, searching for something to say, and then I heard a sigh.

"You probably think he's a coward. Ricky," Peter said. "You probably think he should've just come out with it. Maybe he should've. Maybe he is a coward."

"That's not true!" I countered, cajoling, comforting and correcting all at once. "You remember his first game after the story—*my* story—was published? He showed a lot of guts."

Peter nodded. "Yes. Ricky told me what you did, how you tried to help him."

It was a madhouse, I explained to Peter. Fontana arrived early—nine a.m.—to avoid the flocks of reporters that he knew would be waiting for him. But I arrived at eight thirty among the last reporters to reach Citi Field. Hung over, without a moment's rest, and almost too tired to return the smiling congratulations from Rule, Crane, and Callahan for the astonishing scoop that I had spent all night turning into the most important sports story in the history of the *Tribune.* I hadn't checked my phone, abuzz all morning with calls and texts from colleagues, friends, my parents, and TV news producers who wanted exclusive access to me. I wasn't ready to be part of the story. But I had no choice. They stared when I arrived. As my three buddies congratulated me, whispers and nods among the other reporters—most of them were strangers to me, and Citi Field for that matter—indicated that I was the newsmaker.

Suddenly, a sense of unbelonging enveloped me. I realized how much I had let myself go. That's the man who turned up this epic story? Surely they wondered. Not much of a man with a days-old beard, rumpled clothes, sagging everywhere. I was the ugly, fat lotto winner who drew a lucky number in my Fontana scoop, the only luck I'd ever had. Meanwhile, the TV reporters were splendid in movie star makeup over cover girl faces. They were born lucky.

I leaned against a railing near the players' entrance to the ballpark. I gratefully sipped his coffee when Callahan offered. Then, with the other ninety-seven members of the press who had traveled to Queens that morning, I waited.

I was dozing when the shouting began.

"There he is!"

"Ricky! Over here!"

"Ricky, what is your reaction to the story in today's *Tribune?*"

"Is the article true? Are you gay, Ricky?"

"Ricky, who was that man with you at the bar?"

"Have you told your teammates?"

"Ricky, how long have you known you are a homosexual?"

When I stepped up on the railing to peek over the crowd, I saw him. He wore jeans, a beige cap, and a tan windbreaker with a Nautica logo on the back, which I plainly saw as he turned and walked away from the crowd in the parking lot. The reporters shouted louder. Finally, when he was thirty yards away from us, he stopped. The sportscasters ceased their shouting. He turned to us and walked back toward the stadium, shoulders sagged, as the throng remained silent, reloading their cameras and throats for another volley. He reached us, and the shouting began anew.

Peter interrupted. "You guys caught Ricky by surprise. He didn't expect so many of you so early."

"Neither did I," I admitted. Every local affiliate had sent a reporter and a cameraman. Vans from Fox News and CNN and MSNBC, mobile satellites reaching skyward, parked haphazardly on the curb facing the players' entrance. Fans, too—dozens of New Yorkers came to watch the tumult from behind blue wooden police barricades. I could barely see over the crowd that swarmed around Ricky. And I could barely think with all that shouting.

"Ricky, are you a homosexual?"

"Ricky, have you told Grey and your teammates?"

"Do you live with another man?"

A fan shouted, "We love you, Ricky!" to hoots and cheers from the gallery.

"Is the man in the photo your husband?"

At last Fontana said, "I refuse to answer any questions about my personal business."

As if they didn't hear, the members of the press continued.

"When were you going to come out, Ricky?"

"Ricky, are you religious?"

"Do you expect fans to welcome you?"

He repeated, "I refuse to answer any questions about my personal business."

The shouting continued, the questions the same. Fontana stood defiantly, shaking his head, but saying nothing. My booze-addled brain was throbbing from the racket, so in frustration I shouted, "Ricky! I have a question for Ricky!"

The reporters hushed. After all, I was the ace who had scooped them all, the fellow who had gone overnight from anonymity to the most notable byline in the New York sports press. Though the

Tribune would close in two days, my sudden fame would allow me to start a blog that had more visitors from its inception than Crane's popular corner of the *Times* sports section online. Damn right they shut up when I spoke!

"Ricky, in February you told me that you thought you could break DiMaggio's streak and hit four hundred. Well, you've broken the streak. So are you willing now to make any predictions about your final batting average?"

He almost smiled. Almost.

"Sure, I stand by my word. I can hit four hundred. But no matter how well or how poorly I hit this season, I want to help the Mets reach the World Series. I've said that all along."

Crane decided to take advantage of the silence.

"Ricky, what do think the impact of your sexuality will be on the gay, lesbian, and transgender community in the United States?" Crane asked.

Fontana shook his head. "No more questions, thanks." He walked into the ballpark as the shouting resumed. The interrogation followed him into the stadium and echoed unanswered.

Later that afternoon, Fontana addressed his teammates before that night's game against the Padres. Sammy Olmos, the Mets equipment manager, told me afterward what Fontana had said, reading from a small scrap of paper.

"I just wanted to tell you guys that everything you've read in the papers today is true. I am sorry that I have had to keep secrets from my teammates, but I felt that I deserved my privacy. I am also sorry that my struggle to maintain my privacy has not only caused some unpleasant confrontations with the press in our clubhouse, but also made me a bad teammate. I haven't been as welcoming as I should have been to some of you, and most of you deserved better. I hope you see me as the same ballplayer and the same man you thought I was yesterday."

Fontana did not look up from his notes as he spoke. When he finished, he gazed around the room, and, to his relief, his teammates were still there, listening.

He turned to his locker and began to lace up his spikes. Stunned, some of his teammates drifted back to their lockers without a word. But most walked over to Fontana and embraced him. An enthusiastic crowd of Mets surrounded his locker and shook his hand, congratulated him, encouraged him, thanked him, and promised him that he would not be alone in his struggle for privacy. Some of them, Olmos noted, volunteered to stop speaking to me. Fontana did not encourage them.

"Actually, my son came out to me last year," Olmos added. "I didn't speak to him for weeks. Eventually, I got over it. But if my son was half as eloquent as Fontana when he told me, I would have hugged him on the spot."

While his teammates swatted lazy fastballs around the ballpark, Fontana took batting practice alone in the batting cages beneath Citi Field. He arrived in the dugout moments before the game began. Jason Meyers and Mets Media Relations had done all they could to convince the team's TV network to treat this as just another game. Still, when the public address announcer read the lineups before the anthem, there was a wild, raucous roar when Ricky Fontana's name was spoken. Not cheers, not jeers, just collective, swelling noise over a smattering of applause. Mets fans didn't know how to react.

As his teammates charged onto the field, Fontana followed, head down, sprinting to his position in right field. Sitting in the press box, I heard boos. My heart sank. The game had sold out. Had thousands of fans paid to jeer Ricky Fontana? Yet as he reached the outfield, a cheer rose from the stands that overwhelmed the booing. One minute became two and the intensity of the applause never wavered until the fans in right field stood and began to chant in rhythm, "RI-CKY! RI-CKY!" Fontana turned to them and doffed his cap. At that moment, Fontana and I both dared to hope that life after my article would not be as bad as we feared.

Chapter Eight

How few of us could understand the plight of the gay ballplayer! Surely, however, the gay sports fan can empathize. The male homosexual, according to bigoted orthodoxy, is a man drawn to the interests of women. Yet the gay fan pursues the pastimes of men. Thus he is a man playing a woman pretending to be a man, like a drag queen who keeps his moustache. Most perplexingly, his manly pursuits are unironic. His ball cap is no go-go boy costume fireman's hat, his jersey is no biker's leather. He is just a fan who could be any fan except he isn't just any fan because he's a fag.

A faggot fan who fits in nowhere. Homophobe straights suspect he's a pretender, and skeptical gay comrades wonder why he cares for a pointless game.

Yet there are millions of gay fans, devoted supporters of every team in every major sport. Now their devotion encircled one athlete.

A great cheer arose in the days that followed my infamous article. Gays, lesbians, and their allies exhaled. Finally, He had arrived, the equalizer, the hero. Hey, we can play, said Ricky Fontana without saying anything except the loud declaration with his bat that he could not be daunted by his secrets spilling forth. He went three for four on the day my column was published.

Every other gay athlete fell short as an idol. None were as famous as Ricky, as photogenic, as supremely talented. So requests to meet him, interview him, just one quote, they flooded his agent and Mets Media Relations. ESPN interviewed me for a feature called "The Wall Falls: Ricky Fontana Breaks the Last Barrier in Sports." I noted on the broadcast that Italians had worshipped DiMaggio and Jews named Sandy Koufax as heroes who lifted their people. Now, gays were taking to the airwaves and editorial pages to declare: Fontana has proven that we can do anything. Once, Negro Leaguers were demeaned by comparisons to whites; Josh Gibson was called the black Babe Ruth. In a column to rebut such analogies, I wrote, "Pujols and Tulowitzski, Braun and Stanton—if they're lucky, one day they might be known as the straight Ricky Fontana."

Many assumed that Fontana would embrace his role as gay America's champion. Any day now, I thought, would bring a press conference where he proudly announced his sexuality. Then he would hoist a vulnerable people on his shoulders and go forth joyfully as their hero. Any day now, I thought.

My column launched a news sensation. Coverage from national newscasters and political talking heads bloated my ego. Still, more important to me were the sportswriter colleagues who ran with my story on their beats. Every columnist and hack blogger had an opinion. Even journalists in minor league towns took up the story of baseball's unofficial second integration. In Spokane, a reporter asked Carlos Jackson if he regretted calling Fontana a faggot. Jackson told her to fuck off.

The on-camera interrogation of ballplayers yielded a three-category list of major leaguers: those who supported or embraced gay teammates, those who objected to their presence, and the noncommittal. It is my belief that most players who declined comment actually feared or reviled homosexuals, yet they were too savvy (or shy or cowardly, depending on your point of view) to invite rebuke from journalists who are generally a socially liberal lot.

Much of the negative reaction came in the form of religious condemnations. Joe Lippincott, my colleague at the *Tribune*, thanked me for my column. He said, "Folks who believe that homosexuality is sin ought to know that we can't root for Fontana." Devout players such as Houston's Allan Westcott and Keith Karar of the Yankees said they were dismayed that a role model like Ricky Fontana could be openly gay (even though Fontana had made no public statement since my column). Some wished Fontana well, though they hoped he would eventually see the harm in his lifestyle. Colin Lynn of the Seattle Mariners said he thought Fontana could be cured with prayer.

Still, many other players simply objected to playing alongside a gay man.

Kurt Farthing, pitcher, Arizona Diamondbacks: "Baseball is a brotherhood. You can't have a functioning team if players are worried that teammates are going to make a pass at them. Homosexual players should stay in the closet."

Lou Scott, outfielder, Washington Nationals, on the chance his teammates might be gay: "I'm sure that possibility means most of the team will shower at home now or at the hotel. Whatever. Cuts down our water bill."

Izzie Guillermo, manager, Miami Marlins, on his initial reaction to the news about Ricky Fontana: "I said to myself, that's funny. He hits like a real man."

Later, the MLB Commissioner's Office fined Farthing, Scott, and Guillermo for their remarks. Guillermo (and several of his players) seemed especially surprised. During a postgame interview, Guillermo noted that he had not used any anti-gay slurs. Still, Major League Baseball wanted to make a point that intolerance, no matter how ambiguous, would not be tolerated. Guillermo was an easy target. In 2007, Major League Baseball fined him for calling an umpire "a big fat faggot." A reporter asked Guillermo if he'd be more careful now about using such terms. He snapped, "I won't say shit ever again. Fuck it. Izzy gonna take a vow of silence, no more stories about me."

Three days after I outed Fontana, from the Park Avenue offices of baseball's commissioner came this pronouncement: "Major League Baseball is proud that our national pastime reflects our nation's diversity. Any public discourse by MLB players or personnel intended to alienate or slander fellow players is not in the spirit of fair play and will be punished."

Fontana remained silent. So did his team. On the day of my column and the following day, the Mets took the unprecedented step of closing the clubhouse to reporters and barring the media from the field. The dead air became almost as big a story as Fontana's sexuality. Sports networks and New York news affiliates broadcast live reports from the Citi Field stands. They interviewed fans and beer vendors and ushers, anyone who would opine on camera about gays in baseball because Mets players and the front office weren't talking.

Peter Morgenstern revealed the reason for the hush up. On the night my column was published, Mets Media Relations Director Jason Meyers summoned Ricky Fontana to his office. According to Peter, Meyers wanted Fontana to hold a press conference before the next day's game to announce he was gay.

"It's true, isn't it?" Meyers asked Fontana. He nodded.

"Aw, Ricky," Meyers exclaimed. "Why couldn't you tell us?"

"Because it's none of your business," said Fontana.

But to the Mets public relations guru, a gay superstar was indeed the team's business and very good for business indeed. The Mets strove to be the everyman foil to their crosstown rivals, the blue-blood Yankees. To broaden the team's appeal to New York's Latino audience, they pursued Hispanic superstars like Johan Santana, Carlos Delgado, and Carlos Beltran. Under the leadership of Meyers's predecessor, the team was rebranded as "Los Mets" in advertisements. Players wore jerseys with the Spanish title during practice. Now, Meyers saw another audience to win over. Gay fans might be the ultimate baseball swing voters, undecided about their affiliations because prejudice and cultural pressures persuaded so many that sports were a heterosexual realm. Meyers told Fontana he envisioned promotional nights for same-sex couples, co-sponsorships with LGBT organizations, team fundraisers for marriage equality and anti-bullying groups—all he needed was Ricky Fontana to cooperate.

Meyers was an intern for the Mets in 2002 when rumors about a gay baseball player sizzled in the New York media. Speculation centered on one Mets player: All-Star catcher Mike Piazza. Meyers, dumbfounded, watched the team prepare for the most bizarre press conference in baseball history. Piazza told reporters, "I'm not gay. I'm heterosexual…I can't control what people think. I date women."

Now Meyers asked another Mets star to tell the world he was gay.

"Say that you're proud to be gay and you're proud to be a Met," Meyers said. "And it'll be 1947 all over again." That year was the first a black man played in the major leagues. He was Jackie Robinson, infielder for the Brooklyn Dodgers. The Dodgers moved to Los Angeles in 1958 (breaking my father's heart and millions more), so the Mets dubbed themselves the protectors of Jackie's legacy. The grand hall at the entrance to Citi Field is named the Jackie Robinson Rotunda. Perhaps, Fontana thought, Meyers fancied himself a new millennium Branch Rickey, the brave Dodgers executive who hired Robinson to break baseball's color barrier.

Fontana would hear none of it.

"We could be pioneers," Meyers insisted. "Think of what it'd mean to fans. Especially gay fans." But Fontana refused. He would make no public statements, and he would grant no interviews about his sexuality. Meyers pleaded with Fontana to reconsider. He proposed two days of media silence so Fontana could think over his decision without being hounded by reporters.

But Fontana told Meyers what he said whenever someone stopped him outside the ballpark and gushed about how much it meant to root for a gay ballplayer. He said, "I'm just a fucking ballplayer. Not a gay ballplayer. Just a ballplayer."

On the third day, the media ban was lifted. And for the third straight day, the crowd of reporters and cameramen exceeded eighty people. That evening also saw a rare appearance by Cameron Everly, an injured outfielder who was making his first—and only—visit to Citi Field that season. Mets fans ruefully remember Cam as the stocky slugger who signed a three-year contract and then, during his second week with the team, tore several muscles in his lower back. He never played for the Mets again.

Everly was an outspoken homophobe long before he had a gay teammate. "Being gay is wrong," he told *New York* magazine in 2010. "Two women can't make babies. Neither can two men. That's not right. We as a society shouldn't support that." So when he arrived at Citi Field with his agent to settle a contract dispute, no one was surprised when he walked into the clubhouse to greet his old teammates and spotted Ricky Fontana and sneered.

The two had never met. Still, Fontana recognized Everly and did his best to ignore him when cheers of "Yo, Cam!" greeted Everly.

He entertained the audience that crowded around, outfielder Sam Caple told me the next day. Everly endured playful pokes to his midsection, where he had added a few pounds during his convalescence. Someone remarked admiringly about the dime-sized diamond he wore in his ear, and Everly bent to offer a better view. Then he noticed Fontana sitting quietly on a couch watching the clubhouse television. He brought his finger to his lips—Sssh!—and his eyes and his bejeweled ear sparkled. He winked. Then he placed one hand on his hip. He hung his other hand limply in midair with his elbow against his waist. Then he sashayed over to the couch and swished past Fontana, twitching his behind as he walked, toe to heel. As he passed Fontana, Everly said in a girly screech, "What's up, girlfriend?"

Then he snorted and walked away, shaking his head.

Carlest, Monan, and Esperanza laughed uproariously. Several more of Everly's welcoming committee tittered. The color in Fontana's face deepened, but he did not turn his face from the television.

Everly's mocking, which Peter described during my first interview at his apartment, was not unexpected. But Peter's claim about manager Grey Mason, that shocked me. Mason was a popular figure in New York, the grandfatherly face stumping for used car dealers and borough charities and pasta restaurants in local commercials. Fontana had once been his favorite. Whenever Fontana lashed a base hit, Mason would turn to his coaches and say, "That's my boy, Ricky!" In the midst of the streak, Mason slipped a few times during interviews with the press. "I was pulling hard for my boy—Ricky, that is—and he came through tonight when we needed him," he said to us after a game in May when Fontana doubled home the winning run.

Peter and I agreed to meet again early the next morning to continue my interview. I didn't sleep much that night. Folks like me who covered the game considered Mason to be one of the most sympathetic, player-friendly managers. That he could resent Fontana for his sexuality seemed impossible. He never showed any proclivity toward religion, I explained to Peter. He never took part in the pre- and post-game prayer circles with the devout players.

Peter said, "Just a plain old bigot, I guess. Doesn't need an excuse."

In the private world of the baseball clubhouse, managers are surrogate dads. They are aprons to catch the spills when factionalism and cliquishness bubble over. Managers defend beleaguered players from the media. Men in my profession respect their decrees about clubhouse access without exception. But Mason had abandoned that role on Fontana's behalf. Fontana was on his own to be chased and bullied. Ricky probably didn't miss the man who knocked up his mother and left before Ricky was born. Still, his manager's rejection, I realized, was the second time that Fontana lost a father figure.

I never thought I would see Eusebio Hernandez again, but there he was. It was my second day of interviews with Peter Morgenstern. Peter and I were in the kitchen of his Williamsburg apartment, each of us searching a bag of sweeteners nabbed from coffee shops for our preferred brand. Then Seb wandered into the kitchen. Sleep drooped his eyelids. He wore only boxer shorts and a slim tank top.

"What do you want, honey?" Peter asked.

"Lighter," Seb croaked. He was twiddling an unlit cigarette. He did not greet me. He stared past me as if I didn't exist.

Peter fished a lighter from a drawer and tossed it to Seb, who wrapped himself in a coat by the door and stepped out to the stoop where Ricky and Peter had shared their fateful kiss.

That Seb didn't acknowledge me was, of course, unsurprising and not worth pursuing with Peter. I had tried to contact Seb several times, but my calls went unanswered. His agent explained that Seb was understandably furious with me. After Peter convinced him that the two of them would have more control over Ricky's story if they spoke to me—and assured Seb that I was, against all common sense, sympathetic to Ricky's cause—Seb agreed to a short interview after New Year's Day.

But two weeks earlier, he wouldn't even offer me a glance. So I said to Peter, "It's nice that you have someone to comfort you now that Ricky's gone. A good friend of Ricky's, I imagine."

"Seb was probably Ricky's closest friend, actually. He took a much more commonsense approach to his sexuality, really. He announced to the team he was gay and accepted that some of them wouldn't care and others wouldn't have anything to do with him. Rumors got around, of course, so most ballplayers knew about Seb, and Ricky sort of looked at him like a big brother. Ricky wouldn't mind that we're hooking up."

"You and Seb?"

Peter nodded.

"Really?" I asked. And then like a little kid, "Gee…"

Peter didn't discuss it further, and I didn't press him. I didn't want to pry further into the personal business of the man whose life I had already made so difficult.

"Why didn't Ricky just come out?" I asked.

"I asked him the very same thing," Peter said. "It would've been so much easier if he did it on his own terms."

"During the off-season when nobody's paying attention, yes, it would have been discussed all winter while Ricky could hide from the spotlight. So why did he keep the secret?"

Peter asked, "Do you know any gay men besides me and besides Ricky?"

I remembered Bobby McNamara, my freshman roommate, so I said with certainty, "Yes, of course."

As he placed a mug of coffee near me, he asked, "And are you frightened of us? Have you ever been?"

I recalled one day when Bobby McNamara returned to our dorm room after class. I was reading on my bed in only boxer shorts. He greeted me, sat at his desk, and opened a textbook. All of a sudden I felt naked and observed, and although Bobby paid me no attention, I went to my closet and chose a T-shirt and jeans to wear, muttering about how chilly our room had become. But being modest about your body doesn't make you a homophobe, I decided. Neither does the discomfort I felt when I arrived early at a post-finals party at my history professor's house and saw him kiss his partner good-bye. I was only a kid, then, just out of my mother's house. I couldn't stop staring at them as they held hands. Well, how often do you see two men touching like that, I asked myself.

"Frightened? No, absolutely not," I answered with less conviction. "Why?"

"I'm lucky," Peter said. "My parents accepted my sexuality as soon as I came out, and nearly all of my straight friends shrugged and treated me the same. My high school even had an LGBT Society. So the reaction to Ricky's sexuality is something I didn't get and wasn't prepared for and still don't understand."

I nodded. I didn't know what else to say.

He continued. "After the first game following your column, the pitcher Adam Carlest called his wife. He asked her to make an appointment with his physician. As soon as possible."

"Why?"

"Carlest wanted to schedule a blood test."

"Why? How do you know all this?"

"Mick Kelleher overheard the phone call and told Ricky," Peter said. "Mick said that Carlest thought he had contracted AIDS. Do you know anyone like that, who thinks we all have it or something?"

Carlest, that nitwit. Peter didn't have to finish the story; the ignorance of Adam Carlest—New York's own John Rocker—was a running joke among the Mets beat writers. I once witnessed his idiocy firsthand at an offseason charity function. Jason Meyers attended the fundraiser with Carlest and pitcher Oscar Ferrera. After the event, Meyers struck up a conversation with Carlest. Meyers, who is Jewish, asked how Carlest's recent contract negotiations had gone. Carlest responded, "Well, we asked for $2.5 mil per year, but they jewed us down to 2.3."

Kelleher sat in the bullpen watching Carlest fidget. Usually, he cracked jokes, teased rookies, talked baseball with Mick, or studied the stat sheets until the call came to warm up. Dazed, Carlest wandered the bullpen aimlessly, silently, clearly disturbed. Kelleher asked, "Are you all right, Adam?"

"Yeah, yeah, I'm fine," came the answer.

After Jackie Rios grounded out to end the game, Carlest grabbed his glove and hurried into the locker room, where he tore open his locker and fished out his phone. Kelleher entered as Carlest hastily fled the clubhouse. Curiosity prevailed, and Kelleher followed.

Tucked into a corner in a quiet corridor, Carlest spoke hurriedly into his phone. "Hello, honey. It's me…No, we lost…No, I didn't pitch…Probably in an hour…Listen, I need you to do me a favor. Call Dr. Towers…No, I'm fine. I just need to be sure…I'm fine, really. It's just that, well, you know that kid Fontana? He's a queer…Yeah, you know. How could we?…Right. Exactly…He told us tonight…Well, I share a locker room with the guy…No…No… Dammit! Don't you get it? We shit on the same toilets! We use the same showers! This is baseball, dammit! We spend all day sweating, spitting, and bleeding all over each other…No, I'm not sick. Look, I told you…No…I just want our own doc to arrange a blood test… For what? For what? What do you think?…Who knows where that filthy faggot has been?"

Mick poked his head into the room, where I was interviewing Grey Mason.

"Where's Ricky?" he interrupted. "Anybody seen him?"

Ricky was long gone. Sweaty and sticking to his jeans and cap, he was already in a taxi, shrinking into the leather seat, zooming down the Brooklyn-Queens Expressway on the way to Peter's apartment.

"The next day, Mick warned him: Stay away from Carlest," Peter said. "Ricky didn't need to ask why."

Even though he was on pace to have the best season in baseball history, Fontana's skills were an afterthought to the New York press. After the Padres beat the Mets the following night, the local sportscasters met the team in the locker room as they did after every game. But the questions had nothing to do with baseball.

Adam Carlest and Henry Monan's lockers were cozied into the same corner, and the two bullpen-mates had become fast friends. Monan, a strict Southern Baptist, sometimes teased Carlest, a devout Pentecostalist, by stumbling around the locker room speaking in tongues, eyes rolled back in his head. But the two were often seen around the city together at charity events. Carlest, a short, balding bookworm, was never without a paperback novel when he traveled, and though he liked to quote the Book of Revelations, he tore through Tom Clancy and Clive Cussler. His manager once fined him when the bullpen coach caught him reading an adventure novel tucked between the pages of the scouting reports.

After Fontana's second game out of the closet, Dick Rule thrust a recorder under Monan's sweat-dappled face.

"Mr. Rule! What can we do ya for?" chuckled Carlest.

"Adam!" said Monan in a loud but conspiratorial whisper, "You can't make jokes like that no more since Fontana joined Team Pink." He turned to us. "That's off-the-record, guys. Now whaddya wanna know, Dick?"

Rule smirked and continued, "Do you think baseball is ready for a ga—er, um…homosexual ballplayer?"

"Oh, you mean that question was directed at us?" Monan asked with a guffaw as he tossed that morning's *Daily News* on the floor. Over a photo of Fontana in mid-swing, the back-page headline screamed: IS BASEBALL READY?

"I want the players' and the fans' perspectives," Rule explained.

"Well, the fans said their peace last night," Carlest said.

"And again tonight," Monan exclaimed. "Another ovation for Ricky Fontana!" He glanced at Carlest. "We say, good for Ricky."

"Definitely," Carlest said. "He always puts the team first. Wants to help us win. His double really got us back in the game tonight, and it's too bad we couldn't score him."

Crane interjected, "So you fellas have no problem sharing your locker room, your clubhouse, your dugout with a gay man?"

Carlest turned beet red. Monan said, "C'mon now. Can't we just talk about the game? This is baseball, not politics."

Rule seized the moment. "Do you think Fontana will be a distraction to the team?"

Monan said, "No comment."

Callahan jumped in. "How do you expect Yankee fans to respond tomorrow?"

Monan: "That's for them to decide."

Me: "So Grey tells me you've been working on a cutter. When should we look for that new pitch?"

Monan, relieved: "I'm still trying to get better command of it. I think a few more side sessions, and I should be ready to throw the cutter in a couple weeks."

Rule: "Adam, did you or any of your teammates suspect Fontana was gay?"

Carlest: "No comment. No."

We were really having some fun. I decided to take it a bit further.

Me: "Do you think that other men you've played with—perhaps even other players on the Mets—are gay and have not come out of the closet?"

Monan: "No comment."

Crane winked at me. He wanted the last laugh. "Does Ricky ever bring his partner or his boyfriend to the games?"

The pitchers were stunned.

Crane: "Or do you think he *might* be dating someone else on the team?"

Monan looked as if he had tasted shit. "No more questions, guys. We don't want to talk about it. We're here to play baseball. No more."

Fortunately for those of us with stories to write, other Mets were more generous with their comments.

"Did Ricky Fontana address the team about his homosexuality?"

Mick Kelleher, catcher: "Yes, he did. And he has the support of almost all of his teammates."

"Do you think Major League Baseball is ready for a gay ballplayer?"

Eddie Lee, outfielder: "It depends. Ballplayers, we're just regular people. Some folks are uncomfortable around gays, and some aren't."

"How does Fontana's sexuality change your view of him?"

Oscar Ferrera, pitcher: "Who gives a shit as long as he hits the goddamned ball? I know I'm not hurting anyone's feelings by saying that this team has got to score more runs."

When we had all clicked "send," when our laptops were closed, when the stadium lights were a shadow in our giddy memories, we four wordsmiths found an empty booth at our favorite pub. And we laughed. The nerds had bullied the jocks; four doughy sportswriters had cowed two muscled toughs. Readers flocked to my new blog for more of Ricky Fontana's secrets, but I had resolved to use my byline to protect him. I kept my *Tribune* press pass and followed the Mets on the road at my own expense for the chance to be a hero to my hero. "To us!" Callahan toasted, and he lifted his glass.

"No," I said. "To Ricky Fontana!"

"To Ricky Fontana!" we cheered as we drained our whiskey.

Callahan, the quiet one, surprised us all.

"Ri-cky! R-icky!" he chanted rhythmically, softly. "Ri-cky! Ri-cky!"

Rule joined in, but louder. And then Crane, shouting. And finally I joined, and we four bellowed, "RI-CKY! RI-CKY! RI-CKY! RI-CKY!"

Peter couldn't help but laugh as I described the relieved faces of the patrons of Carrickfergus Pub as the barman escorted us out, still chanting, "Ri-cky! Ri-cky! Ri-cky!" as we each made our way home at two thirty a.m. to sleep off our celebration and prepare for the first game of the heated interleague rivalry between the Mets and the Yankees.

"That game the next day," Peter said, no longer smiling, "That game was brutal."

Fifty-three thousand fans had tickets to the game—a sellout at Yankee Stadium. Ten thousand of them arrived early, a big crowd for late-morning batting practice. Ricky Fontana walked onto the field at eleven thirty a.m., bat in hand. A fan behind the third base dugout spotted him. When he saw the number six on Ricky's black warm-up jersey, the fan grabbed the cardboard sign he had brought to the game. He rolled it into a cone, and, holding it to his mouth like a megaphone, he roared shrilly, and the whole stadium heard him stretch his vocal chords to reach the deep, broad tones of former Yankees public address announcer Bob Sheppard, "Now batting, number six six six, Ricky *Fag*tana. Number six six six."

A discernible titter arose from the grandstands. The offender lowered his cone, looked about the sparse crowd proudly, high-fived his buddy, took his seat, and sipped his beer as if nothing had happened.

Fontana froze. His shoulders clenched, his face locked in a wince, clutching his bat against his chest, like a colonial thief bound in the stocks, he was unable to move, petrified in a moment of public humiliation. He finally sagged loosely, took a few weak practice swings, and walked into the batting cage to take his turn.

He missed the first three pitches.

Thoroughly penetrating the cautious applause of visiting Mets fans, a cascade of jeers met Fontana when he was introduced for his first at bat. Callahan and Crane and I looked at one another in disbelief as thousands of contemptuous mouths curved into boos. Fontana was shaken, striking out twice and popping out weakly to third base. The Mets lost nine to two.

"He didn't speak to me very much during that series," Peter recalled.

"I'm not surprised," I said.

"But that wasn't nearly as bad as the Boston series," Peter said, looking angrier than I had seen him. "I'll never understand the reaction Ricky got in fucking blue-state Boston! Fucking gay congressman Boston!"

"You can throw tolerance and political correctness out the window," I said. "When it comes to baseball, Boston fans hate anyone from New York. My friend Joe covers the Yankees for the *Tribune*. He wasn't the least bit surprised by their reaction. After all, he told me, you can go to Fenway Park and buy a T-shirt that says, 'Jeter sucks' and on the back 'A-Rod Swallows.'"

I paused to see if he wanted me to go on.

"And there's another shirt that simply reads 'Gay-Rod.' And one more that says, 'Jeter has AIDS.' That one is a bumper sticker too, I think."

"And people wear this shit in public?"

"Oh yes," I continued. "And that's nothing compared to what they actually *say* to the opposing players."

❖

"Good God!" Mick Kelleher whispered to himself. Through the bus window, the Mets catcher saw the boys, seven of them, all but one in navy blue caps and red jerseys. The last boy wore a royal blue shirt. Orange text on the shirt read "Fagtana plays for the Pink Team!" The boy stretched the shirt so his reflection glared off the side of the Mets coach bus as it pulled into Fenway Park. The boy was twelve years old, Kelleher told me later, or he couldn't have been more than fourteen.

Kelleher turned to his left cautiously. Had Fontana seen the boys? No—he was staring blankly at the floor, nodding his head to the beat in his headphones. When he caught Kelleher's gaze, Fontana took out his earbuds. And he smiled.

"Wow! Fenway Park!" said Fontana in awe. He stared at the brick facade and the green wall jutting majestically skyward, its inside face pocked by liners off the bats of Ted Williams, Carl Yastrzemski, and Dustin Pedroia. "You know, I've never been here."

Kelleher was distracted. Two more fans—a pair of ruddy, round-faced men—were hailing the bus, one holding a sign with an amateurishly drawn cartoon of a man in a Yankees cap sodomizing a man in a Mets cap. Mick turned back to Fontana quickly, doing his best to block the window with his shoulders. He grabbed Fontana's arm, perhaps a bit too hard. Fontana grunted and looked puzzled.

"You mean it?" Kelleher squeaked. "Never been to Fenway? Wow, man. You grew up so close by."

"I've probably been to every ballpark in Rhode Island—every field where there's a diamond and a backstop—but, no, I've never been to Fenway. After he got out of the Army, my dad played semipro ball—he was a pitcher—and my mom once came to a game of his near here when I was very small, in Worcester, I think. But I've never been here."

As Fontana spoke, the Mets sitting nearby hushed and listened. Fontana in a full-fledged conversation—now *that* was a rare spectacle. Precious, even, to those who had done so much to befriend Fontana before my article and since had been his silent protectors, guarding him against unrelenting reporters and teammates and opponents who feared his sexuality and resented his talent. Jackie Rios peered over his coach seat to hear Fontana's story. Oscar Ferrera and Fontana met as minor leaguers. But chatty, charming Ferrera had never gotten more than five words out of Fontana and gave up on calling him a friend. "Now that he's the Second Coming of Babe Ruth, he'll never talk to us," Ferrera told another Met as the rookie Fontana tore through the majors. But as the bus stopped in Lansdowne Street traffic, Ferrera leaned around his seat to hear him. Even Carlest and Monan quit their argument about New England's best golf courses to lend an ear. Fontana ignored the attention, or he was unaware.

"Once I picked up a bat as a Little Leaguer, I spent every spring, summer, and fall playing ball. I traveled all over looking for Little League, Pony League, Sandlot League, and pickup games. I played hardball with kids five years older than me, and I played softball with retirees. Anything to keep swinging. My grandma or my Aunt Chrissie, they shuffled me all over the place. I never took my spikes, my glove, my bat out of the trunk of their car. I knew I'd be on the road the next day, looking for a game. Never went to any major league games, actually, until I was drafted. What's the point, I asked myself? Nothing I could learn by buying a ticket that I couldn't learn better holding my own bat and glove. You know what I mean?"

"Your dad was a ballplayer? Did he ever make it to the Show?" Kelleher asked.

"And he was in the army," Ferrera exclaimed. "No wonder you always sing the anthem!" And he started to hum "The Star Spangled Banner."

"No, that's not it. He was drafted by the Yanks. Dropped after two seasons at Norwich. Played semipro ball with a losing record and couldn't catch on anywhere. Only met him once when I was seven."

"I'm sorry, man," Ferrera said. "I mean, same shit happened to me. Pops left when I was six. Then he shows up at my big league debut. No joke. He bought a ticket and sat in the grandstand, beer, hotdog, pennant. He snuck down to the first row and waved to me after the game. I gave him the ol' one-finger salute, you hear?"

Ferrera shriveled his face into a nasty grimace and flipped his middle finger. Fontana laughed, more like a giggle. Funny, Kelleher remembered, to see the kid acting like a kid.

The bus stopped outside the players' entrance to the ballpark. The Mets stood, collecting their gear.

"Already you beat your old man," Ferrera said, juggling a book and two issues of *Sports Illustrated.* "He ain't never made it this far."

"Nope," answered Fontana. He fixed his headphones in his ears and grabbed his bag. To Kelleher's relief, the buzz of digital music filled Fontana's head, and he didn't hear as he walked off the bus one of the round-faced men holler, "Hey, Fontana, you *fucking queer!*"

I told Peter, "Harvard and B.U. and Tufts students—members of their gay and lesbian clubs and such—went to the game that day in droves. There were many banners and signs supporting Ricky and cheers from the cheap seats. Enough to drown out the boobirds—at least it sounded that way from the press box."

"Where is that?" Peter asked.

"Above home plate."

"I was at that game," Peter said coolly. "I was sitting on the first base side in the outfield."

"Yeah, right field. You must've had a good view of the Green Monster, eh?"

Peter looked confused. "I didn't see him. That was the first time I traveled to see Ricky in a road game."

"You picked a good one," I offered hopefully. "Ricky went four for four. The last double he hit, I remember it smacked off the

Monster—that's the wall in left field—with this mighty *thwok*! The whole ballpark echoed."

"That was also the last time I went to see Ricky in a road game." Peter frowned. "Sure, I remember those kids, the LGBT clubs. I also remember that from where I was sitting, the fans were abusive—just awful—to Ricky. I mean, it was only a few people, but he could definitely hear them. Then some guy started chanting, 'Yankees suck!' which confused me, of course—the Yankees weren't even *playing*. But his chant spread and soon everyone was doing it, everyone, and it got louder and louder, but between chants, the fans in the first row, *inches* away from Ricky, pointed at him and chanted 'So do you!' and soon the whole first base outfield section was chanting 'Yankees suck! So do you!' at Ricky. I was mortified. I wanted to…kill…those *fucks*."

He spat the last word and a drop of saliva landed on his glass coffee table. I wiped it with my sleeve, and he thanked me.

"He heard every word," Peter continued. "He was a wreck that trip. We had all these plans. While we were in Boston, we were going to visit the museums, see all the touristy crap, and have some *fun*, enjoy the nightlife, all these things we couldn't do in New York without watching our backs. But I couldn't get him to leave my hotel room. He ordered room service and watched TV. He didn't say much. He didn't touch me. He barely *looked* at me. A fine romance, really."

Perhaps Fontana's anxiety explained his performance. He struggled in the remaining games in Boston and his season average slipped to .389. The Mets lost all three to the Red Sox. Their fortunes dipped with their right fielder's spirits as the Braves swept a series against the Rays and took a five-game lead over the Mets.

But not everyone in Beantown berated Fontana, I explained to Peter. On getaway day, a young man in the bleachers hoisted a sign whenever Fontana strode to the plate. Not many noticed him amidst the jeers, but eagle-eyed Crane scanned the crowd between pitches, as if he knew the source of a compelling story could be found among the hecklers. "Lookee there," he said, whistling between his teeth while Fontana took the plate. Crane pointed and handed me his binoculars. A teenager, probably from a nearby college, with a scraggly mop of brown hair and a chin-hugging goatee, held aloft a sign that read, "Marry me, Ricky."

"Cute story," Peter said snidely. I didn't think of Fontana as an object of desire, but to many gay men—and, of course, all those women—he was simply gorgeous. Peter didn't seem like the jealous type, but I realized that my anecdote could stir up bad memories.

"I'm sorry," I said. "It must have been hard on you having so many lust for him."

"No," Peter said. "I didn't care if other men wanted Ricky. I made it clear to him that our relationship was not exclusive. After all, he was practically a teenager and I was only twenty-seven. We were much too young to do the whole dating thing."

"But you lived together. And made him breakfast. And picked up his clothes from the floor. Sounds pretty serious."

"We cared about each other, it's true. But I always thought that I was just one stop on Ricky's journey. I mean, he was so famous and wealthy and he came from such a different world. How could we ever have anything in common? Besides, I know that not everything he told me about his nights on the road could be true. I mean, do you really think he traveled the country and didn't try to get laid?"

CHAPTER NINE

Sex made Ricky Fontana. His mother, when she was seventeen, saw a man and had to have him. Their one night together produced Ricky, and their codes combined to determine that their son's sexuality would make him unlike most men. His first desires arrived when other distractions could have pulled him away from baseball. A friend tried to lure thirteen-year-old Ricky to join his band. A gift that Christmas from Celeste—a Sony PlayStation—tempted him indoors during practice. But the sudden and unexpected longing he felt for other boys (and the derision he knew he would endure) drove him to the diamond. The ballplayer: an easily crafted identity, all he'd known since he first picked up a bat. This was Ricky Fontana until he met me.

Sex made Ricky Fontana a ballplayer, and I made sex his story. Nobody would care if my column revealed that Fontana held some other extraordinary and immutable quality. A beautiful voice, math savantism, a facility with foreign languages—who cares? These would be dull feature stories unread by all but a few fans curious about a photo of Fontana in a choir, at a chalkboard, or scrawling Kanji characters with Ichiro Suzuki.

Fontana had spent his life making himself a sexual object. He worked tirelessly toning his brawn, though he wasn't especially vain. Muscles were the tools of his craft. A ballplayer must not only be strong, he must also be quick. Fontana had thousands of stringy tendons and sinews to reinforce. These small muscles smartened his grip on the bat and allowed him perfect poise to bounce off his toes and attack any pitch. His body was an instrument for baseball's controlled violence, but to many it was also irrepressibly sexual. *Sports Illustrated* shot a cover portrait during his rookie year that Fontana sorely regretted. It showed him chest-up in a sleeveless shirt, sweaty and smeared with clay, bat slung over his steep shoulders, eyes intent on the observer. The magazine cover was sold as a poster, a best seller at Mets Clubhouse Stores. After my column, new shoppers by the hundreds—men, mostly—purchased the photographed fantasy that suddenly seemed more attainable. All his work to be a pinup!

Sex made Ricky Fontana a human being. Whaddya know, he kisses cute blond boys! I took the photos that proved he was just like you and me, his fame notwithstanding. Because even those humans who resemble gods spend much of their time thinking about fucking.

He tried to resist. Sex was inconvenient to Fontana. Being gay seemed incompatible with the identity that he had crafted through years of dedication and practice. As a ballplayer, he was Michelangelo's *David*—a perfect specimen. Fontana believed that heterosexuals at best think gay men are inherently silly. My column put a feather boa over the marble masterpiece.

Yet libido, a powerful force even in men as disciplined as Ricky Fontana, inevitably bowled over his better instincts. Once, in the showers after a minor league game, he found himself staring at a teammate's penis. Fascinated more than aroused. The loose meat was as black and long as a railroad spike. When the man attached to the cock saw Fontana staring, he predictably called Fontana a faggot and reached for a towel. But actual sex would have to wait; Ricky had games to play.

They lived on the road—minor leaguers hauled between towns where there were no paparazzi and many eager girls. To his bush-league comrades, Fontana thought, the true sport was fucking. His teammates came knocking for him. With knuckles on the door, they called him to the hunt, "Ricky? You coming out tonight?"

No, I think I'll stay in.

My legs are killing me.

I'm going over scouting reports.

I've got a bad cold.

Eventually, they stopped asking. Still, Fontana watched them prepare for their safaris with scientific fascination. They were to him a different breed: confident, proud, and unafraid, knowing the look in a woman's eyes like Ricky knew the spin on a curveball.

When the knocking came, Fontana wanted to open the door. But he couldn't. So he didn't. Instead, he pretended he didn't exist. He turned off the lights. He sat in the dark alone. He dug in his brain, searching those gray wrinkles for answers—*Why am I the way I am?*—but finding only echoes of the bat and ball. Frustrated, he lay in bed in darkness exploring himself. His blood raced and his mind surged with thoughts of other players. When he finished, he hated himself. He told himself he was better off practicing his grip on his bat: knuckles aligned, thumbs straight, fingertips loose.

One night, his roommate returned with a woman. He opened the door and the tipsy ditz tumbled into the room. Ricky's roommate followed, stopping suddenly. The woman giggled. The roommate whispered harshly, "Shuttup!" and yanked her by the arm into the doorway. Fontana had not heard them. Grand even in wrinkled and stained boxers, Fontana stood on the bed. Grunting. Thrusting. Rhythmically driving his hips. His eyes—Greg Reynolds would never forget Fontana's distant stare. Sweat poured down his face, dripping onto the bedspread.

Fontana was swinging an imaginary bat. He strode in his bare feet, twisting his torso as he brought his arms through the strike zone. He grunted as he finished each swing, his arms flapping during his follow-through. Then he collected himself and swung again.

"Let's get out of here," Reynolds whispered to his midnight snack.

"What's a-matter with that guy?"

"That's Ricky. He's a little weird. Probably a fucking faggot."

The following night, Reynolds was a faggot—at least that's what Carlos Jackson loudly proclaimed moments before Fontana charged onto the field and flattened him. As players from both teams pulled them apart, Reynolds slapped that fucking faggot on the back and said, "Attaboy, Ricky. You're the man."

❖

After a day off, the Mets returned from Boston for a ten-game home stand. As the scribe who outed the most famous man in America, I found myself that week enjoying free steaks and on-the-house champagne in my hometown's fanciest chophouses, sharing cigars at hotel bars with admiring colleagues, and, most memorably, a carriage ride in Central Park with Crane and two pretty cub reporters from the *Times*. Still, I thought of Tara while playing footsy with my carriage-mates and imagining my face in caricature on the wall at the Palm. Since I last saw my wife, I had written exclusively in my final *Tribune* columns and my new blog about Ricky Fontana, his contributions to the team, his steadfastness, his stoicism, his "blue-collar bravery," as I called it, a "working man's romantic duty to his craft in the face of so much uninvited attention." I printed each blog column and mailed it to Tara at her parents' house in Rochester. (She moved home after our separation.) To each clipping I attached a note inviting her back.

She opened and returned the first letter without a response. Each subsequent letter came back unopened, addressed in her handwriting to "Mister Jeremy Rusch" with a new stamp. An adhesive stamp. She hadn't even bothered to lick them.

Ricky, too, was writing. Long, lonesome love letters arrived on postcards from hotels in major league cities. "No, I'm not going to show them to you," Peter told me with a smirk. "Some things we shared should remain private." But Peter showed me one letter from late June. Fontana described how he had been hit in the shoulder by a pitch that night. On his way to first base, he was sure he heard the pitcher call him a faggot.

During his hitting streak, Fontana became a provocation to some of his teammates, who envied him. The more attention he received, the more desperately he tried to escape it, and the more fervently some jealous players resented him.

Envy spread, first among teammates and then to opponents. It festered throughout the spring, and then split open with the news that Fontana was gay. We watched—me, ashamed, Peter, horrified—as

Ricky Fontana's fellow ballplayers abused him before a national audience. Fontana said little to Peter about what other players did or said to him. He told Peter that it wasn't worth his concern. "I'm not going to let it distract me," Fontana said. "So why should you?"

During the first sixty-two games of the season—the miracle streak—Fontana was struck by a pitched ball only five times. After I wrote my infamous column, twenty-two pitchers hit him; eight of them did so more than once. The increase cannot be coincidence.

For all his gifts with the bat, Fontana was not a fast runner. He stole only four bases during his rookie season, and three of those he swiped as the trail runner in a double steal. But once he was gay to the world, some pitchers suddenly feared Fontana's speed. Many times when he reached first base, a pitcher would try to pick him off three, four, five times. In one game, Rockies pitcher Pascual Martinez threw to first base eleven times during one at bat. After the sixth throw, his own home fans booed Martinez for delaying the game.

Many readers have asked me why pitchers threw over so often to catch Fontana. Were they trying to make the gay ballplayer look foolish? The answer, I think, is more sinister. Fans who watched carefully saw several instances when Fontana would dive headfirst to the bag only to be kicked or stepped on by the first baseman, who could always claim he did so accidentally. Fontana took to wearing batting gloves fitted with extra padding to protect his hands. When Peter asked him why he drew so many pickoff attempts, Fontana simply said, "I think they like to see my face in the dirt."

As Fontana's batting average soared that summer—by the All-Star break he was batting .402—another statistic surged: his strikeouts. During his first season, Fontana struck out only thirty-eight times, a ludicrously low total that drove sabermetricians to equally ludicrous praise. But during his second season, Fontana struck out seventy-five times. Fifty-five of those strikeouts occurred after I revealed he was gay.

In forty-four of those fifty-five strikeouts, he struck out looking.

The significance of that discrepancy cannot be overlooked. Almost every other major leaguer strikes out looking as often as swinging. Fontana's outstanding batting eye indicates that he was statistically less likely to watch a third strike than the average player. To say that the sudden increase in strikeouts had nothing to do with anti-gay bias is ignorant—the claim itself is homophobic.

In fact, the Major League Baseball Commissioner's Office was concerned about on-field bias against Ricky Fontana. Under the condition of anonymity, an MLB official told me that the Commissioner's Office formed a committee to examine umpire bias against Fontana. The official claimed that seven umps were questioned for suspicious calls. In one case, a strike called against Fontana was so far outside that the catcher for the opposing team exclaimed, "Really?" In another game, Fontana was hit by a pitch— everyone on the field heard the ball strike his uniform, and replays show the umpire had an unimpeded view of the pitch. But when Fontana started to jog to first, the umpire called him back. Fontana refused to argue. He doubled on the next pitch.

Peter said he did not know why Fontana didn't fight back sooner. "Oh, he was mad," Peter said. "Furious. He knew he was getting screwed. But Ricky told me he had no recourse." Peter didn't understand why. But baseball fans know that when an umpire makes a bad call, the manager confronts the ump. And while many Mets players, fans, coaches, and even the groundskeepers berated umps for poor calls, never did Grey Mason emerge from the dugout to argue with an umpire. Then again, neither did Fontana himself. He told Peter he had nothing to gain.

One sweltering, windless afternoon in July, the Mets arrived in Miami, peeled off their sweat-stained street clothes, and lazily buttoned their road grays for a night game against the Marlins. And though he limped a bit from a pitch that had drilled his thigh in the previous game, Fontana was at the ballpark early, stretching his sore leg, shagging flies, and dodging reporters. Composed, even when he returned to the clubhouse and found the word "faggot" scrawled on his locker in fielder's eye black. Fontana asked Fredo, the clubhouse assistant, for a towel to wipe it off. Expressionless, resigned but defiant, undisturbed and undistracted from his pregame routine, he quietly asked the nearby newsmen not to mention the incident, and we consented. He answered our questions about baseball banalities and nothing more.

In the third inning that night, Fontana alertly seized an outside fastball with the end of his bat, too good to miss, and swatted it into right field. Hubie Rhodes was up next, and he chopped a grounder to the Marlins shortstop, Bryan Bell, who fielded the ball and ran to second base. Instead of leaping to avoid the sliding runner, as infielders commonly do, Bell threw the ball to first and stepped toward Fontana, crouching. His knee collided with Fontana's shoulder. Even over the crowd's roar of collective shock, a shriek reached my ears from the infield where Fontana lay writhing on his back, clutching his collarbone. And through it all, Bell's eyes never left first base. Finally, he stepped away from Fontana and returned to his position, his back turned to the Mets trainer, who chugged onto the field to examine Fontana, still prone and moaning.

During Bell's next at bat, Mets pitcher Oscar Ferrera threw a fastball at his elbow. Without a glance at the pitcher, Bell took his base while Ferrera glared. Catcher Mick Kelleher asked the umpire for time out. He jogged to the pitcher's mound and slapped Ferrera on the ass with his mitt. "Nice job, Ozzie," Mick said.

Later, Kelleher couldn't recall another moment when a teammate retaliated for an attack on Fontana. "Even the ones who didn't hate Ricky were too scared to fall out of line," he told me. "I'm a backup catcher with bad knees. I don't have more than a season or two left. But I understand how a guy with ten more years of good baseball wouldn't want to take sides. Ballplayers are a religious bunch these days."

Ricky Fontana had a magnificent season, but how much better could he have been had he not been cheated? How many hits did spiteful umpires take away? How many more runs could he have scored without bruises and scrapes from his abusers? How much better would his concentration have been if he had worried only about hitting the ball instead of defending himself?

We'll never know.

Since I put the news in print that Ricky Fontana was gay, his team was the most popular traveling attraction in baseball. Against teams that failed every year in Pittsburgh and Kansas City, the Mets sold out weeknight games. Many fans came to cheer Fontana, but others came to deride him. While owners of struggling ball clubs welcomed the sellouts guaranteed by Fontana's arrival, games against the Mets became a security nightmare. During one game in Philadelphia, fans threw garbage at Fontana. It happened again the following night. Opposing teams began to hire extra security when the Mets came to town.

One day in early July, I left for the ballpark in Cincinnati after guzzling a few beers to offset the tedium of an insignificant game against the Reds. But I sobered up quickly when a few blocks from the ballpark I found a man selling T-shirts from the trunk of his car. He offered me one that read "AIDS: Kills Fags Dead" above Fontana's portrait. He bragged that he had sold seventy-five shirts that day.

In Phoenix, Fontana listened silently to catcalls from the stands. Two men in garish makeup and long blond wigs hooted at him ("Hey, pretty boy!"), and every time he ran to the outfield between innings, they stood and danced and jiggled at him in tube tops and short-shorts.

Thankfully, just as prominent in the stands were fans with signs proclaiming support for Fontana. I noted to Peter that I often saw Fontana's supporters arguing with neighboring fans, even coming to blows. Often Fontana's most vociferous fans would be forced to leave their seats after Fontana's second or third at bat. They could only take so much abuse from homophobic fans.

A Mets public relations gaffe underscored the widespread admiration for Fontana. Paul Callahan noticed in early July that the Mets Clubhouse Store had a new item for sale: pink Mets T-shirts with Fontana's name on the back. The shirts were sold in both men's and women's sizes. Fontana was the only player whose name appeared on a pink shirt for men. The *Post* had the scoop, and the Mets had a debacle—the team tacitly implied that Fontana's gay male fans would think pink clothing is really cute.

"We had to sell those shirts," Jason Meyers admitted to me. "A fan designed his own version online and started selling them out of a cardboard box on the corner of Eighth Avenue and Nineteenth Street. He sold thousands in only a few weeks. We sent him a cease and desist order, but we honestly loved his concept. They're our top sellers!"

Peter purchased a men's medium. There were pink shirts in the stands in Baltimore, I told him, when the Mets arrived for an interleague series.

Now Peter interrupted our recollections. He had never revealed to anyone but his new lover Eusebio Hernandez what happened to Ricky in Baltimore. "Shocked him, humiliated him," Peter sighed. "My poor Slugger!"

Something told me he wasn't talking about Fontana finding his swing again at Camden Yards. I followed the drooping Mets, losers of three in a row, into Charm City, where Fontana's sudden hitting torrent incited his mates to three consecutive victories against the Orioles. But during that trip, bigger news arrived.

"The All-Star voting was announced during that series," I said. "Ricky got more votes than any other player, as I recall." I smiled at Peter. Fontana had surely been proud.

Peter wasn't smiling. Of course, I knew the implications of what occurred at the All-Star Game. But even that wasn't why he frowned. Peter began his story. Noontime in Brooklyn: The sunlight off snow filled the room with white as Peter spoke, words singed by fury, punctuated by clicks of his jaw and flares of his eyebrows, the fierce whites of his teeth and eyes, which never left my face as he told me a story about my hero, a man we both loved, that nobody had ever told before.

In his hotel room, Fontana peeled off the bandages. He had collided with the Orioles second baseman, sliding to beat a hard lob from outfielder Ray Robbins. "Safe!" cried the umpire, and Fontana had a double. Four hours later, his shoulder ached. Purple, then he pressed his finger into the bruise, and it became yellow, then red, then pink. He pressed harder. The pink depression paled. Harder.

The bruise was white. Harder. Colorless now. Harder. Suddenly, Fontana's vision blurred. He yanked his hand from his shoulder. The burning twinge faded while the bruise went pink, red, yellow, and purple.

My flesh can bruise, but my mind is a rock, he thought, shrugging and flexing his chest. *They can't hurt me. They can't hurt me. They* won't *hurt me.*

He balled his hand and pounded his fist into his forehead. *My mind is a rock.*

He stared into the mirror, admiring the redness on his brow.

I destroyed the ball today. I'm the league leader in batting. Hitting .399 as of tonight. Remember me? I hit in sixty-two consecutive games this year. That was me. I destroyed the ball tonight. Had those Baltimore fans groaning

("Fag-got! Fag-got! Fag-got!")

and their pitcher shaking his head

("You got lucky, *maricón*.")

and my teammates cheering

("Man, that ass pirate can whack 'em!")

When all is said and done, I'll be the best hitter there ever was. No record will be safe. I'll be the best there ever was.

Oh shit. Am I crying?

He saw that he was.

But there was a knock at the door.

Fontana wiped his face, threw on a bathrobe, and went to the door.

"Hello, handsome."

Fontana's jaw dropped. The greeting came from a tall, dark-skinned woman. She wore a hot pink, shoulder-length wig and a strapless dress, tight from her breasts to her knees. Her legs were firm, cut from stone. She had a tiny waist. Thick hands and short, colorless nails. A thick nose and a cleft chin. Broad shoulders, too.

"Well, aren't you gonna invite me in?" she pouted in a childish lilt delivered in a rumbling bass.

Fontana never knew what to do with females. He had only been close to one—his mother—and held the rest of womankind to a non-aggression pact that he honored by ignoring them, their bizarre odors, their frail bodies, and their non-affiliation with the world of baseball. But when confronted by one, he was a scared boy, too awkward to say or do anything except step aside and let her into his room.

She sat on the bed. She stared at him. He didn't move. She opened her purse and emptied it on the bed.

"I brought some toys," she said, shuffling through a menagerie of colorful plastic phalluses, rubber balls strung together like a string of pearls, condoms, a set of handcuffs, and what looked like an infant's pacifier with a long, tapered, rubber nipple. "Hope you don't mind the mess."

She smiled at him. Fontana saw that she was missing a tooth. He had not yet moved from the doorway.

"Don't be shy," she said, standing, swaying her hips as she walked toward him. "I'm not gonna hurt you. Unless you ask."

That gap-toothed grin again!

She reached him and grabbed his hand. He felt a stirring beneath his bathrobe (*Oh no! Oh no oh no oh no*) and his blood pulsed.

"What's wrong?" she cooed. And then she removed her wig. "Like me better now?"

He was bald. From his eyebrows to the nape of his neck, he was shaved clean.

Fontana fell backward against the wall, but the bald man came toward him, grinning like a clown. He reached into Fontana's bathrobe, found his target, and grabbed. Fontana pushed him off, and the bald man fell to the floor.

"What the fuck is wrong with you?" the bald man yelped. Then Fontana heard titters from the hallway—he had never closed the door—and suddenly, he understood. "You're not even paying for me. Your boys are, you fucking loser."

"Get out!" Fontana roared. "Get out! Get out! Get out!"

And he kept bellowing, again and again, while the bald man skulked to the bed, collected his toys and his purse, gathered his wig, and, cradling everything in his arms, fled from his room. Fontana stopped screaming. He heard the heavy footfalls of the prostitute in the hallway, and then he heard more steps, also running, and then the sound of two doors closing. Fontana peered into the hallway. The prostitute, adjusting his wrinkled dress, caught his eye and spit, "Fucker!" as the elevator arrived and he walked inside. He listened. From Carlest's room, laughter.

Fontana did not realize he had once again forgotten to close the door until the bellhop arrived.

"Sir? Are you okay? We have had some complaints about yelling from your room, sir. It's very late. Can you keep the noise down? Do you need me to help you up, sir?"

But in a puddle of shivering sobs, Fontana didn't answer.

"When he collected himself, he called me," Peter said. "He swore that nothing else had happened between him and the whore. Still he kept apologizing for cheating on me. Can you believe it?"

"You said that Ricky wasn't much of a lover. But those are the actions of a loving, loyal guy."

"He could be much of a lover," Peter insisted. "The secret that we shared, our intimacy, became a burden. He got nervous. He insisted on taking taxis everywhere and kissed me with one eye open, looking for someone who might recognize him."

I shifted guiltily. Then I wondered if Peter saw me fidget, and I stood still.

"Then his hitting streak began," Peter sneered. "And he was never the same. One day, he came here directly from the stadium, a wreck. I did the best I could to calm him down. But still he paced mumbling that somebody was going to find out about him, and then he'd never be able to play baseball again. Finally, he collapsed on my bed."

Peter said that they lay together for more than an hour, silent, and they kissed now and then, and for the first time in a long while, Ricky did not think about baseball. He smelled in Peter's breath his mother's scent, the smell of home, and Ricky arched his back to meet more of Peter's hand and take in more of his breath. Soon he fell into a waking dream of falling, but he wasn't frightened of hitting the ground, he told Peter later, because he tumbled through memories of home until at last he hit bottom, safe, warm, asleep.

Peter said, "The next morning I woke up, and he was gone. Hours later, I got a phone call. He was in a cab on his way to the hospital, ranting about colon cancer. He was sure he was dying. As you know, it was just an ulcer. Still, he had no peace."

❖

There was a saying among the political reporters at the *Tribune*: As the wind blows, so goes Sailor Sam. War hero, erstwhile peacenik, reborn Reaganite—New York Governor Sam Schiller changed with America. The Boomers who fitfully seized control of the country largely admired him, even those he had lost on one of his sharp political turns.

But his love for baseball never wavered. He wore his Yankees cap to the navy recruitment center where, at age seventeen, Schiller used his brother's driver's license to enlist. There were no pinups tacked to the top of his bunk aboard the *USS Daniel Webster* in the Gulf of Tonkin. Instead he hung a photo of Mickey Mantle, a clearer representation of the America worth defending than a pair of tits. When shrapnel shredded his ribs in 1969, the first thing Ensign Schiller asked upon awakening from a morphine haze was if the Yanks had reached the World Series. They hadn't, though the team honored him with front row seats on opening day 1970. By then his hair was shaggy, his cheeks whiskered. Schiller had spent the winter planning his first congressional campaign. His war hero status put his name on the Democratic ballot for the district that included Woodstock, New York. But his newfound antiwar politics won him votes. Schiller sang with Pete Seeger and got high with Wavy Gravy. He lost the election but earned headlines and admirers. Four years later, he ran again and won. He threw out the first pitch of the 1977 season at Yankee Stadium to raucous cheers.

Then God called. With a second term and a second wife, Schiller made new friends: Billy Graham and Jimmy Swaggart. Born again politically and spiritually, he shocked his constituents by switching parties in 1981. Voters punished him in the next election. But Schiller had correctly read the political winds. The Reagan administration called him to service, and he spent the eighties rising quickly through the Department of Defense. After four years as Dick Cheney's Assistant Secretary of Defense, Schiller followed his boss to Halliburton and then back into politics with the second President Bush. In Rudy Giuliani's box seats during the 2009 World Series, the revered New York mayor urged Schiller to run for governor. With Giuliani's energetic campaigning, Schiller easily won. He wore his Yankees cap when he took the oath of office in Albany.

Sailor Sam loved to campaign more than he liked to govern. So during Ricky Fontana's rookie season, Schiller decided he would run for president.

The following spring, Governor Schiller cheered on Fontana's streak like any other baseball fan. In the midst of his presidential campaign, he asked aides to have the Mets box score ready at every morning briefing. Schiller's run at the White House was hopeless by June; poor showings in key primary states doomed him while Fontana was still in the closet. Still, Schiller stayed in the race. As his prospects faded, Schiller abandoned his stump speech for fiery ad-libbed denouncements of America's moral wasting. He decried abortion, pornography, and gay marriage in spit-punctuated speeches. Pundits surmised that Schiller bloviated in order to win more airtime. Extra exposure and a well-timed tilt rightward could make him an attractive running mate to Republican frontrunner Mitch Haller, a socially liberal Nevada senator.

Or maybe he meant the names he called Ricky Fontana: deviant, scoundrel, pervert. Perhaps such were the demands of his spirituality.

Schiller first targeted Fontana with an off-the-cuff remark at a rally in Des Moines. A reporter asked the governor if he'd heard the news: Ricky Fontana was gay. "What a shame," Schiller exclaimed. He told the surprised newsman, "Ricky Fontana is a great hero. But his lifestyle choice isn't one we ought to encourage to our young people."

The response from the media and liberal Americans: outrage. A writer at Deadspin.com scoffed, "Retrograde Yankees fan Sam Schiller showed his true colors: yellow." A Politico commenter declared the official end of Schiller-for-President: "Any hope for Schiller to attract swing voters who remember his more moderate days has been dashed." Trending on Twitter in the first week of July was the hashtag #schillerdouchebag.

On July 9, I convinced my former assistant Tony to work for me again. I needed his help managing my new blog and social media, which had since the *Tribune* closed earned more than enough readers to afford his salary (and my rent). As the cheers for Fontana turned to jeers, Tony told me, "I don't get it. What's the big deal? We have gay mayors, gay congressmen. Every network, it seems, has a show with a gay character. Why the fuss about a gay ballplayer?"

Schiller answered the question. A broad segment of Americans indeed feared the implications of a gay baseball star. The abusive bleacher bums were not a bigoted fringe drawn from the backwoods to the ballpark to boo the faggot champion. Resistance to gays was everywhere because homosexuals were everywhere, and many Americans saw the omnipresence of gays as a threat. Or else they felt comfortable laughing at mincing characters on TV but could not abide a gay man who played the American game. In an increasingly female-friendly society, the cultural significance of sports as a non-romantic bond between men cannot be overstated. Baseball is the sacred sport of patriarchy, a gift from fathers to sons. Few aspire to the flitty stereotypes of reality television. But millions of boys dreamed of being Ricky Fontana.

Governor Schiller's stance against homosexuality predated Fontana. Liberal blogs had for years referred to Schiller as The Ayatollah for his blustery rhetoric. One year earlier, Schiller gathered a coalition of governors to demand a ban on gays in the military. Later, he moved unsuccessfully to eliminate New York's state tax deduction for gay marriages. And he failed to rally support to bar homosexuals from the Transportation Security Administration (his infamous campaign against "gay airport pat downs").

Though he found few supporters for these crusades in Albany or Washington, Schiller was a folk hero to many of his countrymen. Ordinary folks who cared little for the opinions of professional bloggers or self-styled political sophisticates, they adored him.

Clever Sam Schiller knew that Fontana could represent a nation changing too fast. The indignity of American culture was as much the target of Schiller's campaign that July as the stagnant economy. Decorum had given way to vulgarity, and tolerance had devolved into unruliness. And the name of a gay man was on the backs of thousands of American boys. Kids copied Fontana's toe-tap swing at their Little League games—that was distressing enough for voters to boost Schiller to second-place finishes in the summer's final presidential primaries. He had never officially withdrawn from the race, and on July 10, he revealed his strategy. That day, Schiller announced he would abandon the Republican nomination and run as the presidential candidate for the Tea Party. His well-funded PAC and instant endorsements from six Tea Party-affiliated governors and congressmen made his third-party candidacy instantly viable. Republicans groaned. Liberal pundits seethed.

On July 12, the Mets played a nationally televised game against the Braves. They lost eight to four. Ricky Fontana made the last out, a sharp line drive caught by the left fielder. Moments after the broadcast's final shot of Fontana kicking the dirt in disgust, viewers in Ohio, Pennsylvania, and Florida heard the voice of Fontana's most enthusiastic detractor: "I'm Sam Schiller, and I approve this message."

Now every night, Mets beat reporters broke the baseball-only rule that Fontana insisted upon during interviews. "What do you think of Governor Schiller's comments?" we asked him until he relented.

"I wasn't going to vote for him anyway," he said with a smirk to laughter from the gallery.

Still, a week before the All-Star Game, Schiller surged ahead of the Republican nominee in nationwide polls.

Chapter Ten

We expect more of athletes.

Actors and musicians screw up. They drink; they get high; they cheat on their wives or they beat their women senseless while drinking or getting high; and they swindle, lie, and steal just like the rest of us. But nobody cares. Sure, we pore over scandal sheets to marvel at their fallibility—so *ordinary*, it makes them seem—but there's hardly ever outrage. Politicians, too. There is a certain sleaze to public service, and the word politics itself has come to describe the art of palm greasing, appeasement, and skillful evasiveness. The president cheats on his wife—so what?

We hold athletes to a higher standard.

Their most modest failures are celebrated in the sports press, in books, and on television. Mickey Mantle's alcoholism, Ted Williams's grumpiness, and Pete Rose's addiction to gambling. These men and their weakness in character serve as parables of human imperfection because they are considered to be as close to perfect as a ballplayer can be.

Some say that we expect more of successful jocks because they excel at obeying the rules. Baseball's laws have no room for interpretation: out or safe, foul or fair, and three strikes, you're out. So we expect ballplayers to be experts at following life's simple rules. Don't drink too much, Mickey. Tip your cap, Ted. Stick to the slots and horses, Pete. But they're only human, and we love to watch them fail. And we love to watch them rise again because maybe we too will triumph.

I disagree with all these theories. I think we expect more of athletes because we cannot do what they do. Not many folks can hit a ninety-mile-per-hour fastball. Few men can make the flight of a baseball curve. But it takes no superpowers to put on a tie and run for mayor. Anyone can walk on stage and speak memorized lines or take guitar lessons. We watch other celebrities and think, *I can do that.*

But nobody—not even one of the other 800 major leaguers—could hit a ball like Ricky Fontana. Who would have thought that, just like us, he was a human being?

❖

He arrived at Great American Ballpark in Cincinnati for the All-Star Game in perfect health, but nobody knew it. Ricky Fontana begged out of the Home Run Derby, claiming his shoulder was sore. He insisted that his injury also prevented him from playing in the All-Star Game, but Grey Mason asked the trainer to examine him, and he pronounced Fontana fit to play. "You'll play in the All-Star Game, Ricky, and you'll do fine," Jason Meyers said sympathetically. "You were the most popular player on the ballot. There'll be boos, but nothing you haven't heard before."

Fontana was terrified. Winning the most votes from the fan electorate meant one thing: He was the most popular freak in a nationally televised sideshow. "I would have voted for me if I was a fan," Ricky told Peter on the phone from Cincinnati. "People are wondering, what does a gay ballplayer look like? People want to see one in a uniform, to see if it fits. Many of those fans who voted for me don't give a shit about my game."

His game was league best. Eighty-three games into the season, Fontana had amassed thirty-six homers and a batting average of .411. The National League's team manager, Gary Fabre, had Fontana batting fourth for the NL All-Stars. During the player introductions, he emerged from the dugout to dueling jeers and applause, two surging waves of noise. The crowd cheered every other player.

The game was eventful from the first pitch. Del Matthews lined a sharp double over Fontana's head, and the crowd roared. As he retrieved the ball from the base of the right field wall, he felt debris falling on his cap. After he threw the ball back to the infield, he found peanut shells on his shoulders. He brushed himself off and said nothing.

His first at bat was a bust. Fontana popped out to left field. The American League took the lead in the third inning, when Jack Simpson smashed a long home run.

"Fontana's due up fourth next inning," I noted to Crane and Callahan. "I wonder if an RBI would silence those boobirds."

In the bottom of the third, the first two NL batsmen failed to reach base. Then Jaime Henriques worked his second walk of the game, and Fontana came to the plate. On the second pitch, he nubbed a ground ball slowly down the first base line. He took off toward the bag.

Some of my colleagues suspect that history will remember what happened next as the most replayed moment in professional baseball.

First baseman Russ Striper charged toward home plate and fielded the ground ball about twelve feet away from the base. Fontana sped down the line. Striper lunged toward him off-balance, leaning forward into the baseline. Fontana swiveled his hips to evade him but Striper's momentum put him directly in Fontana's path. Despite a last-minute twist to avoid contact, Fontana's leg smashed into Striper's head, and both men tumbled to the ground.

Fontana jumped up immediately and looked for Striper. He was sitting up, eyes open, stunned, but unhurt, Fontana decided, so he ran to the base. Striper got up, walked over to Fontana, and pushed him. He shouted three words as he shoved Fontana, three words that fans in the first row heard distinctly. Cameras on the field, in the upper deck, and behind home plate clearly show Striper speaking, and it is obvious, despite his subsequent denials, that he shouted to Ricky Fontana, "You fucking faggot!"

Fontana turned red. He yanked off his cap. He tilted back his head and slammed his brow into the bridge of Striper's nose. Then he grabbed him by the shoulders, and, with frightening ease, threw him to the ground. Fontana dove on Striper and rained blows upon him.

During a fight between ballplayers, usually the teammates of the two combatants run onto the field to separate (or sometimes participate in) the scrum. But at the All-Star Game, teammates are not true teammates; the rosters are culled from the best players on each major league team. So for a moment, the players watched in shock. Nobody had ever seen a fight at the All-Star Game, one player recalled. Finally, two of Striper's mates from the Baltimore Orioles charged onto the field, and then both dugouts emptied.

Their hesitance cost Striper his front teeth.

Fontana landed blow after blow on Striper's face. The umpires were the first to reach them, but none of the refs could wrench Fontana from Striper. Finally, two players, Vernon Gluck and Alfonse Alberto, collapsed on Fontana and pulled him away. They could barely restrain him. His white batting gloves were soaked scarlet. He jerked and twisted to escape their grip, but Alberto and Gluck were not letting go. Instead they began to pull him toward the dugout. They saw Striper's Oriole teammates running toward them, intent on attacking Fontana.

Then the stadium seemed to empty onto the field. Pitchers ran in from the bullpen. The police security detail rushed out of the stands. The fans, who before jeered and yelled, were now almost deafening in collective rage. Spectators jumped the fence, first one at a time, running toward Fontana and his bearers, and then the trickle turned into a flood, a tide of angry people rushing toward the National League dugout. Many players had fled the field into the clubhouse, and police officers filled the dugout, pushing out the rioters, though more and more of them swept onto the field every moment. Two minutes later, the commissioner canceled the rest of the game.

I watched the fans pitch beer and debris on the field. I thought: This is my fault. I have ruined the All-Star Game. I have ruined Ricky Fontana. My place in history alongside him was secure.

Chapter Eleven

In the midst of the streak, when Ricky Fontana was anywhere but in front of television cameras, when his absence was as prolific as his hitting, the producers of *MacAdam Place* came calling. Fearing that the face of the New York Mets was becoming baseball's most talented recluse, Jason Meyers and Fontana's agent pleaded with him to appear on the popular children's show. On June 1, the preschoolers of America watched between spoonfuls of cereal the debut of Ricky Fontana the singer. He warbled a song about sharing to a puppet giraffe named Garth. "What's mine is yours and what's yours is mine," Fontana crooned off-key. "Play that way and get a hit every time."

If he had ever lingered in the clubhouse long enough to speak to his teammates, no doubt Fontana would have endured a good-natured ribbing.

One year earlier, the creators of *MacAdam Place* came under fire when two new characters appeared on the show: a pair of penguins named Chuck and Roger. Religious groups and parent organizations claimed the birds were gay. Chuck painted and Roger danced ballet. During one episode, the puppets hugged when Roger's pet goldfish died. The show's head producer, Gus Van Zyke, responded curtly to accusations that his program indoctrinated young viewers with a pro-gay agenda. "Chuck and Roger are penguins. Chuck and Roger are made of felt," Van Zyke said. "Children understand that. Too bad their parents don't."

Yet only thirteen months later, Gus Van Zyke issued one of the first public denunciations of Ricky Fontana. The morning after the All-Star Game, a reporter from the *Daily News* asked him if he regretted having Fontana as a guest on his show. "I can't say I approve of the decisions that guy has made," Van Zyke answered. "If I had known then what I know now, I would've asked for a different player." Despite the outcry from LGBT advocacy groups at the perceived anti-gay slight, to this day Van Zyke stands by his public statement.

As Peter and I recounted the public detractions of Ricky Fontana after the All-Star Game, Peter remembered that the kids' show rebuke stung Ricky. Little Rocco Fontana, age two, was delighted to see his big brother on TV. Whenever the episode replayed, Celeste would take him to the TV. Rocco would watch and squeeze a stuffed version of Garth, the giraffe who sang the duet with Ricky. Van Zyke promised viewers that the Fontana episode of *MacAdam Place* would never run again. But his mother had not recorded the show. Baby Rocco would not see his two heroes together again.

From a motel room near LaGuardia Airport, Fontana phoned Peter. He had checked in under an assumed name and paid in cash to stay for a month. He told Peter, "Last night, I lost my cool. He spat in my face. I lost my sight. Not from the spit, from anger. I don't remember anything until Gluck pulled me off."

Peter said Fontana felt only regret. He did not try to justify the fight. Still, he had not yet processed the magnitude of his mistake until that phone call. "What have I done?" he said. "All those kids watching, all of them saw me. And what they saw? Oh, God. I need to tell them, I need to say that wasn't me. I lost my temper. It happens, right? To all of us."

Elsewhere, reaction was swift and almost absolute. Few dared to defend Ricky Fontana due to the brutality of the beating. Across the nation, we all saw the same gory photos: Striper prone. Fontana astride him. Blood on the grass and his gloves. Chaos in the stands. The riotous mob chasing Fontana into the dugout. Only sixty-five seconds passed from the moment the ball struck Fontana's bat until he disappeared with his bearers into the locker room, but captured on film and published and broadcast ceaselessly for days after the event in every medium, the minute-long fight became immemorial.

All the while he had hidden his homosexuality, Ricky Fontana had another secret. Under folds of practiced blandness, he had tucked away his temper. But his austerity was skin-deep. He laughed and cried easily, said Peter, and Ricky raged, too, quick to snarl at injustices described in one of Peter's chatty stories or a movie or the news. Wrong man, wrong era—remember he was born an American man of the new millennium. Their tastes are generally insipid and homogenized. Their extreme feelings are explained away as disease and drowned with medication. Technology is their prophylactic against emotion and intimacy. Their opinions are measured by clicks of a button marked like or unlike. Ricky Fontana was a love/hate kind of guy.

One day after the All-Star Game, the popular NewsWatch Network politics program *The Mullins Watch* aired a special episode. Host George Mullins had two guests that evening: Philip Weston, Spokesperson, Gay & Lesbian Anti-Defamation Alliance, and Reverend James Johnson, President, Coalition for the Lord's Will.

Mullins: We've all seen what happened at the All-Star Game last night. Gentlemen, I think the question isn't whether baseball should suspend Ricky Fontana, but for how long? What say you, Mr. Weston?

Weston: I think Ricky was particularly brutal in his retaliation for that homophobic slur. I believe that he should be suspended for ten games.

Mullins: Ten games? That's it? Striper is missing two teeth. That seems a little lenient, don't you think, Reverend Johnson?

Johnson: Absolutely. Ricky Fontana should be given a lifetime suspension from baseball.

Weston: What? That's ridiculous. Striper missed one game with his injuries. And we all know what he said to Ricky Fontana. How could he abide such vicious hate speech?

Johnson: So what? Sticks and stones, Mr. Weston. It doesn't matter what Striper said.

Weston: Doesn't matter? Does—

Johnson: No, it doesn't matter. Fontana should have chosen to ignore him. "Do not resist one who is evil. But if anyone strikes you on the right cheek, turn to him the other also." That's Matthew, Chapter 5, Mr. Weston.

Weston: Easy for you to say. But I wonder how many racial slurs you would have to endure before you dispensed with the Book of Matthew, Reverend. How long would you have to be called the N-word day in and out before you snapped and made a regrettable mistake like Ricky Fontana?

Johnson: I would never strike another man. I'm a man of peace.

Mullins: Are you sure, Reverend Johnson? We all have our breaking points. Don't—

Weston: May I suggest that if Ricky were not a gay man, we wouldn't be having this debate? If he hadn't been the focus of so much attention due to the so-called controversy of his sexuality, what happened at the game would just be two jocks roughhousing.

Johnson: Of course his homosexual behavior had something to do with it. Ricky Fontana chooses to walk a path of sin.

Weston: He *chose* to wha—

Johnson: Let me finish! My great-grandfather, the son of a slave, played baseball, as did my grandfather and my father, who was a shortstop in the Negro Leagues. This game is a precious cultural landmark for millions of Americans, not just me. Therefore, I don't think that as a God-fearing nation we should allow our game to be spoiled for future generations by the likes of Ricky Fontana.

Weston: What do you mean, the li—

Johnson: Will you please allow me to finish? Fontana's fight on national television, on a game watched by millions of children, no less, is a disgrace to the game. Fontana should be suspended permanently from organized ball. But I also came on the show today, George, to announce that myself, Cardinal Moynihan, and several other religious leaders here in New York are petitioning Major League Baseball to ban openly homosexual players.

Weston: This is insane. Nonsense! This violates civil rights—

Mullins: Well, technically baseball is a private organization. Much like the Boy Scouts or even religious groups, they are allowed to ban gays and lesbians.

Johnson: That's right, George. And we've already gathered 5,000 signatures. We expect to bring 100,000 to the commissioner by the end of the week.

Even my colleagues condemned Fontana. The morning after, the *Post* published a front-page photo of Fontana straddling Striper with his fist in midair. The headline banner declared "BUTTHEAD!" and below in smaller text, "Fontana the Shame of New York After All-Star Brawl." "MIDSUMMER'S NIGHTMARE" declared the *Daily News*. "SAY IT AIN'T SO" pleaded Crane's column in the *Times*. Newspapers in France, Germany, Italy, the Netherlands, Spain, and the UK posted a wire service story with the headline, "Homosexual Baseball Player Attacks Opponent." Without fanfare, *Time* removed Fontana from its website as an option for readers to select as "Person of the Year."

I have a close friend at *Newsweek*. He told me that the magazine had been preparing an issue dedicated to gay life in the United States. A portrait of Ricky Fontana had been shot for the cover with the caption MISTER AMERICA. The issue was scheduled to go to press two days after the All-Star Game. At the last moment, according to my friend, the cover was scrapped and a new one was hastily conceived. BASEBALL BARBARIAN, declared the caption to a photo of Fontana being dragged into the dugout, his mouth twisted in a snarl, hair stuck to his sweaty brow, knuckles and fingertips soaked in blood reaching toward the camera, reaching out of the magazine, reaching for the reader's very throat, wild-eyed, dangerous, bestial.

Judging from the online chatter, many fans did not know or care that Striper suffered only minor bruises to his face and started at first base for the Orioles three days after the fight with a temporary dental bridge filling the gap created by Fontana's fists. Nobody knew that Striper told his teammates when he returned, "I'm just sorry I got beat up by a fag on national TV." What we knew was what we saw, and what we saw was a gay man assaulting a straight man.

Two days after the All-Star Game, Major League Baseball announced that Ricky Fontana would be suspended for ten games for "the particularly brutal and violent physical confrontation he initiated at baseball's All-Star Game."

"I hope every player and fan learns from this incident that violence is no way to solve our differences," read a statement from the commissioner. Fontana did not appeal his suspension. He hid in the airport motel while the Mets traveled to Atlanta and Philadelphia. He visited Peter only once, lest he (or Peter) would be discovered, followed, attacked. During his suspension, the Mets lost seven of ten games and slipped into a tie for third place with the Marlins.

Fontana rejoined the team in Milwaukee. Before batting practice, he addressed his mates in the clubhouse. Press members were forbidden. Still, I reported the next day that team sources told me the Mets showed little regard for the apology. Some teammates were outwardly hostile or ignored the speech, turning their backs when Fontana spoke. Nonetheless, he told Peter that he hoped that time (and good hitting) would redeem him. He named Josh Hamilton and Roberto Alomar as popular players who overcame ruined reputations. After he addressed the Mets, Fontana read a prepared apology to the media who gathered to cover his return.

Remarkably, the time off and relentless denouncements did not distract Fontana at the bat. He throttled Milwaukee pitching, and the Mets won all three games. That's the difference between successful athletes and the rest of us: the distance they can create with their minds. Bat in hand, there was only horizon. Ricky Fontana saw no scowling teammates or howling fans—only the earth curling into nothingness where he tried to hit the ball.

❖

After the series in Milwaukee, at the airport, running late, running hard to catch my flight and dragging a suitcase I knew would be too big for carry-on, I decided to stop running. So I walked to the gate agent and apologized for not checking my bag. "No matter," she said. "You already missed your flight."

No more letters, no more games. I asked for a new flight with a new destination: Rochester, New York. And then with my credit card, limp from overuse in restaurants and bars and wherever else friends and flirty women want to be taken after ballgames, I made one final purchase from a jewelry shop in the terminal: a diamond ring.

On the plane, I drank to steady the hand holding the ring that I would offer Tara Lonsdale when I asked her to marry me again. I would vow to be a better husband. She would join me at the restaurants and the bars and even the ballgames. She would be my partner in every sense, not just my entertainment on off days and winter weeks. I sweated whiskey and contrition, both healthy and redeeming. She was every bit as pretty as any would-be conquests, I decided, prettier if I treated her right and took her shopping at the right stores. I rehearsed my proposal all the way to Rochester and in the cab on the way to the two-story brick house where the Lonsdales lived.

David Lonsdale answered the doorbell. My brother-in-law recognized me, and his eyes narrowed. The kid, a loser, I had always considered him, shaggy-haired, in his late twenties, living at home, and dressing with the same floppy and baggy-garbed disregard as teenagers half his age—suddenly, he was a threat, taller than me, lankier, flat where I was pudgy, steadfast and unforgiving, as welcoming to a weary traveler as a flag bearing a skull and crossbones.

"What do you want, Jerry?" David asked.

"Is Tara here? I have to speak to her."

I heard her voice. "Davey, who is it?"

I saw her coming down the stairs from the second floor. Aching, I watched her come, a little girl again in the house where she was raised, padding down the stairs in her bare feet and a baggy sweatshirt and clingy nylon leggings, birdlike, knock-kneed, and all the while I knew she'd never take me back. She saw me, and there was that look again, that parochial glare, the parent, the pastor, the scolding prim with curled back lips. She reached the doorway, but David didn't move, standing between us.

"What are you doing here?" she asked.

I fingered the red leatherette ring box in my pocket and stared at David as I spoke to her.

"I am here to take you home."

"Are you?" she asked. Her common defense: bemusement to mask her anxiety.

"Yes."

"Well, then. I suppose you're here to tell me things are going to be different now. You're going to quit drinking, aren't you?"

"Tara, it will take some time."

David laughed aloud. He gave a scoffing hiss and rolled his eyes for effect. I glared at him. He glared back. Now I had nowhere to look because I was too afraid to meet the eyes of either sibling.

"That's not what's wrong with me, the booze," I said to her knees. "I could celebrate less…passionately, yes. But that isn't the problem. The problem is that I don't have you. Now that I have nothing, I see how much I need you. I won't take you for granted anymore."

"You don't get it," she said, her voice trembling. I assumed she was beginning to cry.

"I'll say," David interjected.

"Go home," she said. "Leave me alone."

I watched her turn and walk away. David closed the door without a word.

❖

"Have you ever heard of a man by the name of Branch Rickey?" I asked to break the silence. Peter and I didn't know where to begin on our third day of interviews. We stared at each other until I found the quiet suddenly oppressive.

Peter shook his head. "Who is he?"

"Branch Rickey was the general manager of the Dodgers, when they used to be in Brooklyn. He was instrumental in integrating Major League Baseball. He signed Jackie Robinson, the first black ballplayer."

Peter looked annoyed. "What does that have to do with Ricky?"

"Everything," I explained. I started to dig through my Fontana file, bursting with papers, including a thick stack clipped together with a note that read All-Star Game. I found what I was looking for. "Aha! Do you watch *The Mullins Watch*?"

Peter looked even more annoyed. "No. I stopped watching the news and reading the paper after the fight. I couldn't take all that bullshit that you people said and wrote about him. And why the fuck would I watch that right-wing trash?"

I handed him a transcript of *The Mullins Watch* episode that featured Reverend Johnson. Peter read it and handed it back to me. "Why are you showing this to me?"

"Because now this will make sense," I said, and then I read aloud from my *Tribune* column dated July 16.

WHERE HAVE YOU GONE, BRANCH RICKEY?
by Jeremy Rusch

NEW YORK -- Six decades after Brooklyn Dodgers executive Branch Rickey broke the color barrier in Major League Baseball by signing Jackie Robinson, the first black ballplayer, baseball may once again become a segregated game.

Last night, Reverend James Johnson, founder and chairman of the Coalition for the Lord's Will, was a guest on NewsWatch's *The Mullins Watch*. Reverend Johnson announced he is circulating a petition. His goal: convince Major League Baseball to ban homosexuals.

"I do not think that as a God-fearing nation we should allow our game to be spoiled for future generations by the likes of Ricky Fontana," he told host George Mullins.

In partnership with Cardinal Eamon Moynihan, Reverend Johnson has asked religious leaders of all faiths and denominations to circulate the petition among their constituents. So far, the reverend claims, he has succeeded. At churches, synagogues, and mosques across the five boroughs, over 5,000 people have lent their signature to organized bigotry.

Reverend Johnson should know better. His father was shortstop "Rapid Roger" Johnson of the Negro League New York Black Giants. Roger Johnson was a bona fide star, batting .312 during a 12-year career for the Giants and the Pittsburgh Grays. Scouts for major league ball clubs enviously watched his soft hands in the infield and quick stroke at the plate, but an unofficial agreement between big league owners to reject all black players, regardless of talent, ensured that white fans would never see the speedy shortstop's skills. He retired two years after Jackie Robinson joined the Dodgers.

Like racism during Jim Crow and the era of whites-only baseball, homophobia is every bit as insidious, vicious—and accepted by a silent majority. And if Reverend Johnson has his way, as racism was once institutionalized, so too could homophobia be as common as separate water fountains, toilets, and baseball teams were for the grandparents of today's black Americans.

I do not mean to excuse the violent outburst at the All-Star Game that inspired Reverend Johnson to take up his cause. Ricky Fontana is not without blame. His poorly planned punches have already damaged more than Russell Striper's face. Fontana outraged millions of fans. He incited a national debate. And he revealed an ugly side to our definition of tolerance. Some of us only extend it to those whose behavior our piety allows us to support.

Branch Rickey chose Jackie Robinson to be the first black ballplayer not because he was talented, but because Robinson was charismatic, courageous, and born to lead. Both Rickey and Robinson were religious men with strong Christian principles, and the Dodgers owner asked Robinson if he could agree not to fight back against the racist taunts and injuries he was certain to face. Robinson agreed, and those who witnessed how he was treated by racist fans and ballplayers know that he possessed indescribable dignity and strength.

Where Robinson succeeded, Ricky Fontana failed. He fought back. Though his baseball skills rank him among baseball's gods, Fontana is just a man. And like Jackie Robinson's teammates liked to say, men like Jackie only come around once in a million years.

When I finished, I was disappointed when Peter didn't seem impressed. I was prouder of that column than any other I've written. I hoped it would redeem me in the eyes of the homosexual community. I had received dozens of angry e-mails, letters, and calls from gays and lesbians since June, but few wrote to praise me or support my assertions. Peter was also unmoved.

"So," he said with a sniff. "Did Reverend Johnson respond?"

Damn right he did, I explained. His assistant called the *Tribune* to set up a meeting in his Harlem office. And thousands of other New Yorkers responded, some with congratulations, but most condemning me. My Mr. Met telephone rang incessantly, and during the next two nights, I received twenty-six calls, all of them to complain ("You're going to hell, Mr. Rusch." "How could you defend that queer boy?" "Another liberal media asshole." "How many blowjobs did Fontana give you to write that story?" "Reverend Johnson is a hero!" "Promoting the homosexual agenda is not your responsibility, Mr. Rusch." "Are you also a fag, Jerry?" "I hope you get fired for this!"). Late one night, one caller told me I was "yet another slave of the Jew media." I explained politely that I'm an Episcopalian, and then I hung up the phone and unplugged it from the wall.

I invited Tony to meet me at a coffee shop, ostensibly to invite him along on my interview with Reverend Johnson. But I needed the company. He listened as I sobbed into a mug and recounted my trip to Rochester. I showed him the ring. I had ruined the lives of two people I loved and admired, I explained to Tony, and none of my best efforts to undo my selfishness had succeeded. When I had finished my coffee and regained my composure, he set about to chide me.

"I told you this would happen," he said. I listened quietly, nodding. I was right, Tony said, to suspect that Fontana's sexuality would someday be front-page news. But I had abused my proximity to him. I should have waited until he was comfortable with his fame, when he wasn't a shy kid whose batting skills alone gained him undesired daily headlines. After each admonishment, I apologized. I admitted to Tony that I should have listened to him on that rainy night in June when I was too lonely to say no and too drunk to know better.

"You really ought to stop drinking," he said.

"Yes," I said. But taking advice from someone so young—a kid still, with a frost of acne on his chin—was more than I could stand. I quickly changed the subject. "I hope you don't think I want you to come with me to Reverend Johnson's office because you're black."

"I don't care why you invited me. I'm psyched to meet him!"

"I can't believe I landed this interview. I'm just a guy with a blog."

"Why?" Tony asked. "He loves publicity, anywhere, anytime, from anyone. Good or bad. Another chance for someone to quote his righteous indignation. Didn't you hear him on WFAN last night?"

Into the lion's den—Reverend Johnson moved his crusade against gays in baseball to sports radio. Fontana's fans were ready. By the dozens they called the station to berate the reverend, scold his sanctimony, question his manhood, his patriotism, his faith. Tony noted there had been a much-forwarded alert online to drum up detractors for Reverend Johnson's radio appearance. (The station also frantically publicized his visit.) The reverend laughed off the abuse. Later, on a conservative radio talk show, he explained his cheer. The appearance on WFAN Sports Radio had earned his online petition thousands of additional signatures.

As we finished our coffee, I asked Tony, "Do you believe he's going to get those one hundred thousand signatures?"

"And more. Maybe twice as many. No doubt."

"How can you be so sure? New York is a pretty liberal town. People were dancing in the streets when we legalized gay marriage. I can't imagine he'll find that many people."

"You were right to connect this issue with Branch Rickey," Tony said. "This is racism reinvented. Tell yourself whatever you want. It can't happen here. Not after Jackie and Dr. King. But you're wrong. Like old-school racists, the anti-gay rights crowd argues that gays and lesbians are fundamentally inhuman. By denying a fact of their birth, that sexuality is inherent, is no different than denying that all men are inherently equal. So instead of Negro men running off with your little white daughter, now we're to fear gays. They're to blame for disease, failing marriages, single-parent homes, and our promiscuous pop culture."

"But only to the ultrareligious."

"Not so. And Reverend Johnson's petition is going to prove you wrong."

The elevator door opened. Tony and I stared at each other in disbelief. Two gleaming marble columns adorned the entrance to the offices of the Coalition for the Lord's Will. The costly stone also lined the hall leading to the waiting room. The office's gaudiness galled me, suggesting a temple to some pagan god.

"Maybe the world just isn't ready for a gay ballplayer," I said to Tony after a receptionist pointed us to two chairs. "The sports weeklies run polls every few months asking that question. The majority of athletes polled say, 'Yes, we're ready.' Bobby Valentine said so in 2002, for Christ's sake. But when you share a locker room and a shower with them, your public tolerance can't compete with your private fears. Maybe Fontana wasn't born for this age. Maybe in twenty years, my column wouldn't have mattered."

"The question isn't, are we ready for a gay athlete?" Tony said. "The question is, why do we have to ask if we're ready?"

"This is never gonna happen," I said, lowering my voice to a whisper. "The commish won't buy it. The reverend is a crank. He must have a campaign cooking. He's running for mayor again. Or congressman."

We heard footsteps and turned to see a tall, thin man, smiling broadly, clean-shaven, with eager, mirthful brown eyes, wearing a navy blue suit with dark gray pinstripes and pointed, polished wingtips: Reverend James Johnson.

Popular—his organization received millions of dollars in donations from a largely working-class following—but controversial—he was twice a failed candidate for mayor—Reverend Johnson is an inescapable New York City celebrity, so it took my eyes a moment to adjust to the idea that he existed outside of the nightly news. He had it all down: the stride, the posture, the smile, and for a moment, I forgot that I twice voted against my political affiliation to cast a ballot against him. His looks, his charm, his sharp dress, and casual familiarity with power helped him to beguile me as well as grow his church from a small East Harlem flock into a powerful political force.

He introduced himself and took my hand between his, shaking my whole arm. He repeated the gesture with Tony. "A young baseball fan!" he said to him. "God bless you! My children prefer basketball and football."

I smiled. He grinned back and tried to pry a smile from Tony with a wink. "And don't get me started on hockey," he said.

I couldn't stifle a laugh. Tony seemed unimpressed.

"I think you'll find a lot to like in my office," he said. And with a hand on Tony's shoulder, he escorted him inside. I followed.

I didn't know where to look first. I found myself staring over the roofs of East Harlem, old brick buildings—some still had chimneys—as far as I could see, like a forest of naked redwoods. Floor-to-ceiling windows, a bright, dizzying view. Baseball memorabilia—photos, mitts, bats, and framed books and magazines—covered the walls. My jaw dropped. The first item I spotted was a deep brown baseball with brittle, fraying stitches. In faded ink a signature read "Lou Gehrig."

I looked at Tony and mouthed "Wow!"

He offered us refreshments. His receptionist brought cookies and bottled water. While we ate and walked around the room, admiring his collection, the reverend spoke.

"Baseball is the greatest game," he began. "As if God Himself created it. Perfect, like nothing else on earth. Think, gentlemen, how different the game would be if the distance between the bases were eighty-eight feet instead of ninety. That tiny difference would make it another game entirely. Why, we'd all worship the best bunters if that distance were shorter! But somehow, some inspired man knew that ninety feet is the ideal distance for a batter to beat out the tough grounders, but not the routine one-hoppers."

Tony and I looked at each other. Tony raised an eyebrow.

"There is a ballplayer to reflect every type of man," the reverend continued. "Hedonists have Babe Ruth. The prideful have Joe DiMaggio. Mama's boys have Lou Gehrig. For men who want to change the world, there's Jackie Robinson and Curt Flood. For perfectionists, Ted Williams. Saints have Roberto Clemente and sinners have Pete Rose. Wiseguys have Bob Uecker and Yogi Berra, Casey Stengel and Satchel Paige. Ty Cobb's for the ornery and Willie Mays for those with indomitable cheer. Ernie Banks for idealists and Billy Buckner for realists."

It's true, I thought. That's not something you can say about every profession. How many demure stockbrokers do you know? How many belligerent librarians? How many sportswriters can you name who know when they've wandered into a cliché?

"Like God's decrees, the creators of baseball laid down infallible rules, but"—and then he pounded his desk for emphasis—"he allowed the creature Man to exact judgment of His laws on earth.

"You see, gentlemen, we are all God's umpires here on earth. Balls and strikes aren't so easy to call, and neither is sin. But I call 'em like I see 'em, and that's why for the good of the game I've created the petition that brought you here today."

Tony and I drifted into two chairs while he spoke. Once seated, Tony piped up. "Reverend Johnson, as a man old enough to have participated in the Civil Rights movement, surely you recognize that your suggestion smacks of segregation?"

"I thought *you* were asking the questions, Mr. Rusch," Reverend Johnson said, sneaking a squinty glare at Tony.

"Well, his question is a good one, Reverend."

"No, the question is irrelevant! Homosexuality is a lifestyle. It's an ideology. It's as much a path toward sin as gambling, drinking, and drug abuse."

I shook my head. "That's not true. Fontana's sexuality is no more a choice than your father's and Jackie Robinson's race."

"How dare you invoke my father, Mr. Rusch, here and in your column. April 15, 1947, was the greatest day in his life. He was born black, and he could not choose to be white if he wanted to. And believe me, he wanted to play in the majors so badly, I bet it crossed his mind."

Tony interjected. "Just like you chose to be a Christian?"

Reverend Jackson glared at Tony down an aquiline nose inherited from an ancestor who had once owned another of his ancestors as property. Tony, chest heaving, stared back with his father's hazel eyes, which long ago had been given to his family by force.

"What are you trying to say?" the reverend asked, his breath whistling through clenched teeth.

"You say that homosexuality is a choice with no proof, no evidence to refute the millions of gay people who don't know any other way to be."

"And where is their proof?" Reverend Johnson asked. "They have no more evidence than I do. But I have one thing they don't: the word of God. The only reason that matters."

Tony opened his mouth to interject, but the reverend filled his ears.

"The Bible—our laws, our society—are based upon the teachings of this book. I'm not naïve enough to believe everything in here is real, word for word, exactly as it happened. But I do know that this is the word of God handed down to Man, and billions of Christians and Jews believe the same."

Just then I thought that being an atheist must be a very lonely feeling indeed, and I was glad that I went to church last Easter. I was about to speak, but Tony interrupted. At least, he had regained his calm.

"Reverend, if the Bible said that being black was sin, don't you think the Negro Leagues would have never existed? In fact, if an apostle condemned blacks to damnation, don't you think slavery would still be legal?"

"That's not what the Bible says, so I don't worry about it," Reverend Johnson responded. "Besides, nobody is condemning gays for being who they are. The problem is that they choose to engage in homosexual activities. Punish the sin, not the sinner."

"I see. So if the Bible condemned *acting* black, it would be immoral to engage in black activities. I could be damned for reading Toni Morrison. Or listening to Miles Davis." Tony looked smug.

"I am a religious man," the reverend said. "I am not a bigot. I am not—"

"What's the difference?" Tony, very calm, asked. "Religion is a set of rules to help us explain what we don't understand. So is racism. We can't know what it means to be another color, so we invent myths and caricatures to explain the experience. The reason one becomes religious or racist is the same: Your parents raised you that way. And the cure for both conditions is knowledge."

"Mr. Rusch, I did not agree to see you so that your assistant could badger me with his amateur theology. Kindly ask him to leave."

I stared at my shoes. I couldn't look the reverend in the eye. Tony had used me, I thought. He had used my access to gain an audience with Reverend Johnson in order to scold him. I finally looked at Tony, but again he didn't let me get in a word.

"Don't worry, Jerry. I'm leaving." He glowered at the reverend as he stood. It was good that Tony left while he still had breath unwasted on Reverend Johnson. Faith like his was indefensible yet unassailable.

"Keep with your own kind in hell!" the reverend shouted to the slamming door.

The reverend tossed a thick stack of paper in my lap. Poor Ricky, was all I could think.

"How many are there?" I asked.

"You're holding a list of twenty thousand names, Mr. Rusch."

I didn't speak for a few minutes—just reading. Aaron Reynolds, Brooklyn. Mitch Nunzio, Brooklyn. John Gheriff, Staten Island. Sara Rodriguez, Staten Island.

Reverend Johnson beamed. "We've had a groundswell of support for our movement. In fact, we've delayed our meeting with the commissioner's office because our expectations were exceeded."

"What do you mean?"

"Thousands of people signed the petitions sent to local churches, synagogues, and mosques. And then we moved the petition online." He grinned. "Thanks to the power of the social media, we've gathered over three hundred thousand signatures."

Herman Jones, Bronx. Justine Cohen, Bronx. David Farvala, Manhattan. Michael McInerny, Manhattan. Nick Armbruster, Brooklyn. Linda French, New Jersey.

"The online petition yielded more than just signatures, Mr. Rusch. An amazing thing happened. People e-mailed from across the country to support me. I've got messages from men and women in at least thirty states. It's like the miracle of loaves and fishes, isn't it?" he asked, laughing.

Rachel Bearth, Bronx. Tina Hudziski, Cleveland. Roberto Pedobrini, Detroit. Charles Martinelli, Manhattan. Penelope Dintea, Omaha.

"Mr. Rusch? Are you still with me?"

"Sorry," I said. "I'm a little…shocked."

"Don't be," Reverend Johnson said jovially. "Fontana angered many people with his brutal display. But he did us a favor. Promiscuity and androgyny are an easy sell. It's a year-round Halloween for gays and lesbians, men dressing as women, women acting as men. No wonder we can't get enough of them, especially young people, in this age of dress up. But bloodshed? Well, that's another story. Ricky showed the world that gays think they are above our laws and customs."

According to polls, a majority of Americans support gay marriage. That meant nothing to the reverend. The self-righteous, by definition, claim the right, but few with more audacity than Reverend Johnson. I was too stunned to react, so he charged ahead.

"Laziness, Mr. Rusch. Laziness prevents men like Fontana from pursuing a life in God's name. It's easy to give in to carnal desires, and it's easy to blame nature. Have you noticed that what was once called sin is now treated as a genetic trait? That guy's not a drunk; he's an alcoholic. He's not a crackhead; he's an addict. Nonsense! You choose to have that drink, you choose to smoke that rock, and you choose to sleep with another man."

A tear—it must've been a tear—itched the back of my eye, but I blinked a few times and stared hard at the signatures below to stifle myself. Harry Bindle, New Jersey. Rehna Andersson, Bronx. Pamela Short, Los Angeles. Lozario Hernandez, Albuquerque. Harvey Biltopolos, Harrisburg. Brendan Copeland, Seattle.

"Ricky Fontana exhibited this point perfectly. A Christian man, a man who did not live his life according to the do-whatever-feels-good creed of the homosexual, would not have struck his detractor."

I had not yet looked up from the list. The reverend seemed unsure whether to continue, but he did.

"We've expanded our presentation to the Major League Baseball Executive Committee," he said. "I've hired a team of psychiatrists to present to the commissioner the effects of hiring openly gay players. I've also recruited several major leaguers—including some of Fontana's teammates—to be pollsters."

Now he had my attention. He smiled, acknowledging me.

"These men are going to survey their fellow ballplayers to find out how many disapprove of homosexuals in the game. An anonymous poll, Mr. Rusch, conducted by their counterparts, is likely to yield results that favor my position, don't you think? Sure, ballplayers have been quoted for years saying that the sport is ready for gay players. But who does the baseball player trust, one of his own or a reporter with headlines to write and newspapers to sell? No offense, sir."

"Okay," was all I managed.

"We think our case will be so solid that the players union will give its support to the movement. A union, after all, can't offend the moral values of the majority of its members. And once the union is on our side, the owners will follow. The commissioner's no fool. He realizes that it is patently unfair to force his employees to accept ideologies to which they are fundamentally opposed."

He paused. I had gone back to the list and reached Saleem Ahmedi, Bronx, and Tyra Kudzi, Manhattan, and Ronda Ilescu, Queens.

"Mr. Rusch? Don't you want to write some of this down?"

I absentmindedly tapped my breast pocket and my digital recorder. Reverend Johnson smiled, nodded, and continued.

"If the union or the league cannot be convinced, then we're taking our case to the people. We'll use these petitions to lay bare the facts. Americans do not want homosexuals in baseball. By permitting Ricky Fontana and his ilk to play ball, Major League

Baseball is not providing entertainment that reflects the values of the American people! So we'll demand a baseball boycott—don't buy any tickets, major or minor league—and we'll call for a blackout. Turn off your TVs and your radios! If that fails, then we'll hit them in the pocketbooks with a call to boycott major league sponsors. We must keep the game pure, Mr. Rusch. Don't you agree?"

The reverend was a showy self-promoter, and there was no telling how much of his scheme he believed would succeed. He was also using me, inviting me to his office instead of Crane, Rule, or Callahan because my byline had eclipsed the rest. This exclusive interview was no honor. My column was the straw at the foot of the stake, and I was the flame. Where be headlines, there goeth the reverend! I found out later he had not a campaign but a new book to promote.

Still, my usefulness to fame seekers wasn't swelling the pit in my guts. That was guilt. My column had transformed an American hero to a public enemy and now an apostate. (In fact, that was the headline of my blog the next day which mocked the reverend's petition: RICKY FONTANA: APOSTATE AT THE BAT.) He deserved better. I had to let his enemies know.

I glowered at the reverend. "If Ricky Fontana's a sinner, then we'll both see him in hell. I've never known a better man."

Reverend Johnson seemed accustomed to a hard stare. He smiled. "Fontana has bigger problems, believe it or not, than heaven and hell. I spoke to Governor Schiller this morning. He is arranging with the Ohio Attorney General to send Fontana back to Cincinnati to stand trial for assault. If God won't clean up our game, then the courts will."

Chapter Twelve

The days between sleep paired and tripled. Rest came in fits of shallow slumber on the team bus, an airplane, a hotel bed. Ricky Fontana hid from nightmares. After his vengeful attack, he spoke to nobody once he took off his uniform. Because they followed him everywhere: fans, journalists, opinions. Some of them supportive, most condemning, and all of them unwelcome. They woke him from a jittery torpor on the morning of July 28. Hours earlier, the Mets and the Phillies battled for fourteen innings before Fontana doubled home the winning run, and the tired visitors claimed victory. But Fontana did not enjoy a hero's rest. A mini mob of Philly fans discovered his whereabouts and howled below the window of his fifth-floor hotel room. The cops came. The crowd fled. Two hours later, they returned.

"FAG-GOT!" they chanted rhythmically, "FAG-GOT!" in the derisive singsong that hated sportsmen with two-syllable names have come to know. Again, the cops came, and they arrested five of those too drunk and slow to flee. By then, the sun was already peeking over Philadelphia, and Ricky was too upset to sleep. So he called Peter and apologized for waking him.

"I miss you very much," he said. "I'm sorry for everything. All the trouble I've caused you."

Peter forgave him.

"He sounded like a man who knew he was going to die and wanted to clear his conscience," Peter told me. "After a few more apologies, he hung up. I was so worried about him that I called back later. But the line was busy for hours!"

Ricky hung up the phone and settled back in his bed. Peter's too good for me, he decided. But, relieved by Peter's voice, he let sleep wash over him.

When the phone rang, the first thing Fontana thought was that fans had tracked down his room number. He grabbed the phone and yanked it off the receiver.

"What do you want?" he growled. He heard sobs. "Who is it?"

It was his mother. She told him to turn on the television.

He had just missed the news. The White House press corps was dispersing, and the news station cut back to its anchor.

"At the end of his daily briefing in the Rose Garden, strong words from the president's press secretary for Ricky Fontana," intoned the newsman. "In response to a reporter's question, he said, 'The president cannot support Mr. Fontana nor can he condone his brutal act of retaliatory violence at baseball's All-Star Game.' The president is said to have regretted presenting Fontana an award for outstanding achievement, and he will rescind that award as soon as possible."

Fontana swore loudly and dropped the telephone.

"They sent federal fucking agents to Rhode Island," Peter told me. "Can you imagine the look on Celeste's face when she opened the door and these G-men were there to collect Ricky's plaque? They took it right off her mantle."

Nobody came to Celeste Fontana's house to retrieve the Amerigo Vespucci Award for "Outstanding Contributions to National Life by an Italian-American." That plaque rests forever in the Cranston dump, Peter explained. It was worthless after a spokesman for the Italian-American Society of New York told a reporter that the group had retracted the award. He told the press, "We must protect the legacy of Joe DiMaggio, a true team player."

Fontana was a fugitive who happened to live and work before an audience of millions. A criminal, he had assaulted another man whose only crime, Peter admitted to me, was "being an asshole." Baseball's punishment, many agreed, was lenient. Talking heads wondered aloud if political correctness compelled the executives who ran the game to respond to a brutal assault with a slap on the wrist. In a long-winded missive, Paul Callahan wrote, "If a straight man assaulted another straight man with such ferocity on the field of play, many observers of the game—this reporter included—believe that the punishment would be far more severe than a ten-game suspension. But the Commissioner's Office fears accusations of homophobia, and a new double standard has emerged. Russ Striper has committed baseball's first anti-gay hate crime."

By the end of July, Fontana had a batting average of .409. And no one can rescind a base hit. Though a few fans threw back the hits that reached the stands, home runs are forever. Nobody could rob Fontana of his achievements on the field, which accumulated at a furious pace.

But it became clear as the weeks passed that some public animosity toward Fontana had nothing to do with his poor decision at the All-Star Game and everything to do with his sexuality.

He had only been gay to the world for six weeks. As Fontana marched undaunted toward Ted Williams's modern batting record—a .406 average—many baseball fans could neither believe nor allow reality: A homosexual man was going to break two of the most treasured records in sports. His violent outburst should have justified resentment of only Ricky Fontana himself. Yet most of the derision he faced after July was predictably indiscriminate homophobia. Fontana personified both the fondest hope and most chilling fear of American fathers: Your son is a major league superstar (the dream); your son is gay (the nightmare).

No longer could Fontana safely flee the ballpark through the stands. Fans recognized him and accosted him, seizing his elbow or shoulder, posing epithets and threats. After a game in Washington, Fontana attempted his getaway through the bleachers, but six men identified him and poured what remained of their beers over him as he fled.

The marriage proposals from smitten girls seemed to stop on the day my fateful column went to press. But Fontana was still getting mail, more than ever before. Many wrote to support him. Some men wrote with romantic overtures. Fontana read none of the letters. Occasionally, a clubhouse attendant would tape an encouraging note to his locker. One read:

Dear Ricky,
I don't watch baseball. I don't know anything about the game. I just don't care for sports. Still, you are my hero.
I cannot thank you enough for your bravery. As a gay man who has just come out to his friends and parents, you are my inspiration. Although I've never met you, I will always think of you as a friend.
With fondest gratitude,
John B.

But many—about two-thirds, according to team officials—of the 900 messages that arrived each day in the team's e-mail were insults, condemnations, and threats.

Dear Mr. Fontana,
I am a mother of four and a longtime Mets fan in California. My favorite player was Ron Darling. But then you came along and I liked you better. I thought you were the greatest hitter. But I can't let my kids watch you anymore because you are a homosexual. According to the Bible, "thou shalt not lie with another man as thou would with a woman." But I am praying for you and I hope that you will turn away from sin.
Delores Markham, Bakersfield, California

Mommie! Mommie! Striper called me a name. Wah wah wah! Silly faggit.

Dear Faget Fontana,
Stay away from Ted William's record. If you're hitting 400 in Philly, I will kill you.

Fagtana:
Get AIDS. Fuck off. Die.

Hi Fag,

Visiting teams stay at the Sheraton Hotel here in Cincinnati. I know where you will be, faget, so you better sit out against the Reds.

In my columns that summer and to this day, I blame my colleagues in part for inspiring the public to turn on Fontana. I did not but certainly should have predicted the response to his homosexuality. Nobody foresaw his outburst at the All-Star Game, and nobody condoned it. Still, irresponsible members of the sports press fed the controversy by describing his sexuality and the Striper incident as if one caused the other. One New York reporter wrote, "Ricky Fontana, the homosexual right fielder for the Mets involved in last week's brawl at the All-Star Game, hit two doubles in a losing effort." Even my friend Dick Rule began one column, "Still embroiled in controversy over his homosexuality and inciting a riot that cancelled the Midsummer Classic, Ricky Fontana had no comment about the presidential award yesterday."

I knew it, and everyone who followed our game agreed: If he lasted in baseball, his greatest achievements were yet to come. Still, after they read the alarmist press, some ordinary Americans could not help but wonder who Fontana was going to assault next.

We who report the news were diverted by only two stories that summer. Now, the presidential candidates and Fontana were players in the same drama. On July 22, supporters hosted a welcome home dinner at the Waldorf-Astoria for Governor Schiller. Reverend James Johnson was a small name on the program. Buried between more notable speakers, he had been invited ostensibly to announce a revival concert at a Queens's convocation center. TESTIFY! NYC would be rich with New York City gospel groups and visiting singers. A citywide call to prayer. "I'm proud to announce tonight that Governor Schiller has vowed to attend," said Reverend Johnson. He detailed the availability of tickets and other notable attendees. Then he concluded, "All are welcome to join us and lift away sin with song!"

From the audience, a member of his congregation whom Johnson had planted asked, "Even Ricky Fontana? Can he come?"

After a few jeers (also from supporters Johnson had coached) the reverend exclaimed, "Ricky Fontana? You said, Ricky Fontana? Satan's pit bull himself? Nose out the window, ridin' shotgun with the devil. Sure, Ricky can come. All are welcome!"

The governor's remarks were a trimmed version of his stump speech, abbreviated so nobody's dinner would get cold. Then the questions. The third came from a *Post* reporter, "Is there any truth to the story about criminal charges against Ricky Fontana?"

Governor Schiller said, "If the player he attacked presses charges, I will cooperate with Ohio in seeing Fontana arraigned like any other suspect in an assault."

Peter told me, "Ricky didn't leave the team hotel on the next road trip in Pittsburgh except to go to the games. He was sure there'd be police waiting for him."

So Peter sent him care packages. One day, Fontana returned to his room to find a box from Peter: books. And a note. "You'll never be alone if you've got one of these to keep you company," Peter wrote. The box contained *In Cold Blood* by Truman Capote, *Catcher in the Rye* by J. D. Salinger, and *Huckleberry Finn.*

A week later, Peter found a box on his stoop containing three paperbacks: Babe Ruth's autobiography, *If I Had a Hammer* by Hank Aaron, and *Say Hey* by Willie Mays.

Ricky was, Peter said, an old-fashioned romantic. He wrote letters to Peter in messy cursive—Fontana did not trust e-mails or text messages, which lived in fuzzy, ethereal space where they could not be protected or destroyed.

Peter looked uneasy when I asked about Fontana's letters. "He wrote about the future," Peter said. "Life after his playing days. The problem was, that future always included me."

"And you didn't want to be part of his plans?"

"I wasn't sure," Peter corrected me. "I knew his crush on me was more than a crush, but how could I bring it up? He had nobody else."

No friends, no family. He hardly spoke to Celeste Fontana, whose daycare company had lost clients when they learned her son was that baseball player from the news.

Still, Ricky Fontana had millions of new admirers.

As reaction to the beating bled from sports blogs to political publications, unlikely fans cleaved to Fontana. They had never watched an inning of baseball, but now they knew him and what he stood for. Bullied kids, burnouts. Skaters in Washington Square Park wore his uniform. Even the hipster kids in Williamsburg. By August, Peter noticed Fontana's name on their backs. The locals who had not recognized Ricky on jogs or trips to the bodega donned fashionably distressed Mets T-shirts.

When the Warped Tour rolled into Randall's Island, two bands unintentionally dressed in identical outfits. Each member of two punk rock acts wore white Mets jerseys with Fontana's number six.

Up went his name on the menu of a West Village bar. The Fontana was an orange-and-blue cocktail of bourbon, Cointreau, blue curaçao, and Champagne "that will beat your ass bloody."

Jason Meyers noticed a run on camouflage Mets T-shirts with Fontana's name from the team's online store. Gay and lesbian military personnel bought them in droves, as did the self-styled resistance fighters at nationwide protests against corporate greed.

When a theater workers union went on strike, Fontana was there. Ten of his jerseys on the picket line.

When the Chinese premier spoke at the United Nations, Fontana was there. On the backs of several demonstrators demanding a free Tibet was the number six Mets jersey, a symbol of righteous revenge.

Fontana was there. "Hello, my little sluggers," said Lady Gaga to her fans at Madison Square Garden. "If you can't hug 'em, then slug 'em!" she said as she launched into song, tearing off her Fontana jersey and tossing it into the frenzied crowd.

My journalist comrades and I missed the heroism in Fontana's bloody beat down. He said no. No to bullying, no to hate, no to turning the other cheek. Where some saw reactionary fury, others saw righteous indignation. Hubris delivered daily humbled a champion—Americans love that story. Fighting back is part of our national character. Fontana swatted Russell Striper to the ground, and many Americans cheered.

❖

Like my hero, I scarcely slept during those weeks. My beat was burning, Fontana was in every section of the paper, and with interview requests, television appearances, I was winded. But just as Fontana kept hitting, I drank nonstop. Everybody wanted to have dinner with me to talk about Fontana, and I rarely paid for a round that summer. When someone else was buying, I never said no.

I learned later how many of those nights out with colleagues became shameful scenes that I wouldn't remember. Drunk and making passes at female colleagues or waitresses, sobbing about Tara, blubbering slurry opinions. My addiction was industry gossip. Like Fontana, my secret was out.

Finally, I discovered what it was like to be hounded. For weeks, Joe Lippincott, my colleague at the *Tribune*, called me from his travels with the Yankees. I had stumbled into him one evening at *Trib* headquarters while I was absolutely blotto. After that encounter, Joe called me regularly to check in. He lauded the virtues of Alcoholics Anonymous. He implored me to come with him to a meeting. He said I needed to get right with God. I politely told him to fuck off. "Keep your crusade against sin," I said to Joe. "Take it on the road with the governor!"

During the second week of August, the Reds came to Citi Field for three games. The Mets won the first game nine to two. Fontana came and left the ballparks like a shadow, only seen by reporters long enough to smack two singles for the victors. The next day, he swatted a double and a triple in a losing effort. Moments after the final out was recorded, Paul Callahan and I sprinted outside to see if we could catch Fontana before he fled. Clutching cups of coffee (which I Irished up a bit with snorts of Bailey's), we waited together, shivering on a brisk Indian summer evening. At the time, of course, I didn't know that Fontana had decamped Brooklyn for the nearby airport motel. And when he spotted me and Paul, Fontana retreated back into the ballpark, ducked out another exit, and walked to his hideout.

Then, he got lonely and we got hungry. Paul and I took a taxi to Peter Luger's steakhouse in Williamsburg, not five minutes away from where another cab dropped Ricky Fontana later that night.

Lightning struck twice. I was in a taxi on Bedford Avenue, looking for the right spot for a solo nightcap (and, I'll admit, also hoping for an improbable glimpse of Fontana). Already drunk. Callahan had spent every bill in his wallet on a porterhouse for two and more beers than we could count. Pink and pickled, he bid me good night. Shortly after eleven p.m. in the cab, I saw a man walking down the street. He was alone and carrying a pizza box. Wearing a tan hat pulled low over his brow, he was tall, handsome, and hurried. I asked the cabbie to pull over to the curb next to him. There was no doubt that by some stroke of destiny I had stumbled upon Ricky Fontana.

"Need a lift?" I asked when I rolled down the window.

He looked too shocked to be angry. "Okay."

He got in, and emotion overwhelmed me. I didn't know what to say, and I didn't greet him. For a minute, there was an uncomfortable silence. The driver interrupted.

"Hey there," he said. "I won't charge you for the extra passenger if your buddy gives me a slice."

Fontana laughed. He opened the box and offered pizza to the cabbie.

"Where you headed?" I asked Fontana.

"North Tenth Street. You know the spot."

"You're out late," I noted.

"This was the only place open," he said, pointing to the box. He paused, and his nose wrinkled. "Been drinking, eh?"

"Yes, a little."

He leaned to get a better look at my face. "So it's true what the guys say about you," he said. "You know, you shouldn't drink so much."

"Okay," was all I could manage.

We didn't speak for a minute or two.

"Ricky, I just want to say I'm sorry."

"Aw, fuck it, Jerry," he said, looking too exhausted to be moved by my contrition.

"Fuck it?" I repeated.

"Yeah, fuck it. I'll get by."

"Oh."

"Thanks to you, I know they'll remember what I am. But because of you, they'll also remember what I've done. You gave me a goal. If I never play another game, they'll remember me for reaching it. Do you see?"

I nodded.

"Do you want some pizza?"

I was too drunk to say no. He gave me a slice and I began to eat ravenously. A bit of tomato sauce dripped onto my pants. *Feeds me and forgives me. Hallelujah!*

As I took a tissue from my pocket to dab the spilled sauce, it tumbled from my pocket, the red box. For weeks, I had been meaning to pawn the ring that I bought for Tara. But each day I found something better to do—usually heavy drinking—to distract me from the errand.

"What's that?" asked Fontana, pointing to the box.

"Engagement ring I am going to sell," I said. I opened the box. "An heirloom from family I never cared for."

"How much you want for it?"

I woozily stared him down. Nothing in his eager brown eyes betrayed insincerity.

"You really want it?"

"Yeah, yeah! My mom's birthday is tomorrow, and I never got her a gift."

I didn't have to think about a price. "Just take it," I said, shoveling it into his lap. "For you, after everything I've done, it's the least I can do."

"Oh, man!" he exclaimed, grinning widely. "You sure? Thanks!" He grasped my hand and slapped my shoulder. He stank. To escape us, Fontana had not showered after the game, and the smell of nine innings, one double, two singles, and three trips across home plate lingered on his body. He was batting .403. His hands felt massive and strong on my arm. I realized I had never been this close to him alone.

"Pardon me, sir," Fontana said through the plastic divider to the cabbie. "Please pull over at the next corner."

"Okay, pal," said the driver, who, I noticed for the first time during the trip, was wearing a Mets cap. When he leaned forward to answer his ringing cell phone, I saw the number six on his back.

The cab slowed and stopped.

"Well, enjoy the rest of the season!" Fontana said.

He gave me his hand.

"You too, Ricky. Good luck!"

I shook his hand. Large and small, young and old, beautiful and plain, we were nonetheless alike, I noticed as we touched. Unsure of ourselves, no! More: Abusing ourselves, sabotaging our happiness. We had reached the pinnacle of our professions, yet we could not celebrate. Someone stole the dance floor from beneath our feet, plank by parquet plank. But it wasn't my wife or homophobic fans that spoiled our celebration. Drinking was my ruin. And Fontana's curse was shame and secrecy. We met now at the bottom.

"Good night!" we said to each other simultaneously and smiled, and then he got out of the cab and walked into Peter's building. That was the last time I spoke to Ricky Fontana. And I was too goddamned drunk to remember it the next day. Six weeks later, I quit drinking. I told Tara that I quit because I wasn't actually sure I'd shared a taxi and pizza with my hero. What mattered to her was that I was sober. She moved back to New York when I showed her my ninety-day chip. But I'll always regret having nothing to prove that my chance good-bye with Ricky Fontana wasn't a dream except for a tomato sauce stain on a pair of brown corduroys.

❖

On August 18, the Mets played the Astros in Houston. In the bottom of the eighth inning, the Mets took the field losing by three runs. Fontana stood in right, waiting for Oscar Ferrera to finish his warm-up tosses. Then he heard the fans to his left shouting. Two men, shirtless, rushed onto the field. Wobbling, unsteady, and drunk, they dashed a crooked path toward Fontana, who froze. Two security guards followed. As the fans neared Fontana, the guards tackled them to the ground. Seconds later, six Houston police officers came to their aid. And though they were pulled off the field shouting and spitting toward Fontana, the two men, brothers William and Samuel Brown of nearby Everett, Texas, claimed after the game that they "just wanted to shake the faggot's hand." Both men were jailed and fined for disorderly conduct.

The mood was tense the following night though the game was not. Houston deployed one hundred extra uniformed police officers to Minute Maid Park. "God hates fags!" declared protestors' signs outside the stadium. The cops didn't chase two young fans who pelted the protestors with trash.

The Mets bombarded the Astros pitchers with nine runs in the first three innings. Fontana contributed two hits. But while the Astros batted in the sixth inning, another fan charged the field.

The incident began when two drunks in the right field stands exchanged insults. Then they came to blows. As the crowd craned to watch the fight and the cops rushed over to end it, Tyler Wheeler decided now was as good a moment as any to carry out his mission. It was, he told police detectives later, "A mission that God gave me, and how am I supposed to turn down the Lord?"

He checked his pockets. He adjusted his belt. He untied and tied his shoelaces with a double knot. He left his seat. Without taking his eyes from Ricky Fontana, he walked from the sixth row of Section 110 near third base. Wheeler followed the curving walkway until he neared where the two brawlers were flailing at each other. He casually walked down the steps toward right field. Nobody stopped him; the cops and ballpark security were climbing over fans and empty seats to contain the fight. Wheeler reached the first row. Then he spilled over the railing and ran.

Again, Fontana froze.

Sergeant Luke Lawson was the first to spot Wheeler. He heard a woman shout, "Look, he's running onto the field!" and turned to see Wheeler tumble onto the grass, get up, and sprint. Sgt. Lawson ran to the railing. He knew he would never catch the running man, who was ten yards from Fontana and closing. Then the man drew an object from his pocket. A metallic glint caught Sgt. Lawson's eye, and he knew he had no choice. Calmly, but without another second's hesitation, he remembered later to the Houston chief of police, he straightened his moustache with his forefingers, reached for his belt, and drew his pistol.

Sgt. Lawson fired two shots at Tyler Wheeler. The first grazed his buttocks, but the second found its mark, piercing Wheeler's calf and shattering his fibula. Wheeler fell to the ground, crawled a few more feet on his hands, and stopped. His last memory before fainting was screaming. Thousands of screams. The multitude fled for the exits, leaving only those too terrified to move, or too curious, or both. Twelve fans were injured in the scramble to escape.

From the press box, I heard the Astros and Mets radio and TV announcers screaming into their microphones, retired ballplayers and wonky, analytical sports network figureheads suddenly pulled into deep water by history's undertow, struggling—as I would later—to find words to describe the waves of people crashing against each other. Rule gazed over the field, breathlessly repeating, "Holy shit," and Callahan sat quiet and white. Crane panicked, shaking me, asking me what had happened, was Fontana okay, who was the guy on the field? I thought of Tara and how much I needed her now and would need her tonight to explain how all this could happen and how it couldn't possibly be my fault, could it?

The police found a knife with a nine-inch blade in the grass where Wheeler fell.

CHAPTER THIRTEEN

No one is stopping you from doing what you want to do. Not the man with the knife. Not the gargoyle faces screwed into jeers, or the governor, or the reverend.

Ricky Fontana could do the utmost. Eusebio Hernandez didn't need to say so at Mickey Maco's restaurant. He had never known anyone with a sturdier will than Fontana, who would have what he wanted and needed no reminders to seek it. A man less determined would have thrown down his bat for fear another madman would reach him blade-first.

But Ricky was in the lineup for the next game.

I thank God every day that He blessed Ricky Fontana with such strength.

The attack seemed to gather his resolve. A Houston judge had not yet arraigned Tyler Wheeler before Fontana swatted his next home run. For the next six days, he sent baseballs helter-skelter across National League outfields. Throttling almost every pitch, a fury of intent. Fontana called Peter from St. Louis. "Just get to the last day of the season, that's all I want," he told Peter. "Then we can be together."

Swayed by Fontana's resilience after the failed assassination, public opinion favored him again. Wheeler's sin trumped that of his would-be victim. The rural Texas boy—only twenty-one, barely months older than Fontana—had for years shown signs of schizophrenia. According to online chatter, Wheeler was himself battling homosexual urges. Shame and self-hatred, some surmised, inspired the attack.

Even teammates who had been detractors rallied around Fontana. Mick Kelleher was surprised after one game to find Fontana sharing a locker room bench with Henry Monan. The reliever who'd teased Fontana for joining "Team Pink" was scrolling through websites on his iPad. Fontana listened, nodding, as Monan explained the virtues of various makes of recreational vehicles. Homophobe and homo side-by-side, knees touching.

Of course, Fontana spoke hardly a word about the incident. How did he feel about the attack? "Well, I'm here, aren't I?" How should Wheeler be punished? "That's not for me to decide." Are you worried about future attacks? "Can't worry about what I can't prevent."

Peter told me, "He was scared; he stopped sleeping. I sent him some Xanax, and he started sleeping again. That was the process. I don't know what went on in his head. He said he didn't want to be a bother to me."

The pills helped him relax. On Xanax at night he became the star of a one-man show at the Providence Civic Center. Ricky Fontana sings the best of Billy Joel, presented for a limited engagement at the Skyway Motel in Queens. Technical difficulties, ladies and gents. A knock at the door brought the pizza deliveryman and an intermission. Then, after dinner, in went his earbuds, and on with the show.

The courts determined that Wheeler was too crazy to stand trial. The public found others to blame. Tony streamed radio talk shows on his laptop. Scores of callers complained about Reverend James Johnson. He had, some claimed, created the climate of hate that provoked Tyler Wheeler. Two days before TESTIFY! NYC, the reverend's revival in Queens, an anonymous gang of online swashbucklers hacked the website of the Coalition for the Lord's Will. They replaced the reverend's homepage with a photo of a man ejaculating on another man's face.

Twelve hundred protestors swooped upon the Flushing Convocation Center on the first day of TESTIFY! NYC. There were as many Fontana jerseys as Guy Fawkes masks. Endless shouting, an unbroken rhythm of chants. The newsmen loved it. Cameras trained on the protestors as the visitors arrived, stunned.

Before the reverend appeared, he had already lost the media's attention to the barbarians at the gates. Who were they? The protestors I interviewed seemed mostly to be young and included many gays and lesbians. Still, they represented a more diverse cross-section of New Yorkers than I expected.

And why shouldn't anyone or everyone be angry? Especially the young ones. An American toils unabashedly for success on earth in addition to his heavenly reward. A century of growth enriched previous generations and promised their children comfort and fulfillment. Nowadays the prospect of wealth was all but dashed, and the afterlife seemed still less likely. Our leaders bickered over how to spend debt. Jobs gone, opportunities spent, and heroes struck down one by one. So they had converged on Wall Street and screamed for a future that resembled a comfortable past. So they flooded the streets again on August 25 at the opening of TESTIFY! NYC. They were ready to shake the enemy by his collar, whoever he might be.

To the center of this maelstrom of blame came Reverend Johnson. The first worshipper took a knee at TESTIFY! NYC only a week after the Wheeler attack. But in the preceding days, the reverend persisted in baiting Ricky Fontana. Did the attack move the reverend to reconsider his public remarks against him? "Well, I don't think the boy should be killed, of course not," Reverend Johnson told a reporter two days earlier. "But if he had died, I know where he'd be now. Let's just say not in heaven staring hungrily at the cherubs."

As the chauffeur opened the door to the reverend's limousine, a glass bottle shattered against the car. Reverend Johnson ducked into the arms of burly bowtied bodyguards. But he could not hide from the abuse. "Your God is dead!" "Leave Ricky alone!" "Homophobic asshole!"

I was there, in the midst of the mob, digital recorder thrust toward the swarm of men shielding Reverend Johnson. Yet I couldn't reach him, couldn't get near. The swell of irate objectors pushed me back as they moved in. A small but determined phalanx of policemen pushed back the protestors, and the reverend's entourage swept past the heavily guarded door.

I could not catch my breath. I reached into my pocket for my flask. No one predicted this response, no one could have, not even the most dedicated followers of the online groups who organized the Days of Rage, as the protestors described their movement online: "In protest of Reverend James Johnson's homophobia, Governor Sam Schiller's pursuit of criminal charges against Ricky Fontana, and a political climate that abets intolerance and superstition."

At the press entrance, I showed my pass to an unsmiling man who looked like somebody's cellmate. "Raise your arms," he commanded. I lifted my arms to be frisked. Precaution was necessary, I understood. The thug patted my hips, the small of my back, and stopped when he reached my armpits. "What's that?" he asked, tapping my heart.

From my breast pocket, I removed my flask. Brimming with bourbon at nine a.m., it was six or seven sips lighter now.

"Get the fuck outta here," said the guard.

"Okay, I'll leave this outside," I said. "Watch it for me? This belonged to my father."

"Man, this is God's house," came the answer. "You think you can walk in here with booze? No, I say you can't get in with or without it. Go home."

"I have to get in," I whined. "I'm Jerry Rusch, the sportswriter. Don't you know who I am?"

The guard shrugged. He explained that I could watch the sermon on the closed-circuit TVs in the lobby. "But you ain't going no further after this stunt."

From inside, applause. Reverend Johnson was mounting the pulpit. The guard looked away for a moment when another guest offered his ticket. I ducked aside, but the guard saw me and seized my collar. Maybe it was the whiskey, but I didn't stop. I pulled forward like a dog towing his master. So the guard took my arm. His comrade saw us and grabbed my other arm. With unsettling ease, they lifted me from the ground. The guards carried me, legs flailing for the earth, into a small anteroom. Glowering at me, one of the watchmen phoned his boss.

I sat on a folding chair, head in hands. From the lobby televisions, the reverend's voice pealed. "Do you sense him, millionaires? Do you bow to your Creator? We are all millionaires, rich with His blessings!"

Halleluiahs filled the halls. My head throbbed, and I could not stifle urgent sobs. The guards wrinkled their noses at my blubbering. They turned their backs to me and watched the door. The black-clad men didn't speak, and the sermon seeped into the room. "Bless us all," said the reverend, "Bless this coalition of Christians, Jews, and Muslims gathered here today to affirm our faith. For all faiths are endangered!"

Into the room came the event's security chief, a wiry, rusty-haired retired cop. He asked for my press pass and driver's license. I gave him my wallet. Still sniffling, I watched wordlessly as he fished for my identification. He explained that my choices were to leave now or to leave later in the back of a police car.

As he returned my license, four baseball cards fell from my wallet. The security chief pinched the corner of one of them gingerly and lifted it to my face. Ricky Fontana smiled. He had scrawled his messy signature across his home white uniform. I had asked Ricky for the autograph during his rookie season. For my nephew, I told him. The card hadn't left my wallet since.

"Can I keep this?" asked the security chief. "This guy's my favorite, no matter what he did."

Outside the Flushing Convocation Center, chaos. Police pushed back the furious, chanting gatecrashers. From behind the policemen, worshippers howled back at the Days of Rage protest. I asked a young man taking pictures what had happened. He showed me blurry photos of a mob. A few dozen Ragers had broken through police barriers when an SUV arrived that allegedly contained Governor Schiller. They banged on the windows, he said, and somebody bludgeoned the side view mirror with a wooden sign. The governor was already inside the building. Still, the protestors had dented his ride back to LaGuardia Airport.

Just then, a hearty cheer rose from the Rager crowd. "Let 'em see, let 'em watch," I heard somebody shout. The protesters parted. Thirteen costumed men. They faced the police line and the neatly dressed worshippers who had stopped behind the cops to yell damnations. A troupe of guerilla performance artists, they called themselves: twelve young white men in short tunics and sandals. In the center, a black man in long flowing robes, dreadlocked, wearing a close-shaved beard and moustache. His wrists were tied to a plywood cross. Fastened around his waist: a black rubber penis.

One of the disciples fell to his knees before the cross. He stroked the veined sex toy. The crucified man thrust and gyrated his hips. From behind the police, the worshippers howled. Then the fake fellator kissed the penis. He rose, bowed to the black Jesus, and stepped aside. Another wispy disciple took a knee and faced his master.

Now the howls heightened. The police turned to restrain the outraged worshippers. "All hail the faggot antichrist!" screeched a protestor in a Fontana jersey. Uproarious cheers from the rollicking Ragers! Cameras rolled and flashes clicked. The police barreled toward the performers, and the protestors stepped aside. NYPD arrested all thirteen members of the pornographic flash mob for public indecency. Uncensored video of their act would garner over 500,000 hits online before the evening was out. The protestors laughed. In the video, they can be heard laughing as each apostle took a knee. That laughter launched ten thousand editorials and weeks of airtime for talk show blowhards.

I wasn't laughing. As I left the scene, I said under my breath to the guffawing protestors, "I was never one of you."

Nor was Ricky Fontana. He wouldn't hear of the protest for days. He took no questions from reporters on the Mets road trip that week. When Peter mentioned the black Jesus viral video, Ricky was indifferent. He was more eager to discuss *The Heart is a Lonely Hunter*, the latest loan from Peter's paperback library.

Had he read my blog, Fontana would've known my feelings. The sanctimony of his detractors dismayed me, but so too did the crassness of the Days of Rage. Everyone else with a New York byline chose a side to condemn. My seemingly noncommittal stance earned me plenty of nasty e-mails. Stick to sports, said my readers.

Ricky Fontana didn't read my column. After Carson McCullers, he moved on to *A Tree Grows in Brooklyn.*

On August 25, Governor Schiller withdrew from the presidential race. For weeks, the press had obsessively covered every comment Schiller had made about Ricky Fontana, and Republican nominee Mitch Haller seized the chance to lambaste his rival for conservative votes. "When I said that the Governor should keep his eye on the ball, I meant the economy," Senator Haller joked. After weeks of sinking poll numbers that ended in the debacle at TESTIFY! NYC, Schiller's three largest financial backers withdrew their promised support for the campaign's stretch run. Instead their money would go to Haller, a safer choice to defeat the incumbent president. SAILOR SAM SAYS SAYONARA announced the front page of the *New York Post.* Said that day's *Daily News* editorial, "Governor Schiller spent the summer defying claims that he was just the political flavor of the week. Then next week came and proved him wrong."

Many saw Schiller's departing remarks as a warning to Fontana. The governor declared, "I am leaving the presidential race to fight for American values and return our country to its moral center. The rule of law must be upheld—at all costs."

The next day, vandals left their mark for Reverend James Johnson. Employees of the Coalition for the Lord's Will arrived for work to find a spray-painted face on the doors of their offices. Ricky Fontana gazed from the glass facade. Below his portrait, eight stenciled letters. In drippy paint, the caption spelled "Apostate."

The graffiti inspired front-page outrage in New York. In the days to follow, the same vandals (or copycats) sprayed the stencil portrait on six churches in three boroughs. Cops chased two daring idiots down Fifth Avenue at three a.m. after a cabbie spotted them attempting to deface the door of Saint Patrick's Cathedral with Fontana's face.

On August 29, Fontana went three-for-five at Colorado and raised his batting average to .401. No batter had breached a .400 average so late in the season since John Olerud in 1993. That night, the Republican National Committee convened in Denver to nominate Senator Haller for president. At a press conference that night in Albany, spectators booed Sam Schiller during his address to officially endorse Senator Haller. CNN cameras found a man in the crowd wearing a Fontana jersey giving the Governor a thumbs-down.

On September 3, Governor Schiller arrived at Long Island's Hofstra University to deliver the matriculation address. Seated among the incoming freshmen were twenty-four seniors. Shortly after Schiller began to speak, one of them rose, shouted, and unfurled a sign that read "Hands Off Our Bodies, Governor Schiller!" Campus security pulled the screeching student outside. The governor continued. Minutes later, another student stood and bellowed at Schiller for recent anti-abortion remarks. On went the interruptions throughout the speech. A protestor stood, shouted, and left with security. Twenty-four times.

All twenty-four students wore T-shirts featuring the "Apostate" stencil.

Whispers on so-called news websites—that's all it was. A source inside his defunct campaign claimed that Governor Schiller would have revenge. For Fontana's face appearing everywhere as his White House run faltered, the governor would punish Ricky Fontana. Schiller was trying to persuade Russ Striper to press assault charges. So said a rumor widely published on September 15.

I dismissed the notion on my blog. Collusion between Striper and Schiller made for a nifty narrative. My sources in Baltimore told me that Striper would never press charges. He was too macho, they said, too bigoted to be a gay man's victim, too proud to let lawyers swing back for him. "Besides, what punishment could Fontana receive?" wrote a colleague at the *Baltimore Sun*. "A slap on the wrist, probation. No judge would give him jail time for a months-old dust-up."

❖

Few expected the Mets to succeed. The doubters surely included the architects of the MLB schedule. Good teams are often pitted against each other in the final week for maximum drama (and TV ratings). The Mets, however, were marooned in Pittsburgh for the season's final series. I was also stranded there for four games that were supposed to be meaningless because the Pirates are perennial non-contenders.

Still, led by Fontana, the Mets foiled skeptics and won the first three games. Meanwhile, the Milwaukee Brewers, ahead of the Mets for the final wildcard playoff spot, lost three games, which improbably gave New York a shot at the playoffs.

Of course, the team's achievement seemed secondary. The baseball-watching world was more enraptured by a statistic: .406. The lofty batting average that Fontana brought to Pittsburgh— nobody had hit so high in more than seventy years. Achieving that mark would mean Fontana that season would surpass another baseball immortal: Ted Williams, the last man to hit .400.

Hours before the season's final game, I wasn't sure if I'd be there to see Fontana go for the record. Three days sober. Miserable and shaking. I had not been without a drink for so long since high school. Normally, I started my workday with a shot of whiskey from my father's flask. But now the flask was home, under my bed. The minibar looked mighty tempting. I remembered when I had finished off every wee bottle stashed in my room, usually by myself, since Tony needed only a few drops of something stronger than cider to get sauced. What happened next became my most vivid memory in years. After I showered and dressed, dizziness overcame me. I crawled onto the bed. My head spun. My stomach lurched. I tried to steady my head with my hands, but spasms shook them, and my fingers flickered like a catcher signaling a pitch.

Somehow, I reached my phone. We had spoken twice since I had quit. Now, Tara didn't answer. Will she ever forgive me? I panicked. Suddenly, the air-conditioner sounded like whispers— secretive, condemning voices—and I thought I was going mad so I called her again, and again she didn't answer, and I sobbed when her voice mail picked up, but I didn't leave a message. I had no choice. I threw myself off the bed and shuffled on hands and knees to the bar and tore open the door and grabbed the first bottle I found (vodka) and emptied it into my gullet. But my stomach refused. My face flushed. My guts burned. My ears popped, and my vision seemed to dim and lose color. That's when I tasted my lunch against the back of my throat. I ran for the bathroom and ducked my head in the toilet and vomited.

I purged and finished purging, and then I wept as I had never wept as an adult. I realized that every other tear I had cried as a grown man had been shed while I was drunk, which made me cry harder. I could not imagine a more ridiculous scene: a balding fat man with a nose too big for his face, head in a toilet, cold water stinging his nostrils and soaking his eyebrows. Then, a lucky break—my phone rang. I stumbled back to bed, where I had left the phone.

"Jerry, are you there? I saw you called. I heard crying, I was scared."

I wiped the water from my face. "Yes, I'm here. I'm fine."

"I still worry about you," Tara said.

"Please, please, please don't worry about me," I told her. "I'll be fine." Then I quickly ended the call, but not before I blurted, "I love you!"

I brushed my teeth and changed my shirt. I left for the game.

When I reached the ballpark, the news had just broken. Russ Striper had filed assault charges. Governor Schiller assured fans that Fontana could play in the season's final game. Still, he told reporters, the state Attorney General had informed the Mets that Fontana was expected to surrender to NYPD the next day. I would be waiting for him at One Police Plaza, as would dozens of news crews. The governor knew that every network would cover Fontana's perp walk.

I was wrong. Schiller was not above vengeance. And he waited to break the news on Fontana's day of triumph.

Fontana arrived at PNC Park that afternoon with a smile. He calmly told the press that he would only answer questions about baseball. Then he grinned. "Okay, fire away!"

No pressure. No matter what happened, Ricky Fontana would finish the day as the first .400 hitter since Ted Williams, but, "I'm damn sure gonna try and beat his average anyway," Fontana told us. Like a musician watching the measures pass before his solo, he was radiant, ready for his moment, and when he noticed me among the throng of reporters and TV newsmen in the Mets clubhouse, Fontana did something I've never seen him do before: He winked!

Outside the ballpark, beneath signs that read "No Scalping," men drawled to the crowd, "Who needs tickets? How much will you pay for history?" Wary cops on patrol watched with grins as baseball-mad tourists from New York paid hundreds—even thousands—for tickets.

During the nightly news, anchors on NBC, ABC, Fox, and CBS promised viewers that the network would interrupt their prime-time fare to broadcast Fontana's at bats live. That morning, the president's press secretary assured the White House media corps that the president had not rescheduled that evening's budget address because of the game. The president had urgent unforeseen business that evening.

Breathless viewers and listeners and fans at the ballpark knew, every one, that Fontana needed two hits to break the record. But the Mets needed more than hits. They needed to win, or else the team would lose the wildcard spot to the Milwaukee Brewers, who played in Florida with a one-game lead. If Milwaukee lost and New York won, the Mets would be the last team to reach the playoffs.

In the bottom of the first inning, Ricky Fontana was scheduled to bat third. The leadoff hitter, Jackie Rios, popped out. Fontana walked out of the dugout into the on-deck circle. He took no practice swings, standing, waiting motionlessly as Sam Ellis grounded out to third base. Boos—I heard them with my own ears!—echoed from the upper deck as Fontana took the plate, but then the announcer's voice boomed across the stadium, and when his name was spoken, fans rose and shrieked.

Fontana reached the batter's box and stopped to fix his gloves. Andrew Yates, the Pittsburgh catcher, said, "Ricky, we're gonna pitch to you today. Allie's got his good shit working. But good luck."

"Thanks," Fontana said, and he adopted his batting stance.

Allie Thompson, the Pirates starting pitcher, looked bored during the ovation. His eyes rolled like the nasty chest-to-knees curveball he threw, which he called his "yacker," a deadly pitch. Finally, the batter, the catcher, and the umpire were ready. Thompson threw a fastball past Fontana for strike one. Next came the yacker. It died before it reached its target and bounced on home plate. Another fastball, outside. With the count in his favor, Fontana was looking for a fastball and instead Thompson threw that wicked curve. Fontana missed it by a mile. But during the swing, his first of the night, the stadium glowed with camera flashes. "Shit, shit, shit," said Dilly Leonard, playing third for the Pirates, momentarily blinded and rubbing the glare from his eyes.

The next pitch was a fastball, and I thought I saw Fontana's eyes light up the moment it left the pitcher's fingertips; Thompson had left the pitch too high. Fontana swung and corked the ball down the left field line. I heard from the luxury box near me Mets owner Alan Turner screaming, "Go, go, go!" as the ball soared through the air. It ricocheted off the top of the wall. By the time it stopped bouncing, Fontana was on second base, a double, his first hit, a stroke that raised his average to .407. The fans thrashed. Motion and noise vibrated the press box, and the wild crowd leapt and pumped their fists in waves of joy, frothing into a foamy noise, a single scream, "Aaaaaaaaaaaiii" it went, as the shortstop threw the ball back to Allie Thompson. Fontana called time out, clapped his hands, and handed his batting gloves to the batboy.

He didn't score. But in the bottom of the second inning, the Pirates plated two against Oscar Ferrera on three pitches flayed deep into the outfield gaps by George Ayala, Germain Stinson, and Gunnar Jorgen, the G-spot, as the Pittsburgh fans referred to their lineup's powerful core. New York flopped in the second and third, going down feebly on twelve Allie Thompson pitches. But the Pirates scored again in the fourth. Ricardo Guerren smacked a line drive that sneaked over the right field wall, a shot that cleared the yellow line at the top of the fence by the distance between the lines on your fingertips, a lucky shot. The home team had a three to nothing lead when Ricky Fontana took the plate in the bottom of the fourth. There was one out. Before his name was announced, the fans rose. Again, the big building echoed with their three-part rhythm, a waltz-like cheer. "Fon-tan-a!" and "M-V-P!" filled the air.

There was no drama; Fontana saw to it on the first pitch. He swung hastily but still made contact and blooped the ball off the end of his bat into the outfield grass. The most historic hit of his career, and yet, for Fontana, an undeserved hit: a cheap Texas Leaguer. Still, the moment the ball hit the ground and Fontana touched first base and the record was secure, the umpires called time out. Dozens of cops ran onto the field, and just in time, because spectators rushed the field again, as they had during the All-Star Game. But now instead of calling for blood, they cheered his name. "Ricky, Ricky! We love you!" one man cried as he was dragged off the field by the cops and the public address announcer intoned, "Ladies and gentlemen, the new modern batting champion, *Ricky Fontana*." The ballpark erupted into cheers and applause while the Mets and the Pirates players left their dugouts to form a queue near first base.

Fontana embraced each man, teammate and opponent. The commissioner and Ted Williams's son pushed through the line followed by cameramen and Jim Wallace of Fox Sports TV. The commissioner announced that the Baseball Writers Association of America had for the first time elected a unanimous Most Valuable Player to be named during the season. Two men in tuxedos hauled out the MVP trophy and handed it to Ricky, who hoisted it aloft and began to laugh. Jim Wallace thrust the mike under Fontana's chin. Only laughter echoed across the ballpark speakers. Wallace held the mike steady for a moment and when it became clear that words had failed Fontana, Wallace looked awkwardly to his cameraman for instruction and ran off the field. The Mets hoisted Fontana on their shoulders and carried him around the infield while he clutched his trophy to his chest.

"Where are you going?" Crane shouted, but I barely heard him over the din. I turned and sped for the door of the press box, into the hallway, and past the guards keeping fans from our workspace. Now deep in the bowels of the stadium, I panted. Noise thickened the air, and every sound seemed indistinct as I floated, hardly aware of my own footsteps, out of the tunnel and into the stands. I clapped my hands to my ears. My sickness rubbed my nerves raw. Once my ears were covered, my nose took over and I smelled booze everywhere. I shivered, and though each step forward seemed a monumental effort—a fat man to my left, cheering, was holding his cup crookedly and golden drops of beer spilled everywhere—I pushed through the crowd, knocking against a woman, stepping over a child, ducking under a man with a toddler on his shoulders, until I reached the seats closest to the field and a better view of Fontana. He was still holding his trophy perched atop the shoulders of Sam Ellis and Doug Spiedler, his teammates, who paraded around the field. They passed me. Fontana's face was bright red. His cap had been knocked off, and the embraces of fans and teammates had untucked his uniform. He looked like a messy little kid, hair unkempt, face streaked with sweat and tears, clutching his plaque like a lost toy found again.

Then, a jeer. A woman, in her thirties, blonde, wearing too much makeup and a white cardigan over a Mets T-shirt, cupped her hands to her mouth and booed. She was standing almost immediately to my right.

"You bitch," I screamed. "What the fuck is wrong with you?"

She shrank. A man, tall and angry, leaned around her.

"What did you call my wife?"

My finger in his face, I shouted, "Bitch. Booing Fontana at a moment like this. I can't think of a better word for your wife."

"You fucking asshole," he said. "Look at the scoreboard. That's why she's booing."

He thrust his finger toward the out-of-town scoreboard in right field. Next to the score of the Marlins and Brewers game, which until Fontana's at bat had been tied in the ninth inning at two-two, appeared the letter F: final. The Brewers won three to two. Even if the Mets won that day, their season was over.

Now Fontana was on the ground again looking for his cap. A bat boy brought him another as the umpires hurried the players back to their dugouts. The Pirates defenders returned to their posts. As they returned to the dugout, a few of the Mets noticed the scoreboard. The team saw the F, and their shoulders sagged. Fontana heard Sam Ellis shout, "Fucking fish. Couldn't help us out." The game resumed and the next batter took the plate. Fontana stood on first base and seemed to droop. I could scarcely imagine from his dour expression that only moments before he had been rinsing Russ Striper's bloodstains from the grass with tears of joy.

There were no tears after the game, which the Mets won seven to four, but plenty of regret. The first questioner at the press conference for Ricky Fontana asked if he was proud to break the two records in the same season.

"I'm proud," he said glumly. "But we lost."

He answered questions for twenty-five minutes, and finally he spoke unprompted into the microphone. "I'm ready to go home now," he said. "If you'll excuse me, I would like to get dressed." And he left the podium.

His miracle season was over. Ricky Fontana batted .408. He hit fifty-eight home runs. He drove in 148 runs. He had hit in sixty-two consecutive games. He left a major league ballpark for the last time as the best hitter who has ever played the game.

There he was, the record-breaking hero, in Peter's bedroom. Peter had arrived not long after a taxi had dropped off the new National League MVP at his apartment. Peter watched Ricky quietly, unnoticed. The Slugger's clothes lay in a rumpled pile on the bed. Fontana grabbed a shirt, tucked the wrinkled sleeves behind, folded the shirt in half, and laid it gently in a suitcase. He fished through the pile, found two bleach-stained socks, placed one over the other, and folded them. All the while he packed haphazardly, he hummed along to the tune in his headphones, shaking his hips to the music. Cute, Peter thought.

His wardrobe filled the suitcase. As Fontana grunted and strained to zip the overstuffed bag, Peter sneaked behind him, pulled off his headphones, and said, "Here, let me help."

They closed the bag. Fontana sat on the suitcase and Peter lay on the bed. Neither spoke.

"Where are you going, Slugger?" Peter pouted. "I thought the season was over."

"We're getting out of here," said Ricky.

"We? Where? Don't you have a date at Central Booking tomorrow?" Peter winked.

"We are going to buy an RV and drive. Nobody will find us on the open road," Ricky said dreamily. Then he saw Peter's confusion. "Or we'll fly. Maybe go to Italy, where my family's from, Calabria. Then Rome, Venice, too. As long as we end up somewhere they play baseball."

"Mmm, a European vacation sounds nice," Peter said.

"Not vacation. For good. I'm not going to jail. I'm not playing ball for people who hate me."

Aghast, Peter asked, "You're running away?" Ricky nodded. "And you want me to come?" Fontana nodded again. "I can't," Peter said, taking Ricky's hand.

Fontana jerked his hand away. "You're not coming with me?"

"No, of course not. My friends are here. My family, my job. Look, you have nothing to run from. You're not going to jail. The lawyers for the Mets will see you maybe spend a few hours reading to school kids."

Fontana seemed to shrink. Slouched and defeated and still sitting on the suitcase, his legs dangled off the bed but didn't reach the floor, and he looked to Peter every bit like a little boy. His face shriveled, lips trembling. He *is* a little boy, thought Peter.

Poor kid.

"But we're in love," Fontana said with defeat and desperation.

Peter clung to his arm and said, "We've known each other for only a few months. And we've only lived together for a few weeks. You're not even twenty-one, Ricky."

As Fontana's face melted from dejection to horror, Peter realized he had made a mistake. So he said, "Of course, I love you, too."

Fontana reached into his pocket, opened the red leather box, and removed my ring. He dropped to one knee.

"What the hell are you doing?" Peter asked.

"Marry me," said Ricky.

"What?"

"Marry me," he repeated.

"Are you kidding?"

"No."

"Jesus, Jesus, Jesus."

"I don't want him," kidded Fontana. "I want you."

"God. Why?"

"I have heard people say that love makes you weak. Yet with you, I feel strong. Powerful. Bigger! Like I could reach into the sky and stir the stars with my bat."

"Oh, Ricky. Where did you read that?"

"Marry me. I have asked you, and you haven't answered."

"You've lost your mind. No. We're not in love. Jesus Christ!"

"Why not?"

"I'm not ready for this."

"You're seeing someone else?"

"A few people. Just now and then. Nothing serious!"

Eyes ablaze, Fontana stood, balled his fists, and took a step forward, but Peter held his ground.

"You've been seeing other people, too," Peter shouted, his breath condensing on Fontana's chin. "Haven't you? All those nights alone on the road."

Fontana was too flabbergasted to respond. His fingers relaxed and his arms went limp and his shoulders slumped. The little boy was back, and Peter fought the urge to snicker at how his curveball had made Ricky's knees buckle.

Ricky remembered: No one is stopping you. At dinner during spring training, Ricky admitted to Seb that he wanted very much to ask out the shy fair-haired man Seb had introduced him to at a party.

But he had heard that Peter was Seb's ex-boyfriend. Over burgers at Mickey Maco's, Seb gave Ricky his blessing: No one is stopping you from doing what you want to do.

Nobody, that is, except Peter.

But Fontana gathered his strength. One last swing. "I could have any man in this city, or any woman. How could you say no? You could be mine."

"What do you expect?" Peter asked, with less defiance. "I'm not much older than you. We're too young to pine for each other while you're traveling for six months. I thought you understood that."

"All right," Fontana said, resigned. "Okay. Yes, okay."

"But I still care about you," Peter said. "Very much."

That's when Fontana began to cry. Peter didn't know what to do, this giant man crying, so he cried, too, hot tears like kerosene, his face was on fire. Fontana, bright red, was also aflame.

Peter kissed him. They made love. Fontana left Peter's apartment soon after. Neither Peter nor I have seen Ricky Fontana since.

Epilogue

Tara said that during our six-month separation she thought of me every day. She said it hurt more to ignore me than it did to be ignored and overlooked and disregarded. But one day Tara received a letter from me that she could not crumple. It contained a plastic badge congratulating me for three months of sobriety. Tara decided to come home. I told her I had learned to cook since she had left (though not very well), and I had been sleeping on one side of the bed, as if to leave room for her, as if she would come home at any moment, as if she had never left. So she stayed for good.

In sobriety, Joe Lippincott was my guide. Before he became a Christian, he was, I learned, addicted to cocaine. I recalled Joe's two-month sabbatical from the *Tribune* in 2005. Joe explained that he had spent the time at an upstate New York rehabilitation clinic. After a particularly bad bender, Joe didn't come to work, and Earl Driggs smelled a rat. He used a flathead screwdriver to pry open Joe's desk, where he found "a fucking epic stash of cocaine that would shrink Tony Montana's nuts." Driggs wasn't mad. "I was confused," he told me. "Where the fuck did Joe get the money for that blow? I know how much we pay him." He kept Joe on paid leave while Joe met the men who helped him, and me, to get sober.

Since the moment we are born, we face the unknown. We have to choose to face it; when our mothers offer us our first spoonful of solid food, we can refuse. When we're sent to pre-school, high school, and leave home, when we make love for the first time, there is fear and excitement in choosing the irrevocable future. Such was my journey to sobriety. Life without booze wasn't easy—at first, even the simplest tasks left me helpless. One morning Tara found me crying because I ran out of razors but I had to shave and get to work. I used to drink when I was unoccupied, so boredom was new to me. Writing sober was also a challenge. When I drank, I was eloquent, Shakespeare in corduroys. Like the drinks washed my vision with some miracle detergent, booze made my brights brighter, and every shadow seem deep, intense, and fascinating. Each triumph was Beethoven's Ninth and each failure Mozart's Requiem. It's no way for a man to live. Like an unremembered dream that steals a sleeper's peace, alcohol pinched years from my life. I woke up on the day that I was born again like an unrested forty-something child.

God took me back without question. I listened for Him, and He spoke. I heard His encouragement. I was on the right path: piety, sobriety, faith. I learned new indulgences. No drink satisfied me like shaking the preacher's hand on Sunday. Only baseball compared to that pleasure. Reverend Johnson was right: The game is not unlike religion. Faith and fandom lift my spirits and connect me to an enthusiastic community. I am part of something larger than myself.

The men who cured my alcoholism make no claim to my transformation. Neither does Joe. I turned to God for help, they tell me, and He gave me what I asked for. Tara gave birth to our first son only weeks before this book went to press. Many times while I was writing this manuscript, frustration overcame me, and I stopped writing. Then I would call her into my office. I threw my arms around her hips and pulled her to me, cradling my son's first cradle, and I covered her cheeks in kisses, one for each little pigment speck, a gesture of a perfect love to mark each imperfection. Then I would write more.

I fall in love too easily. I can't help it. That's what Joe says. Addiction is in my blood, and I'm helpless to staunch the flow that began when I had that first drink of Daddy's whiskey at age nine. When I make a mistake, I still think God is punishing me. And while the fate of Ricky Fontana makes me doubt Him sometimes, I've prayed every day since I stopped drinking. I pray for Tara and my son. I pray for myself. But during the time I spent to put these words to paper, I found myself repeating, God Bless Ricky Fontana!

Although God gave me the courage to face the unknown, there is one unknown, the ultimate unknown, which we have no choice but to face. That is death. It's when we face death that can be a choice, and, according to the front-page headlines on every newspaper in New York, Ricky Fontana chose an afternoon in December two weeks before his twenty-first birthday.

At the time this book went to press, his body had not been found.

People often ask me if I think Ricky Fontana killed himself. I doubt it, though I understand why suicide is the widely accepted explanation for his disappearance. There was something self-destructive about his notorious head butt. Also, gay men are statistically more likely to commit suicide than straight men, and many fans—even those who came to the ballpark to jeer him— would admit that the public humiliation he endured could drive anyone over the edge. He was a kid, really, so it's easy to assume that Fontana was just another teenage suicide. While some teenagers think the world is out to get them, the world really was gunning for Ricky Fontana.

Baseball's John F. Kennedy—if the assassin Tyler Wheeler had been faster, then Ricky Fontana would be a martyred symbol of youth and history altering possibility. And we would all be guilty. We who booed him, we who judged him, and me, who exposed him.

We want to believe that Fontana killed himself because he alone would be to blame. The suicide victim is also the perpetrator. No matter how badly we tormented him, we could pass off his suicide as an illness. Depression killed him. A faceless disease took Ricky, one among millions, nothing special, no martyr, just a page in the obituaries. Game over. Tomorrow's another day. Play ball.

But Ricky Fontana is alive, I think. I have no way of knowing for certain. I will keep looking for him. I need him. Baseball needs him. We need him to forgive us. We need to give him another chance.

❖

On the day after his record-breaking season ended, Ricky Fontana officially became a fugitive. Rule, Callahan, Crane, and I waited for six hours outside One Police Plaza. Fontana never showed. Police searched his hotel room and Peter's apartment. They questioned his teammates. Nobody found a trace of him.

Another media firestorm: Ricky Fontana on the lam! The same oldies DJ who resurrected the Joe DiMaggio song during Fontana's streak revived another hit. "There's a man on the run! Go, Ricky, go!" the DJ screeched. So began the return of "Band on the Run" to the top of the charts. The song by Paul McCartney and Wings played ceaselessly on New York radio and shot up rankings of online sales. Thousands of gleeful callers kept the tune in rotation.

Governor Schiller threatened him. An NYPD spokesman vowed to catch him. The Mets publicly urged him to surrender to the police. But Fontana stayed gone.

His song faded out of radio rotation. Fans turned their attention to football. My colleagues and I assumed Fontana would show up to spring training ready to deal with the legal consequences, or else he'd surface beforehand during the dead of winter to face a judge while baseball fans hibernated.

Fontana had been missing for three months when Dan Sutherland called. The private investigator phoned me one night before I left for Florida to cover my first spring training as a full-time blogger. Sutherland said that Celeste Fontana had not heard from Ricky since November. On November 21, three weeks after the Yankees won the World Series, Reverend Johnson held a press conference to announce that he had gathered over 700,000 signatures to ban gays from baseball. He demanded that Major League Baseball take action. The next day, the Commissioner's Office released a statement: "Baseball has always been a tolerant game and a national symbol of progress. Americans from all backgrounds, religions, and lifestyles play our game. Major League Baseball will bar no man from the sport on the basis of his race or creed or sexual preference."

Celeste called Ricky when she read about the commissioner's decision in the *Providence Journal*. Ricky answered the phone—the first time in weeks they had spoken. Fontana told her he was grateful for the commissioner's decision. He said he loved her and ended the call. Celeste had not been able to reach him since.

I told Sutherland that I had no reason to expect that Fontana wouldn't report to the first practice of the new baseball season. But Fontana didn't show up at the Mets practice facility in Port St. Lucie, Florida. His agent, his mother, and Peter had no idea where to find him. Celeste filed a missing person's report with the New York City Police Department, and Ricky Fontana officially became, as the detective in charge of the investigation called him, "the living dead."

Dick Rule got wind of his disappearance before I did. The next day, the *Daily News* published a graphic with Fontana's portrait on the side of a milk carton. After two more days, the Mets fined him. Fans were riveted; the sportswriters laughed. Most of us assumed right away that the Mets had fined a dead man. "He's killed himself, for sure," Crane wrote to me in an e-mail. "It's only a matter of time until a neighbor smells his corpse."

Fontana remained a phantom haunting the imaginations of fans, players, and writers during spring training. No one on the Mets spoke of him publicly. All we heard from his teammates was a four-word statement from Mick Kelleher, "I hope he's okay." By the end of March, Major League Baseball was in an awkward position. The most talented player in the game was missing; should he be mourned? Would the Mets wear black armbands or his uniform number embossed on their caps? Would the flags at the ballparks be at half-staff on opening day, and should the public address announcer ask the crowd for a moment of silence to remember Ricky Fontana? And if they did, would he be booed even after his supposed death?

The commissioner didn't need to make a decision.

The new season was three days old when a jogger spotted a badly decomposed body on the New Jersey shore of the Hudson River. The corpse was once a white man, over six feet tall, with brown eyes and black hair. For one afternoon, New Yorkers believed that the mystery of Ricky Fontana's vanishing had been solved. He had jumped from the top of the 300-foot-high Palisades cliffs near Weehawken, New Jersey, and fell to his death in the river. The *Post* website ran a photo slideshow of forensic investigators rappelling down the cliff face to examine sandstone outcroppings where no doubt a suicide would have left samples of his blood and hair before he hit the water.

But the next day, the news came through: Jesse Bloom was an overdose. His heart stopped during a methamphetamine binge, and he fell into the Hudson and floated downriver. He had been missing from his home in Peekskill, New York, for two months.

Still, even though rumors of Fontana's suicidal plunge into the Hudson proved false, most had already decided that he was dead. There was no on field commemoration by Major League Baseball, but the Mets lowered flags at Citi Field on opening day. For the rest of the spring, the team wore a black number six on their uniforms. The National Baseball Hall of Fame and Museum in Cooperstown, New York, draped black velvet over the display that housed the bats, uniforms, and spikes Fontana used when he broke Williams's and DiMaggio's records. Beneath a gold-framed portrait in oil of Fontana, the Hall of Fame placed a placard reading "Forever Young."

A week after opening day, Celeste Fontana held a private funeral service near Ricky's childhood home in Cranston, Rhode Island. There were no reporters present. None were invited. Neither was Peter Morgenstern. Crane and I speculated that the rumors were true: Until my column was published, Celeste Fontana did not know Ricky was gay. She has to this day refused to speak publicly about him. Days later, Peter hosted a memorial dinner at his apartment for Fontana's friends outside of baseball and even some of his teammates. With kindness and forgiveness beyond my understanding, he also invited me back into his home to remember the life of Ricky Fontana.

Why couldn't he return Ricky's love? Peter answered before I could ask. He had wondered for weeks since Ricky disappeared if he had done wrong by him, and he feared his rejection had spurred Ricky's suicide. "I hardly knew him," Peter explained. "He seemed impenetrably shallow. I spent our time together stumbling around in the dark looking for a door. Behind that door I expected to find another Ricky, the real Ricky. But there was no door."

Peter asked me to speak at the vigil. I told his friends that Fontana had become what he always wanted to be: a legend. Though he is preserved in photos and video, he doesn't seem real now, and he will only be a legend to future ballplayers and fans. Ricky Fontana will live forever between the living and the dead.

I refused to give up. On my blog that spring, I drummed up from loyal readers enough money to offer a $10,000 reward for information about Fontana's whereabouts. Thousands of letters and e-mails arrived. Someone spotted him in Chicago in the stands at Wrigley Field on opening day. A child swore she saw him at the San Diego Zoo. Two men from San Bernardino, California, claimed they had slept with him in February. I even received a letter from a Yankees fan in Rome, Italy, who was sure Fontana had gone to his ancestral home in Calabria. "It is common knowledge here in Italy," he wrote. Only one message caught my attention. Someone with an anonymous e-mail address wrote and claimed he or she worked at the Bank of New York. The writer said that Ricky Fontana's checking and savings accounts had been emptied and closed in December. But representatives from the bank wouldn't speak to me, not unless I worked with the police.

Weeks passed and nothing came of my plea for information. Celeste Fontana was also unsuccessful, Dan Sutherland told me. The public lost interest. The Mets eventually removed the memorial patches from their uniforms, and the boys of spring became the boys of summer. Charles Bussey, the new Mets right fielder, hit ten home runs in the first two months of his rookie season. Despite my best efforts, Ricky Fontana's name disappeared from the newspapers and the minds of fans. Readers and online followers asked me to stop writing about a dead man when twenty-five living Mets were battling for first place.

The baseball season ended without news about the game's best hitter. Then, three days before Thanksgiving, my phone rang. A thick Latin American accent asked if I would like to meet Ricky Fontana. The caller had read my blog, he said, and he was ready to claim the reward.

Like me, Javier Rendon once dreamed of playing baseball. Like me, he couldn't hit a curveball, was too short, and his school teammates in Maracaibo, Venezuela, outshined him at every facet of the sport. Like me, Javy had to find another avenue into the game he loved, but he wasn't a very good writer. But like a good writer sees the world in sentences and paragraphs, Javy also had excellent vision. He could spot baseball talent, and it was to his good fortune that he met and married a beautiful Cuban woman in 1998, the same year Orlando "El Duque" Hernandez fled Cuba and helped the New York Yankees win the World Series. Suddenly, his frequent visits to his wife's family in Havana made Javy's eye for winning ballplayers invaluable to major league general managers obsessed with mining Castro's island prison for talent.

He'll kill me when he reads that. Javy loves Cuba, and he raves about the island's rum and tobacco and women. "But I'm sure I got the best one, Jerry," he says knowingly, showing a small portrait of his wife he keeps in his wallet. He even has kind words for Fidel. "He's a great friend to baseball and was a hell of a player when he was young."

I already knew Javy well thanks to a profile in *Sports Illustrated* published after he recommended to the White Sox a slick-hitting Cuban shortstop named J. J. "Hey Hey" Gomez, who, during Fontana's final season, fell a few votes shy of beating Charles Bussey for Minor League Player of the Year. We met after a Mets-Marlins game in Miami. Between sips of beer, Javy said, "Word is getting round in Cuba about a power hitting *yanqui* who is making the best pitchers look like little boys."

Javy said that the stranger's teammates and coaches in Villa Clara knew almost nothing about him. "He is new to the league, a rookie. He calls himself Pedro Ramirez, but that's got to be a joke," Javy said. "He's a white boy, for sure; everyone says it. He doesn't say where he's from. He doesn't drink. He doesn't chase girls. He doesn't speak Spanish very well. But he's a fucking can't miss hitter."

I peppered him with questions. He answered almost none of them. He had not met or spoken to Pedro Ramirez. He had not seen him play for Villa Clara. Finally, Javy asked, "Would you like to come with me to Cuba? I am going soon. I will take you."

I had to pay my own way. I had to pay Javy's way, too. I had to double the reward money if Pedro Ramirez was Ricky Fontana. But until now, Javy never knew that I would have tripled the money or more if it were true.

I love my country. I hated to go to Cuba, to disobey my government, to spend money and support a regime that legitimized itself only in opposition to my homeland. But I went. Getting there wasn't easy. In fact, most anyone who has anything to do with baseball is trying to get out of Cuba.

A plane ride to Panama. Another to Havana. A night at the home of Freddy and Flora Morales, Javy's in-laws, who fed me and offered me rum and beer that I turned down politely. I was soon the only man at the dinner table not a little bit glassy-eyed and laughing at Javy's colorful jokes that I only vaguely understood with my high school Spanish. Always traveling, suddenly, I never felt so far from home.

Javy, it seemed, was a better scout than a navigator. An hour after we left Casa Morales the next day, we were lost. Javy needed a lot of persuading, but finally we pulled Freddy's ancient Oldsmobile to the side of the road and fished through the glove box for a map. That's when I heard a sound that brought me home, an abrupt click that at once made me fall in love with Cuba. We both heard it: the crack of the bat.

Ten boys, young teenagers, were playing baseball fifty yards off the side of the road. In shorts and T-shirts, some of them barefoot, they played five against five, two outfielders, two infielders, and one pitcher for each team. What looked like the rusted hood of an old Ford served as their catcher and backstop. The game ball was small and blue and rubber, and the bat they used seemed to be the handle of a mop. Still, they played crisp baseball while Javy and I watched them for five minutes before interrupting their lively chatter with a shout and a wave. I thought I had come prepared to barter with them for directions. While Javy asked them the way to Villa Clara, I riffled through my backpack for cigarettes and melted candy bars.

JOSHUA MARTINO

Two of the boys looked at my gifts and laughed. Javy went into his pocket, produced two small foil packages, and the boys' eyes widened. "Cards, cards," they said in English. "*Gracias, señor. Tienen más?*"

As he handed them another pack of Topps baseball cards—the boys tore open the foil ravenously and began arguing over the contents—Javy said to me, "Americans think that cash is king. But I know the true currency here in Cuba is baseball."

We reached Villa Clara by noon. I couldn't help but be stunned and disappointed that one of Cuba's major ball clubs played in a small, run-down park outshined by many American minor league fields. By comparison, the Mets spring training practice field seemed palatial.

Javy seemed to know the manager for Villa Clara, a wizened old man named Cruz who wore a bushy gray moustache. As soon as the words "Pedro Ramirez" left Javy's tongue, Cruz looked panicked and began to babble.

Javy translated: Pedro Ramirez did not show up for the game last night against Cienfuegos. The old woman at the house where he boarded didn't know where he had gone. His room is empty and his things are gone. Do you know where he is? Does your American friend?

But before Javy could answer, Cruz turned to me and asked in broken English, "Where he go? Do you know? I am looking for him. If he want more money, we get it."

"How much money does Ramirez make?" I asked Javy.

"Most every player makes twenty-five dollars per month. Don't look stunned. It goes a long way down here."

Cruz was frantic. Javy asked if any of the other ballplayers knew where to find Pedro Ramirez. He said we could ask them ourselves. Jose Ruiz played first base for Villa Clara. He agreed to speak to me, gladly accepting the cigarettes that the boys had refused. Javy translated.

I asked him to tell me whatever he knew about Pedro Ramirez. Was he an American?

"He was white, definitely. He spoke terrible Spanish."

What did he look like?

"*Guapo. Muy guapo,*" Ruiz began, grinning. Handsome, very handsome. "He is tall and has brown hair and a beard on his whole face and brown eyes. But he is definitely white, yes."

Show me how he batted, I asked. Ruiz set his feet wide apart and held his bat high above his head, his elbow cocked parallel to the ground—just like Fontana.

"What else can you tell me about him, about his game?" I asked. Javy barked at him in Spanish, and then Ruiz answered.

I didn't need a translation. He said, "*Él es el mejor del mundo.*" He's the best in the world.

About the Author

Joshua Martino is a writer from New York. *Fontana* is his first novel.

Books Available From Bold Strokes Books

Oath of Honor by Radclyffe. A First Responders novel. First do no harm…First Physician of the United States, Wes Masters, discovers that being the president's doctor demands more than brains and personal sacrifice—especially when politics is the order of the day. (978-1-60282-671-7)

A Question of Ghosts by Cate Culpepper. Becca Healy hopes Dr. Joanne Call can help her learn if her mother really committed suicide—but she's not sure she can handle her mother's ghost, a decades-old mystery, and lusting after the difficult Dr. Call without some serious chocolate consumption. (978-1-60282-672-4)

The Night Off by Meghan O'Brien. When Emily Parker pays for a taboo role-playing fantasy encounter from the Xtreme Encounters escort agency, she expects to surrender control—but never imagines losing her heart to dangerous butch, Nat Swayne. (978-1-60282-673-1)

Sara by Greg Herren. A mysterious and beautiful new student at Southern Heights High School stirs things up when students start dying. (978-1-60282-674-8)

Fontana by Joshua Martino. Fame, obsession, and vengeance collide in a novel that asks: What if America's greatest hero was gay?(978-1-60282-675-5)

Lemon Reef by Robin Silverman. What would you risk for the memory of your first love? When Jenna Ross learns her high school love Del Soto died on Lemon Reef, she refuses to accept the medical examiner's report of a death from natural causes and risks everything to find the truth. (978-1-60282-676-2)

The Dirty Diner: Gay Erotica on the Menu edited by Jerry Wheeler. Gay erotica set in restaurants, featuring food, sex, and men—could you really ask for anything more? (978-1-60282-677-9)

Slingshot by Carsen Taite. Bounty hunter Luca Bennett takes on a seemingly simple job for defense attorney Ronnie Moreno, but the job quickly turns complicated and dangerous, as does her attraction to the elusive Ronnie Moreno. (978-1-60282-666-3)

Touch Me Gently by D. Jackson Leigh. Secrets have always meant heartbreak and banishment to Salem Lacey until she meets the beautiful and mysterious Knox Bolander and learns some secrets are necessary. (978-1-60282-667-0)

Missing by P.J. Trebelhorn. FBI agent Olivia Andrews knows exactly what she wants out of life, but then she's forced to rethink everything when she meets fellow agent Sophie Kane while investigating a child abduction. (978-1-60282-668-7)

Sweat: Gay Jock Erotica edited by Todd Gregory. Sizzling tales of smoking-hot sex with the athletic studs everyone fantasizes about. (978-1-60282-669-4)

The Marrying Kind by Ken O'Neill. Just when successful wedding planner Adam More decides to protest inequality by quitting the business and boycotting marriage entirely, his only sibling announces her engagement. (978-1-60282-670-0)

Dark Wings Descending by Lesley Davis. What if the demons you face in life are real? Chicago detective Rafe Douglas is about to find out. (978-1-60282-660-1)

sunfall by Nell Stark and Trinity Tam. The final installment of the everafter series. Valentine Darrow and Alexa Newland work to rebuild their relationship even as they find themselves at the heart of the struggle that will determine a new world order for vampires and wereshifters. (978-1-60282-661-8)

Mission of Desire by Terri Richards. Nicole Kennedy finds herself in Africa at the center of an international conspiracy and being rescued by beautiful but arrogant government agent Kira Anthony, but is Kira someone Nicole can trust or is she blinded by desire? (978-1-60282-662-5)

Boys of Summer edited by Steve Berman. Stories of young love and adventure, when the sky's ceiling is a bright blue marvel, when another boy's laughter at the beach can distract from dull summer jobs. (978-1-60282-663-2)

The Locket and the Flintlock by Rebecca S. Buck. When Regency gentlewoman Lucia Foxe is robbed on the highway, will the masked outlaw who stole Lucia's precious locket also claim her heart? (978-1-60282-664-9)

Calendar Boys by Logan Zachary. A man a month will keep you excited year round. (978-1-60282-665-6)